The Boyfriend

Laura Southgate

FLEET
2020

FLEET

First published in New Zealand in 2019 by Victoria University Press
First published in Great Britain in 2019 by Fleet
This edition published in 2020 by Fleet

1 3 5 7 9 10 8 6 4 2

A CIP catalogue record for this book
is available from the British Library.

ISBN: 978-0-349-72630-4

Typeset in Palatino by M Rules
Printed and bound in Great Britain by Clays Ltd, Elcograf S.p.A.

Papers used by Fleet are from well-managed forests
and other responsible sources.

Fleet
An imprint of
Little, Brown Book Group
Carmelite House
50 Victoria Embankment
London EC4Y 0DZ

An Hachette UK Company
www.hachette.co.uk

www.littlebrown.co.uk

for David

At seventeen, here's what I know: a boyfriend falls desperately in love. It's an affliction. He tells you he loves you, how much it's hurting him. Then he kisses you passionately. It would be best if it finished there, but after that, he's going to want to have sex with you. It probably hurts, you probably both cry. And then you're together.

There's another thing a boyfriend's supposed to do: ask you out. Which makes me wonder if Dieter Cohen was almost a boyfriend. But that was different. He asked me, 'Do you like coffee?' and I said yes, even though I'd only ever had Greggs or Jarrah, which I learned isn't real coffee. He took me to Society, the café he used to work at, and ordered me a latte from a tall glass. Which was delicious! But liking coffee together isn't going out.

I met Dieter at the library. He used to take the bus with me sometimes after work. That didn't mean anything though. He just happened to be going in the same direction at the same time. I was off home and he was going to his mate's place across the valley to play Dungeons and Dragons.

Until the incident with Claudia, he gave me guitar lessons too, but it was strictly business, even though every time he repositioned my fingers on the strings I had a minor stroke.

A few weeks into our shelving together, he started calling me 'Liebchen', which means 'darling' or 'dear' in German, which he was studying at university. I can never decide which English translation he might have had in mind, or what connotation. There are so many. For instance, did he mean 'darling' like in the Beatles' song 'Oh Darling'? Because if he did, I had severely underreacted. Or did he mean 'darling' like when my dad, Gary, had enough of my nonsense and said, 'daaarl-ing ...' like a final warning? Well, he didn't mean it like that because that wasn't the tone of his voice. But if it meant something, he wouldn't have said it at all. He'd have kept my darlingness to himself until he found a way to announce it.

When he invited me to his flat warming I thought maybe that was asking me out, the way he kept talking about it in smoko breaks round the back of the library, tilting his bird face to exhale his Marlboro, tapping the ash into the tray with a gentle pat of his forefinger, blinking rapidly. He told me about the records he had lined up to play, the Guinness he'd bought, the varsity friends he wanted me to meet. But that definitely wasn't asking me out, because on that night there was Claudia, literally inserting herself into the barely existent gap between us on the couch and sliding her hand up his thigh.

He showed me his rings the last time we walked together from the bus stop, stretching his fingers out under the sodium street lamps. 'Each ring represents a woman,' he said. 'A woman who broke my heart.' Three rings. I wonder if Claudia will be the fourth.

Claudia is my ring. If it wasn't for her, I wouldn't have a broken heart. I'd still be catching the bus with Dieter, getting guitar lessons from Dieter, watching Dieter smoke. Claudia is the reason I know about staying awake till the birds start, about staying inside all summer because I don't want to offend the people I can't smile at, the people in the neighbourhood who do or don't recognise me, the boys whose voices have dropped since we last spoke, since they made me and Amber and Kathy dance naked to the *Ghostbusters* theme tune. Claudia is the reason I'm not even sure I could form my face into a shape that wouldn't look stricken or sarcastic or sick.

Alison, my mum, isn't too worried. I start seventh form in just a week's time. We have an isn't-this-ridiculous type of conversation, an I-literally-haven't-left-the-house-in-weeks type of hysterical laughter type of conversation. It's a transitional thing. She says that when I get to university I'll feel better. I just have to get through one more year. I've been stuck in this oppressive girls' world too long. All I need is intellectual stimulation and some interesting people, she says. 'And a boyfriend,' I add. 'Oh there's no rush for that,' she says. We agree he's out there. And that's another reason not to leave the house, because what if I see him and I give him the deranged rictus face and it's over before it even begins?

What is a boyfriend? What does a boyfriend do? A year down the track, or two, or three, if anyone asks, it's true, I might not know the answers anymore. But I would call them stupid questions.

Part 1

Going Out

1

At the beginning of my last school term, I decided to give yoga a try. My place was in the back row next to a girl from school, Mandi. Everyone else in the yoga class was old and took it seriously.

'Concentrate on your breath,' said our bald instructor. His penis was visible through his tights.

I was getting into triangle pose, dipping, pointing, feeling pointless.

'Swivel your heads towards the ceiling.'

A guy at the front was concentrating on his breath in an audible way, like he was gathering up phlegm.

'Great work, Donny.'

Yeah, wow. You can breathe in and out loudly.

I glanced at Mandi to see what she thought, but she was staring out the window.

The rest of us were barefoot, but this guy was wearing shoes. Not the latest Reeboks or anything, just these sad old chunky sneakers that had maybe once been white. He was also wearing a hat – a grey-brown beanie, which he never removed.

At least, in between the beanie and the shoes, his clothes were as instructed: loose-fitting, comfortable. As we dipped into triangle pose, his T-shirt flopped down past his shoulder. It was muscular and a tiny bit hairy.

One day he showed up outside school, between me and the school buses chugging out their sad diesel throbs. I had to wear full uniform that day for prizegiving dress rehearsals, and I was steering my art folio case in and out amongst the teachers and the throngs of shrieking third-formers overwhelmed by outsized backpacks. I was anxious to get to yoga so I could change before anyone saw me. But all of a sudden there he was. He grabbed my tie and gave it a little yank.

'Erica,' he said, walking alongside me. 'I've never seen you in this getup.'

'I don't normally wear it. We don't have to in seventh form.'

He pursed his lips strangely, looking me up and down. 'What a shame.'

And so we walked to yoga together.

In yoga class, Mandi and I got the giggles when our instructor said 'pubic bone'. We were supposed to do this weird rocking backbend, but our ankles kicked away when we giggled. We shook on the mats, helpless with laughter.

Donny did it perfectly, breathing his snorty animal breath, because it wasn't funny, of course. He made me see that, the next year. Pressed my pubic bone while I was standing in *tadasana* in my bedroom, adjusting my alignment. That was maybe the first time he touched me there, and the way he did it made me realise it was no big deal. Kind of like when Amber took me to TM with her parents and the guy 'initiated' me while everyone else was chanting with their eyes shut. When it's spiritual, it's pure, like a doctor examining you.

The yoga class was only ten weeks. After that I didn't see Donny properly for a long time. Not that I was on the lookout for him or anything. But he did pop up a couple of times. Once, when I went to a Bovine gig with Tanya, Beth and Amber at the Bongo Bar, I spotted his beanie from across the room. He was talking to a tall girl with blond hair. Outside the postural rigour of yoga he looked faintly lopsided, as if his right side was subject to erosion. Even his face was drawn crooked. When he smiled at the girl his lips parted on the right to reveal his back teeth, tense and eager, like a dog's.

'Shield me,' I said to Tanya, who was sitting next to me on the outside of the booth.

'What is it?' she asked excitedly. 'Is it Dieter? Where is he?'

'It's not Dieter, come on.' I shrank down by her shoulder. 'If it was Dieter you would know.'

'How would we know?'

'If it was Dieter I'd be screaming,' I said in her ear. She smirked.

Beth leaned across the table at us. 'What's the haps?'

I rummaged in my duffel bag and took out my notebook and wrote, still squished side-on to Tanya: YOGA GUY. I showed it to Tanya. She widened her eyes and began to scan the room.

'Show me!' said Beth. Tanya passed it to her. Beth frowned. 'Is he a babe?'

Tanya gave her a pitying look. 'Beth, nobody here's a babe.'

'Except me,' said Amber, rolling a Port Royal.

Beth grabbed my pen and wrote her own note. It said, Tie fetish?!

Tanya saw it over my shoulder. 'Oh – Tie Guy!'

'That's the one.'

Everyone was nodding in unison.

Amber lit the Port Royal. Even though she was directly oppo-site me, when she exhaled I couldn't smell it. The place was so smoky already.

I took a long sip of my vodka, lemon and lime. I'd been trying to ration it till the band started their set, because I was worried someone would notice we hadn't paid a cover charge. The scary doorman had no doubt taken his place at the front behind the girl who was stamping people's wrists. He had a shaved head with a flat top to it. Having a drink in my hand made me fear him less, but I couldn't afford another one.

Tanya grabbed my notebook and wrote me a message: *He's coming?!*

I looked up and, to my horror, Donny was walking towards me with the tall girl at his side.

'Well hello there, Erica,' he said when he got to our table. His smile was wide, like Krusty the Clown's. 'At last we meet! You finished school yet or what?'

I shrugged in what I hoped would be a blasé way. I could sense the looks the others were giving one another. They could wait.

'Erica, I'd like you to meet Calliope here, a visitor from merry England.'

Calliope reached in to clasp my hand. Her hand was boneless and damp. She barely smiled.

'Nice to meet you,' I said.

'Are you here on holiday?' asked Tanya.

'We met at a backpackers' in Kaitaia,' said Donny. 'We've been at large ever since.'

'South Island next,' said Calliope shyly. 'I'd like to see the mountains.'

Tanya and I nodded.

'So are you girls going to university next year?' asked Donny.

'Yeah, I hope so,' I said.

'What'll you study? What's your best subject?'

'I dunno,' I said. 'Maybe German.' German wasn't my best subject, but Dieter Cohen was doing it.

A tap on the microphone. A couple of strums, bursts of feedback. Bovine was starting. Calliope turned towards them. She said something to Donny and began slinking her way towards the front, his hand in hers.

*

10

Afterwards we went to McDonald's. Everyone was discussing the merits of the various members of Bovine.

Beth unpacked her Happy Meal. 'Which one do you like, Erica?'

'I like them all, musically. I don't have a *crush* on any of them if that's what you mean.'

'Ooh, touchy,' said Amber.

'What about your admirer?' Beth asked. 'You got the hots for him?'

Tanya took a long slurp on the chocolate thickshake we were sharing. 'How can she possibly like a guy like that? He's so *decrepit*.'

'Excuse me,' I said, taking the drink off her. 'I do *not* like that guy.'

'Uh – hello? You went bright red when he came over.'

'You're doing it again now!' said Beth.

'That's because it's embarrassing! He's the one who approached me, okay? I'm not interested.'

'Oh, that's right. You only have eyes for Dieter,' said Tanya.

'Dieter Tampon Eater,' said Beth.

'Dieter is a weirdo goth,' said Amber.

'He's into Victoriana.'

'Whatever Trevor,' said Tanya.

'It's not like he wears makeup or anything,' I said.

Tanya smirked. 'Sure, sure. Bet you wouldn't mind if he did though.'

'Maybe I wouldn't!'

'But the thing is, Dieter isn't interested, is he, Erica?' said Amber.

'Yeah, but we know who is,' said Tanya.

'Tie Guy!' said Amber.

'Tie Guy!' said Beth.

*

I saw 'Tie Guy' one other time before I started university, but he didn't see me. It was at the library. He was in an argument with Dieter at the issues desk, a pile of books between them. Dieter stood up. He was shorter than Donny, of a much slighter build.

'Sorry, mate,' he said. 'I can't issue you these books.'

Donny did a kind of karate kick at the desk.

The security guard came along and put his hand on his shoulder. 'Fuck, man,' Donny said as he was escorted out, 'is this a public library or what?'

Dieter sat down. He was laughing, but I could tell he was rattled. He looked small then. If the desk hadn't been there, he'd be injured right now. Donny would've crushed his shoulder in one hand, like a can of Fresh Up.

I never got the full story. Our guitar lessons had stopped with the arrival of Claudia, and Dieter didn't ask me to join him on his cigarette breaks anymore.

It wasn't long after that that he left. He had to devote himself to his studies, was the official story, but I feared it had more to do with alcohol. On one of our last shelving shifts together, he asked me for Panadol. When I pressed for details he only said, 'Debauchery.' I supposed Claudia was involved, but he didn't look happy about it.

2

In my first year at university, I was too busy admiring Paul to notice Donny when he started showing up at German Club. Paul had a yellow raincoat. He'd light up the lift with it. His smile was like that too. So bright, you kind of had to look at him sideways.

We were in the German Club production together. I was in the band playing guitar and Paul was understudy for Dr Faustus. Donny wasn't in the play. He was just in the beginners' class, but he'd started coming along to video nights and cornering people at drinks. We waved at each other across the room once. He was busy enthusing to Fiona Patterson, the leather-jacket-wearing lecturer.

Paul and I started hanging out after rehearsals, taking drinks back to his bedsit. At first we were with other people from the crew, and then it was just us. He never asked me out exactly, or made any declarations. We went to Society for coffee twice, spent a few hours on the phone. It was too easy-going to be significant. Even when we started kissing and taking off each other's clothes, I wasn't sure I could call him a boyfriend yet. He hadn't started acting differently, so nothing had changed.

The first time I slept over at Paul's, I walked downtown afterwards, I don't know why – to go to the bank or something – somewhere hushed and hallowed with other people but nobody asking questions. Not that Gary or Alison would've quizzed me relentlessly. It wasn't that unusual for me to be out all night. I was old enough and they were cool.

My body was humming, not so much like a sports car as a computer or a fridge. Was it anxiety, or some little buzz about sharing a man's bed, whispering weird things in German to each other, skin to skin in the dim light? I smelled of antibacterial soap, which somehow underlined the fact we hadn't gone all the way – we were just clean friends.

We'd slept late, then eaten Weetbix and cheese on toast in quick succession. Paul was out of milk so our Nescafé was black and heavily sugared, and we dressed our Weetbix with watered-down Easi-Yo. He showed me the white plastic cylinder he grew it in.

I was impressed. 'I can't believe you make your own yoghurt. You're eighteen years old.'

'It's actually really easy,' he'd said with a grin. 'Easy with an *i*.'

On my way down Church Street that afternoon, Donny lurched into view, heading towards me on the diagonal. He swung his arm out straight like a school patrol sign.

'Hey – hello there!'

'Oh hi,' I said, trying to give the impression I didn't remember who he was.

'Hey, do you wanna go to the movies with me?'

'Um.'

His eyes were full of manic optimism. 'There's this movie *Brassed Off* that's on at the Rialto. I have a friend who can get us in for free.'

'Um, maybe some time?'

'Come on. Couragio!'

'I dunno. I'm just doing some stuff in town. I didn't really plan on going to the movies.'

14

'You didn't *plan*? Oh dear. You didn't *plan*. Well Erica, in that case I guess there's no hope. No plan! You don't *plan* on getting free tickets to the movies.'

That wasn't exactly true. Some people spent all day listening to the radio so they could get free giveaways. 'I don't know. What's this movie about?'

'It has Ewan McGregor in it, the guy from *Trainspotting*, only he's this clean-cut lad playing tenor trombone. It looks pretty cute. There's a spunky blond actress in the poster with him. She has that peculiar English crispness. Pretty ravishing, I must say.'

'Oh yeah?'

'It's so strange. I was just thinking, I'm bound to run into some lovely soul who'll accompany me to that movie and wow – I run into you, Erica. An even lovelier soul than I could possibly have asked for! Allow me to feel pleasantly refreshed by this moment of serendipity a little longer before you rob me of all hope, wouldya?'

So we went to the movie. We waited in the lobby till there was nobody around and then the guy gave us a nod from behind the popcorn counter. It was the end of the trailers. Donny tugged me into a row near the back and we sat side by side, his warm elbow nudging mine on the arm rest. His body smelled musky and sharp – tea tree and fresh sweat with hints of incense and mown grass.

Afterwards we wandered, blinking, back to where we started.

'You going home now, or?'

'Yeah.'

'Cool. Well,' Donny laughed and scratched his head. 'I'm kind of out of practice with this sort of thing.'

'What sort of thing is that?'

'Uh – going out, you know, with a pretty girl like you.'

Pretty girl? What did he mean? He was a lot older than me. I thought of the English girl he was with at the Bongo Bar last

15

year. Calliope. She was pretty. And young. But perhaps that had ended badly and he was only hanging out with older women now. Maybe he was going out with Fiona Patterson? 'That's okay. I mean, we only went to the movies. I have a boyfriend anyway,' I lied.

'You do?' He looked crestfallen. I was confused. If he'd meant to ask me out, he'd done it completely wrong. You don't just wander into someone and take them to the movies by accident and then act as though it's some big thing.

'I do. I'm going out with Paul, you know, from German Club?'

'Paul?' Donny laughed and shook his head. 'Listen, let's not waste our time worrying about such an unworthy opponent.'

He got a notebook out of his pocket and wrote down his phone number. I didn't have time to think. By the time he'd torn off the page and handed it to me, I'd agreed to give him a German lesson at my house.

3

'Don't deny it,' Donny kept saying. *'Du liebt mir.'*

'Du liebst mich, you mean,' I said.

That was about the extent of our German lesson: love takes the accusative. After that, German gave way to English. Donny closed his notebook and brought his chair close to mine, bypassing the corner of the kitchen table we'd been leaning across. He clutched at my hands.

'Erica, don't think you can hide it. Anyone can see you're in love. I have eyes.'

He did have eyes, and he fixed them on me with a kind of wild intensity that would have been frightening if it weren't so comical. I wrenched my hands from his grip to cover my mouth. I had a smile on the verge of a laughing fit and I wasn't sure I could stop that once it started.

The rest of the lesson, Donny was pleading for a kiss, remonstrating with me for snorting as I prised his hands off my cheeks, smudged my lips away, pressed a hand hard onto his jaw. It went on and on, and even though I could barely suppress my giggles, it felt like a pretty cruel joke that here at last was my passionate would-be boyfriend in the form of a deranged older man declaring in broken German that I was in love with him.

Alison had popped her head round the living-room door when Donny arrived, given him a polite wave. It was after dinner, so she and Gary were probably drinking tea and complaining softly to each other in front of the television. I was in the kitchen helping a fellow student with his beginner German. That was the plan, anyway.

Distraction could be an option. I had learned that from babysitting. *I see you pulling all the pots and pans out of the cupboards. I raise you: making paper hats from newspaper.*

'Would you like a hot drink?' I asked. 'We have tea, Ovaltine, Jarrah?'

He slumped into a dejected stoop. He said nothing, lifting only his head, impressing upon me with his eyes the futility of my attempt.

'I think I'll have an Ovaltine,' I said. 'I like Jarrah, but it's probably a bit late for that. Coffee gives me palpitations.'

I took two mugs from the cupboard and put them on the bench. I thought by the time I'd boiled the jug maybe he'd be ready to choose, but when I went to the other cupboard to get the Ovaltine, he was staring at the ceiling with an alarming intensity. *Gott im Himmel.*

He wasn't exactly good looking. One of his legs was shorter than the other – that was why he had to wear the special sneakers. He'd smashed his right leg up in a motorbike accident when he was seventeen. The doctors had squished the contents of his leg below the knee into a knobbly, calf-shaped tube and hoped for the best. He'd lost about an inch on that side.

Not that looks mattered to me. But his strange appearance made his self-assurance harder to discount. I almost felt sorry for him, knowing how pitiful it is to fall in love with someone who doesn't love you back, but he didn't make it easy for me with all the groping attempts at kissing and his bizarre insistence that I was in love with *him*.

18

He slapped his hand on the table. '*Verstehst du nichts? Ich war –
ich bin . . .*'

'*Auf Englisch?*'

'Don't you get it? I haven't waded through so many years of
solitude, these lonely, wretched years in the wilderness, only
to emerge oblivious to this rare connection that is happening
between us. This electricity, Erica. I feel it coming off you, joining
my body to yours. Why are you denying it?'

'Denying what?'

'Erica, do you mean to pretend that you don't know the effect
you're having? Come on. You're no *cock tease*, if you'll permit me
to use that vulgar term. No, no. Cover your ears,' he said, leaning forward and clasping his hands gently around my head. 'I
believe you are innocent. *Entschuldigen mir bitte.* A case for Doktor
Freud, perhaps.'

I was eighteen. Was I repressed? I had to admit the possibility
that Donny knew better than I did.

I gave Donny his second German lesson at his flat. It turned
out his friend Foster was in Bovine, and they were playing at the
Bongo Bar later that night. Bovine was cool and it was beyond
exciting to see them now I had a friend of a friend in the band.

Donny's room smelled of incense and beer. He had a line of
obscure beers in the middle of the room to choose from and a
bottle of Grant's. 'Take your pick,' he said, and I chose a beer with
a weird cherry flavour and took a seat on the milk crate near the
stereo. He had an impressive pile of tapes stacked up against the
wall behind it.

'That's my record collection, man,' he said sadly. 'I had to sell
everything a couple of years back. But I put it all on tape first. Easier
to move around now anyway. Those boxes weighed a fuckload.'

He didn't try to kiss me this time, just eyed me unblinkingly
and asked me about what music I knew. He only played stuff I'd
never heard of, of which there was a surprising amount.

'You know John Cale?'

I shook my head.

'From the Velvet Underground?'

'Oh yeah? No.'

He smiled and waggled a tape at me knowingly. 'Wait till you hear this. *Vintage Violence,* man.' He put the tape in and fast-forwarded it a few times.

'Check this out,' he said when he found the right pause.

He sat on his futon and watched me as I listened. It was 'Big White Cloud' and as the piano joined the violins it was as if Donny had spiked my drink. John Cale began to sing and my brain was swelling – the room was full of uplifting portent.

I was anxious to take this significant feeling to the gig where I'd meet cool people and begin to be part of something. Maybe someone would even invite me to join their band.

'Can we get going?' I asked when the song had finished.

He smiled indulgently at me, ejecting the tape and tightening it with a pencil. 'These things don't usually start till after midnight,' he said.

We arrived in time for Bovine's last song, 'Stranded', the same Saints cover they did as an encore the first time I saw them. They were playing calmly, like they were doing the dishes, not strumming and hitting and straining at the microphone. The guitarist was in a black T-shirt tucked into black jeans and he was playing power chords like it was no big deal. I jumped and nodded appreciatively, wishing I could get my fingers to go in the right place every time like that. He looked almost bored, but his sweaty brown hair gave him away. That was Donny's friend Foster.

While the band was packing up everybody began to move around. The scary doorman had given up for the night and was skulling a beer by himself. I tried to walk past him undetected on the way to the bar but Donny steered me towards him.

'Erica, this is Sick,' he said, and the doorman extended a hand to shake. He was wearing fingerless gloves, and the ends of his fingers were tattooed with wonky hieroglyphs.

'Gidday, Erica,' he said. 'How old are you, chick? I gotta ask.'

'Twenty-three,' I said, hoping the extremity of the lie would help me get away with it.

He nodded almost deferentially before returning to his beer.

Foster came over to the bar with the bass player, Ben, who looked askance at Donny and started talking to the barman before he could introduce us properly. Foster said a weary hi and gave me a sceptical glance up and down. 'Pleasure,' he said, and turned back to Donny as if he was waiting for more information.

'Foster, man, you're more hermetically sealed than usual this evening,' said Donny.

Foster just raised his eyebrows and turned away to order his beer.

I stood up close to him so he could hear me and said, 'I'm sorry we missed most of it. I loved "Stranded".' I asked how the rest of their performance had gone.

He said it went okay. 'This is the best part of the night so far.' He was smiling, but it was a difficult smile to read.

'Do they pay you?'

'I'm getting paid in beer,' he said. 'Would you like one?'

I said I would.

'What kind do you like?' he asked.

'Anything dark.'

'Hey, what about me?' asked Donny when Foster ordered me a Guinness.

'Get your own beer,' said Foster. 'You barely even made it to the gig.'

'Neither did she,' said Donny.

Foster watched as I dipped my lips in the foam.

'I can't say no to free Guinness,' I said, and thanked him.

It was two years ago that I went to Dieter's party. He'd promised we could go out on the deck with our Guinness later, just him and me. That might have happened if Claudia hadn't scuttled in and stolen him.

Foster asked what subjects I was studying. Philosophy had been one of his majors, too. Now he had a master's in anthropology, whatever that was. He was trying to get it together to do a PhD somewhere overseas next year.

'Basically I want to leave the country,' he said, 'and postpone real life as long as possible.' He excused himself.

Donny was deep in conversation with a woman with golden skin and long dark wavy hair. They were standing very close together and she was touching his chest. His arm gestures were more circumscribed than usual, as if her touch had sedated him.

When Foster came back he had a soft box with a red circle in the middle of it.

I said, 'What's that?'

'It's my Lucky Strikes,' he said. 'Do you want one?'

'I don't think so,' I said. I could feel my face going red. 'Are they what I think they are?'

'I don't know,' he said, grinning. 'What do you think they are?'

'Where did you get them?'

'There's a dispenser in the toilets.'

'Right-o,' I said. So they were definitely condoms then. I felt a pang. He was just another guy scanning the bar for chicks.

He opened the packet and slid out a cigarette. He pointed it at me.

'Oh, I thought—' A fresh wave of embarrassment. 'No thanks. I've never seen those cigarettes before.'

Foster cocked his ear towards my mouth.

'Are these Lucky Strikes particular to this bar?' I enunciated. 'Is it like a special thing they have?'

He smiled incredulously and said no, they came from the United States. 'But they're available worldwide,' he said.

'Why have I never seen them before then?'

'Search me,' he said.

Donny brought over the beautiful woman he'd been talking to.

'Foster – Erica – this is Angelique.'

'*Enchanté*,' she said, beaming and holding her hand out to me. I clasped it in both my hands and gave it a squeeze. I wondered if she expected me to kiss it.

'Hi,' said Foster, taking a swig of his pint.

'Great set,' said Angelique to Foster.

'Angelique here's a big Saints fan,' said Donny.

'Yeah,' said Angelique, nodding appreciatively at Foster. 'Mean cover.'

Foster said thanks.

'Did you know Donny went on tour with them once?' she asked.

Foster raised his eyebrows at Donny, who was grinning shyly at the floor. 'Is that so? Haven't heard that one, no.'

'I didn't know you were musical,' I said to Donny, but he didn't say anything, maybe because it was a stupid thing to say. Punks rejected the whole notion of musicality.

Angelique drained her glass and set it on the bar beside Foster. 'I have to go to work,' she said. She gave me a hug, then gave Donny a peck on the cheek. For Foster, she rippled her fingers into a wave.

After 1 a.m., they turned the music down so we could hear how loudly we'd been talking to one another. The crowd thinned out. Angelique had left, but Foster kept drinking with us.

A pale, red-headed woman came in wearing a fluffy brown jacket. She darted a beguiling smirk at Foster on her way to the bar, but he didn't smile back. She started talking to Sick.

'Foster here is broken-hearted,' said Donny. 'Aren't you, Foz?'

Foster didn't roll his eyes so much as glance up at the spirits shelf.

'What happened?' I asked Donny.

He nodded over at the woman who'd just arrived. She was laughing and gesticulating at Sick. It looked like they were getting into some sort of friendly argument.

'That woman over there carrying out her ostentatious and frankly *incomprehensible* flirtation with Sick is a cruel person by the name of Phoebe.'

Foster half-laughed. 'She's okay,' he said. 'I mean, she's hard work sometimes, but we're friends.'

'That's how she keeps destroying you,' said Donny. 'You're enslaved.'

Foster gave him a look like that was enough. 'A bit warped, don't you think?'

Donny leaned close to me. 'The other day I had to walk Foster home like a dog. He was on all fours, crying all the way. Phoebe, man.'

'It wasn't Phoebe,' said Foster. 'It was Bridget.'

'It was Bridget, but you were crying about Phoebe.'

We stayed at the Bongo Bar till closing. I was hoping Foster would get so drunk that we'd have to walk him home like a dog, but it didn't come to that. The three of us lived near one another, so we walked home together, stopping round the back of the bakery on the way to pick up hot bread. I didn't know you could do that, but the man with the hairnet who came to the door didn't look surprised to see us, he just asked for exact change, and no problem – a loaf straight out of the oven in a crispy paper bag. We took turns cradling it and tugging away at the steamy stuff as we headed up the hill.

Outside Donny's, we stood around in an awkward

triangle on the footpath. Donny's face looked sallow in the sulphur glow.

'Come in,' said Donny to me, but it was Foster who replied.

'Okay,' he said, glancing my way.

'I need to sleep,' I said.

'You can sleep here,' said Donny.

'No I can't,' I said. I couldn't. His room only had one bed.

Foster was shuffling from foot to foot, face to the moon, still holding the remains of the bread. 'Don't let me—' he said to me. 'You do what you like. I'll walk with you if you want.'

'No, no,' I said. 'Let's go in for a bit. Finish the bread.'

In Donny's room, I sat on a yoga bolster and Foster sat on the upturned milk crate. Donny sat on the bed in full lotus, looking like a swami. Without comment or apparent cause, he pulled his notebook out of his cargo pants pocket and jotted something down. When he'd finished, he threw it on the bed and said to Foster, 'You know she's never heard of John Cale?'

'I have,' I said. 'I mean – I have now.'

The two of them took turns at saying names and feigning consternation when I shook my head.

'Warren Zevon?' said Foster, and then Donny dug out a tape and played 'Werewolves of London'.

I laughed at the lyrics and they laughed at my laughing. It was like they were in on some secret, something beyond being older and knowing old music.

I examined the tape for clues. It had a homemade cover, a photo of Warren Zevon glued over some frenzied wiggly lines. Warren Zevon looked a tiny bit like Donny.

We passed a bottle of Grant's around. After a while, Donny's flatmate knocked on the door. She was wearing nothing but a Pearl Jam T-shirt, squinting through her long limp hair into the light. She asked us to turn it down.

'No taste in music,' said Donny when she was gone.

25

'She might just want to sleep,' said Foster.

'Nah, man, she can't complain. Those two are getting through a tube of KY a night. You should hear the racket.'

Foster said he should probably be getting going.

'Me too,' I said.

'You don't have to leave yet,' said Donny.

Foster cleared his throat loudly as he made his way to the door so I could pretend I didn't hear.

It was only ten minutes up the hill to my place, really, if you power walked, but we were tired and unsteady from all the booze, so we meandered.

The first part of the walk was steep. I listened to Foster's breathing in the dark, out and in, so sure of itself. I wondered what he thought of mine.

'Have you guys known each other long?' he asked when we got to a lesser incline.

'Not long,' I said. 'I mean we kind of met last year, at yoga. Now I'm his German tutor. Not like his proper tutor, but—'

'Is that so?' he said. 'Could you teach me too?'

'Sure,' I said, but I didn't know if he was serious.

At about the second-to-last bend before we got to my house, a lone morepork was calling, probably the same one who used to sing to me when I was pining for Dieter Cohen. He'd have to stop soon. The sky was beginning to lighten.

'So – what do you make of Donny?' Foster asked. He sounded uncertain. I could just make out his expression as he passed under a street lamp, but I couldn't read it.

'He's pretty odd,' I said. 'Sometimes I'm not sure if he's really smart or just completely insane.'

'I know,' he said. 'He reads some pretty interesting books, though. I mean, he's not stupid anyway.'

'I guess,' I said. 'I suppose I don't get his angle. What's

so important that he's always having to take notes in that notebook?'

'Probably nothing he doesn't talk about anyway,' said Foster. 'He doesn't exactly hold back.'

'Yeah, but I still feel like I'm always missing something.' I hoped I hadn't said too much. 'But you like him. You seem like a perceptive guy.'

'Thanks. I don't know about that.'

'Because you've had bad luck with women?' I asked, emboldened by the drink.

He snorted. 'Yeah don't – I mean, take everything Donny says with a grain of salt. He tends to overdramatise.'

I nodded. I wondered if, in Donny's mind, tonight had been a date.

'He's not exactly lacking in intensity,' I said. 'It's like he's missing some of the usual settings.'

'Something like that,' said Foster.

'This is me,' I said, pointing up as we approached the steps to my house.

'That looks like a big flat. How many bedrooms?'

'Oh,' I said. 'It's just me and my parents.'

'Oh shit,' he said, stopping. 'You're really young, aren't you?'

'Not really.'

'Yes you are,' he said. 'Believe me.'

As I was walking up the steps, I heard his voice call out to me to be careful. I looked down. He was standing where I'd left him under a lamp, watching to make sure I didn't stumble on my way up.

4

On my nineteenth birthday, I invited a few people round to my house for drinks. Donny and Paul, a few others from German Club, and Amber and Tanya and Beth. Gary set up a barbecue in the back yard for us and left us to it.

'I bring gifts,' Donny said when I greeted him at the back gate. He kept his hands behind his back and insisted under his breath that we go into my bedroom to open them. When we got there, I sat on the bed and he handed me three parcels wrapped in newspaper and green plastic twine.

He stared while I tore the newspaper, smiling and sucking in his bottom lip.

The first gift was a small tub of Vaseline. 'Thanks,' I said. 'Could be useful.' I guessed he was a man of few means so I should be grateful.

The next parcel had a pungent aroma. It turned out to be some Ayurvedic soap made of something called neem, which is antibacterial but natural, not like the kind that Paul used, which smelled like throat lozenges, medical in a cheap way. I couldn't tell if I liked the smell or not.

'To keep thee clean,' said Donny.

The third gift was a mixtape with 'Goodnight Irene' scrawled in loops on the front, circles superimposed over and over in biro to form the letters so intensely that the cardboard looked scoured.

'Thanks,' I said, relieved that I could go back to the party. 'Look forward to having a listen.'

'We'll listen together,' he said, eyes wide.

'Maybe.'

Amber was rolling a Port Royal on the porch when I got back. Donny greeted her. '*Guten Abend, mein Fräulein.*' She raised an eyebrow but kept her eyes on the tobacco.

'Amber and I went to school together,' I told Donny. 'We've known each other since we were thirteen.'

'This is pleasing to imagine,' said Donny.

Paul and some other German Club people were sitting on deck chairs eating sausages wrapped in white bread and drinking beer. Tanya and Beth were squished together midway up the back steps, bent over their rum and Cokes. I couldn't decide which group to approach first so I checked the barbecue. A couple of anaemic-looking vegetarian sausages sat on the grill, but the coals were barely warm. 'Anybody know how to light this thing up?' I asked, and Paul bounded over. He said we needed a taper. 'Some newspaper or something?'

'I've got just the thing,' I said. 'I'll be right back.'

'I'll come,' said Paul, and followed me to my bedroom.

'What's the story here?' he said, looking at the shreds of newspaper from Donny's presents.

'It's weird, isn't it? I'm so prepared,' I said. 'Tapers a go-go.'

Donny loomed in the doorway just as Paul was picking up the 'Goodnight Irene' mixtape. He bowed his head in my direction, his crooked frame bending seductively to one side as he pressed an elbow against the doorframe. '*Dankeschön – für die vegetarian – sausages.*'

Paul gave a short sniff and put the tape down. '*Vegetarische Würste.*'

29

Donny got his notebook out of his cargo pants pocket and wrote it down.

'I'm sorry,' I said, though I wasn't sure why. 'We needed a taper.' I held up the piece of newspaper I'd chosen. 'Let's go.'

Paul went out the door and up the stairs ahead of me. Halfway up the stairs I felt Donny's hand nudging at my hip. He took my hand. We walked like that up the stairs and through the kitchen to the back porch, with him clasping my hand behind my back, like a secret I was keeping from myself.

In the end, it was just Donny and Paul and me, sitting on the floor of my bedroom while Paul tried to explain quarks. He drew a diagram in Donny's book and started jabbing at it with his pen.

'You've lost me,' I said, laughing as Donny took the pen off him.

'Too much rum for you, missy,' said Paul.

Donny got busy with something in his notebook, holding it close to his chest.

'Can you believe I'm nineteen?' I asked, resting my head in Paul's lap.

'You don't look a day over five,' said Paul.

'I'm older than you,' I told Paul, who was eighteen for a couple more months. He put one hand on my forehead, sweeping some hair off it, then placed the other hand slowly and deliberately on my belly. It was heavy and warm. I'm on my way, the hand said. I'll be there soon.

Donny stopped scribbling in his book.

'Care to share it with the class?' asked Paul.

'It's for Erica,' Donny said. I looked up at him. He handed me the notebook with a dramatic glare.

He'd drawn a picture of Paul, long and narrow with big eyes of surprise, bubbles coming unbidden from his outstretched hands. Above the cartoon was the caption, *Quarks a-paulling*.

'Right,' said Paul. He started a picture of his own.

'Let me see,' I said. He was drawing a picture of Donny with big eyebrows slanting down towards his nose and steam coming out his ears.

Underneath he wrote, *Herr Donnmeister*.

Finally, Donny left. Paul and I got into our pyjamas and squished into my single bed. I was hoping we could go all the way this time, seeing it was my birthday, but Paul was put off by Alison and Gary being in the next room. He did his best to entertain me through the flannelette.

The next morning, we ate crumpets with golden syrup. When Gary came into the kitchen, he greeted Paul with exaggerated surprise. He liked Paul. So did Spongecake the cat, and she disliked almost everybody.

5

It was getting dark, and my friends and I were in the Botanical Gardens, getting ready to go into town to dance.

Donny had been chucked out of his flat for not paying the rent. He had come home that afternoon to find his stereo, his yoga bolster and a pile of clothes on the porch. So he was kind of down. While my friends were there Donny and I spent some time on the see-saw, but mostly he hung back drinking his extra-strength beer on a bench overlooking the playground where we swung on the swings and drank our booze on the grass.

Paul wasn't in the mood to dance, and they wouldn't have let Donny in, because of his shoes. So the others left without me and Donny came loping down the hill.

Paul suggested we visit the duck pond. We took what remained of our drinks down there and sat on the concrete, watching the ducks zigging and zagging until they flapped out of the water and built pace, scurrying in panicked circles round the edge of the pond and back again.

The drakes ganged up on a single female and chased her until she was tired of being chased and pecked and jumped on and one of them held her down and another one inseminated her.

The successful drake arched his neck and flung open his wings to scare off his helper.

'Now they'll swap places,' Donny said.

It was late when Paul went home. Too late to go back to my house. I'd forgotten my key and I knew Gary and Alison wouldn't take kindly to getting woken by a knock on the door.

I could have slept with Paul in his bed, but I couldn't abandon Donny, and Paul was getting sick of Donny tagging along anyway. 'Too old to be this odd,' he said, like oddity was the sole preserve of us youngsters.

Donny suggested we go to Foster's place, but I wanted to sleep in the Gardens. We lay down in some pine needles near the children's playground. I tried to flatten myself against the hillside, willing my body to conform like plasticine, but there was no way. 'I'm too cold,' I said. 'I hate the wind.' I jammed my palm into the pine needles. Underneath was dry, hard clay. The wind buffeted my hair, sent gusts up my skirt.

Donny sat up. 'Hey, this is nuts. We'll go to Foster's place.'

'I dunno. We just show up on his doorstep at 1 a.m.?'

'Have some moxie, Erica. You wanna sleep, or what?'

I don't remember what happened when we got to Foster's place, but I imagine Foster was still up, drinking whisky in the kitchen with Ben. I can picture them blinking at us from their seats as though they'd been sitting in the dark and we'd just turned on the light.

Their flatmate, Shan, had left, so there was an empty room. It had a mattress in it. And someone must've given us a sheet.

It was dark in that room. I don't think it even had a lightbulb. I felt out of place lying there under a sheet in my clothes with this strange man, more ominous and exposed even than when we tried to sleep in the children's playground.

33

I lay on my side turned away from him, fists clenched, waiting for him to fall asleep so I could relax, but I sensed that his body was awake and watchful, twanging.

The silence broke with Donny's voice saying my name, only it wasn't Donny exactly, or even my name. He was putting on a weird accent, rolling his r's. 'Err-*or*-ica?' he said, like it was a question. He said it again. 'Err-*or*-ica?' Maybe he was trying to be funny, but after the third, fourth and fifth time it wasn't.

Something happened after that and I don't think I slept. I left to go to the bathroom, and I didn't have any clothes on then, just the sheet. Draped over my head like a madonna, like a cartoon ghost.

In the dark I stood at the sink and let the cold tap run and run. My face was hot, but I didn't cup my hands under the flow. I'd lost function. Out of order, out of bounds. Blank took hold and I became mute, even to myself.

A chink of light spilled down the staircase from Foster's attic room. No doors between us, only stairs. I turned the tap off and listened for a sign.

Then, nothing.

Blank until the next bathroom, a long shower at home with Donny's neem soap. I saw a bruise and I vomited, crouching at the drain hole. Watched my puke wash down it bit by bit till it was all gone, all clean.

Something in your ears. Something to do with the heat. That's what Alison said.

6

This erasure is part of the injury. A loss, a lacuna. Evidential tampering.

Part 2

Moving In

7

I would like to say it was just one thing after another, but unfortunately one thing could not be relied upon to follow any other thing. Some things happened concurrently, sideways or back to front.

It all stopped making sense for a while, because sometimes it has to get worse before it can get better. It's like when you're tidying your room and you start by sorting things into piles on the floor until you can't see the floor at all, you can't find through-ways or exit the room, even on tiptoes, and nobody else can join you in there. 'Hello!' calls a family member from the doorway, smiling encouragement, and all you can do is smile and wave, because for the time being, you're marooned.

Sometimes, you get angry because you can't tell which pile is which, and you've forgotten how to read and maybe you don't even recognise your own face in the mirror anymore. You might start kicking whatever's near your feet, to make some space. Or getting down on your knees and shuffling the paper round in circles and flinging pieces out to the far corners of the room.

Or you could just close your eyes and pretend nothing's there. You can disappear for a while, you and your room, and everything in it.

That's what I did most of all. I stopped noticing. Stopped remembering. But I do know some things.

I know that Donny was there. At Gary and Alison's. He stayed on the pull-out divan in the spare room. I slept downstairs in my room most nights, although I wasn't prudish, so I sometimes shared his bed. Not in a sexual way though. He just kept hanging around because he had nowhere to stay. I guess that had something to do with how things went from then on in.

Can I stay at your place?

No. I don't think that's a question he would have asked.

Alison seemed amused by the whole thing. I overheard her talking about it to her friend in the kitchen.

'Boyfriends?'

'At least two. One of them's set himself up in the spare room.'

'How does that work?'

'Goodness knows.'

And they both laughed.

I hardly saw Gary. It was a slow fade, until I barely knew if he was or wasn't in the house. When I walked past him on the stairs he'd say nothing. No nod, no smile, no greeting.

Once he came into the kitchen when Donny and I were eating toast and he said, 'Oh – sorry,' and turned around and closed the door behind him.

Donny was staying in our spare room, but he wasn't my boyfriend. I could tell you that but you wouldn't believe me. Nobody did.

8

Paul made me Earl Grey in china that looked to belong to an elderly lady and told me calmly he'd been thinking.

'Maybe we'd be better just as friends,' he said. He asked me what I thought.

'I think maybe we already are,' I said.

'And I don't want to lose you, as a friend.'

'There's no danger of that.'

He asked me why I kept hanging round with Herr Donnmeister.

I said I didn't know. It was just happening.

'So it's more him hanging around you, than you hanging around him. Is that what you're saying?'

'Where the hell did this tea set come from, Paul?'

'A second-hand shop.'

'Oh, okay. I thought maybe your grandma gave it to you.'

'I like tea. It tastes better from porcelain.'

'Right. Nothing wrong with that.'

'No there's not. So why are you looking at me like that?'

I hesitated. 'Umm, is this your way of telling me something?'

'What do you mean?'

'Like – I dunno. I mean, it's not your typical blokey mug. I mean, even having a saucer . . . '

He shook his head. 'I'm not gay, if that's what you mean. Men are way too unhygienic.'

'Too unhygienic?' I thought about his antibacterial soap and wondered how highly he'd rated me on the hygiene scale. 'That's a weird basis for your attraction to people.'

'Okay. And?'

'Sure. You don't care what people think, and that's cool.'

He put his cup down gently and smiled as if he genuinely didn't. Paul always smiled through everything. And I smiled back. *Happy happy, joy joy.* I didn't feel like smiling at all. Did he?

'How old do you think he is?' he asked.

'He's in his thirties. He told us, remember?'

'Yeah, that's what he implied anyway. But he's talking about all that punk music and being in London and that's got to be the seventies, which puts him well into his forties by now.'

'There was punk music in the eighties.'

'Even if he is thirty-something, which I doubt, that's old enough. He could be someone's dad.'

'Not my dad.'

I could just see his double bed through the gap between the screen and his kitchenette, continental blanket pulled tight and neatly tucked. It was sad to think I wouldn't get another go on it again. Paul was a nice kisser. The first time he kissed me I was lying on his floor with my eyes shut. I'd felt like I was falling through the floor, and I said so. His mouth had a taste of warm luncheon. I'd relished that kiss, had wanted to prolong it. And everything we tried after that was nice too. But now I realised it was meaningless. Nothing meaningful could end with such a mellow conversation.

'So tell me, Erica, do you find him attractive?'

'You've got to be joking.' I had to be on my way, and stood.

'Herr Donnmeister is calling,' he said as we hugged goodbye. 'It's not like that at all.'

I walked home sad. I couldn't cry. My knees were shaking.

I kept my eyes on the asphalt, on the lookout for tar and dog poo. One step after another, something in me was drying out, heating, forming a crust.

9

Donny was matter of fact about the blood. Not embarrassed at all. Made it quite clear he was only doing it for me as a favour, which made it perfect. Because he wasn't doing it for lust. It was a selfless exchange.

That was all there was to it. Squeaking in, a pushpin through a wet balloon. I had no idea how dead it would be in there. Strange. I'd assumed there would be something to discover.

He took my underpants. But he promised to pay me back with a new three-dollar pair, the kind Calliope had worn on their tour of the South Island.

'White cotton ones with flowers like forget-me-nots,' he said.

'Sounds like little girls' undies,' I said, and he just smiled and shook his head.

I gave him my school tie. Or at least, he took it. He found it dangling on the mobile clothes rack in the sun porch after we did the deed. Poked it through the loops on his cargo pants and tied it in a Windsor knot. His pants were too slouchy otherwise. When he did a downward dog you could see the tops of his briefs. They were the kind of men's briefs you get at DEKA, rolled up in rows inside hard plastic packs. Grey marle, bright red. Teal blue. That's what they called the colour of our school skirt, cardies, blazers, but it dignified the colour much too much.

Donny wearing my tie signalled something about his punk sensibility. If I had worn it then, my own actual school tie, it would have marked me out as a freak.

I decided to cut my hair after that. It was getting tangled in the wind. The sharp ends kept getting in my eyes, my mouth, up my nose. I wanted a sleek bob. So I cut it myself. I put newspaper down in front of the mirror in my bedroom and gave it the chop.

It was hard to tell if I was getting it the same on both sides. The hair was curling quickly as it dried. I got Donny to cut the back. I had his word that it was even.

When he was finished, he stretched his jaw over the scruff of my neck and gave it a gummy chomp. It sent a shock through me like a horse bite.

I felt lighter with my hair shorter. Nothing like a bare neck in summertime. Now when the wind got up, my hair didn't annoy me so much. But I was straight and narrow and my footsteps lacked gravity, as though my whole body could get swept away.

10

We hung out with Foster a lot after that. One day we sat in Foster's attic bedroom, just me and Foster and Donny. It must have been morning, because there was sun in the room, and Foster's dormer window faced east.

Donny noticed some CDs on top of a stack by Foster's stereo. 'Big Star, man. You should check these guys out,' he told me. But it was Foster who chose the songs. He was the one making the CD tray swish and click, he was the one with his fingers on the controls.

He played 'September Gurls' and 'Thirteen'. He picked all the romantic ones. For his sake, I pretended not to notice, but I was touched. When he played us 'Kangaroo', I could see he was tearing up at that song. He didn't want me to see that. When he was emotional, he started looking a tiny bit angry.

Another time we sat up late in Foster's kitchen, listening to *OK Computer*. He'd just bought it. He was talking more to Ben about it than to me or Donny. I'd had the CD for several months already and could have told him which songs were good and which ones he could maybe skip. I could have even dubbed it for him.

I sat on Donny's knee, crying and singing along. Foster poured himself another whisky.

I held out my mug. It had an ad for Mallowpuffs on it.

'Foster, you're my Mallowpuff,' I said.

He shook his head.

'I need more, to get me through the rest of this album.'

'I doubt that's necessary,' said Foster.

'I need whisky. Urgently. As an urgent matter. I'm actually Irish.'

'You're Irish enough as it is,' Foster told me.

'Erica, that's not very Irish, is it?' asked Ben.

'My surname, silly. My many Irish forefathers. As far back as Irish people go. Drinking whisky all the way.'

'Now, now, Miss Nolan,' said Donny, putting on a posh voice. 'You're drinking these poor English chaps out of house and home.'

I got up with the intention of helping myself to the bottle Foster so tauntingly withheld, but I only snatched a moment of verticality before a whirling, crumpling sensation sent me staggering to the toilet. I took the empty mug with me as a souvenir.

'Bed time for the little lady,' Donny said when I came back into the kitchen. He hooked his arms through my armpits and pulled me back.

Ben looked at Foster. 'Fuck, man.'

Foster shrugged.

I croaked at Donny as he dragged me into the empty bedroom, 'I don't want to go in here, I don't like this room,' but nobody heard and I passed out too fast to do anything else.

When I woke up, Donny was snoring next to me on the mattress. It was dark. I crept out to the kitchen for some water. My throat was parched, with unexpelled chunks of vomit lodged in it. The TV was on in the next room, mutely advertising a party chat line that somehow allowed you to play pool with strangers over the phone. I went in and lay down on the couch in front of it and thought about *Seinfeld*.

I wanted to be Elaine but I knew I couldn't be Elaine. I was just Kramer's girlfriend, which meant none of this could last longer than a single episode.

I cried for a while and fell asleep. When I woke up it was broad daylight and Foster was holding a toasted croissant in front of my nose.

'Miss Nolan,' he said.

Donny called out from the kitchen, 'Get it down ya!'

I took the plate and stared at it. My head throbbed. I couldn't look at Foster.

'Think you can manage it?' he asked.

Later, we walked up the road to my old primary school for a game of cricket. Foster and Ben had both been in the 1st XI at high school, so they knew how to bat and bowl. Donny and I, on the other hand, had the barest of clues.

Foster put his arms around me to demonstrate how the bat was held. 'Don't grip it,' he said. 'It's not a club.'

'What are you saying? I'm a caveman?'

'Look, let go. Like this. My hand is barely there. Just the lightest touch.'

Ben and Foster took turns bowling at me. They looked pretty good. It takes a manly elegance to bowl well. We didn't have any wickets, because it was a concrete playground, so they'd erected a pile of beer cans, and shouted 'Yesss!' and 'Ouuuut!' whenever they smashed them.

Donny was fielding, doing gyrating boogie woogie movements to try and put the bowlers off, even though technically he was on their team.

Once I hit it pretty far. It wasn't a six, because it hit the ground, but it was far enough.

'Run!' yelled Foster, and I did. It was one thing I could do. I could run pretty fast.

Donny and Ben sprinted after the ball together. Ben was faster but Donny was closer to where I hit, so it was him who grabbed it and hurled it at the cans just as I was putting my bat down at the stick we were using for a crease.

'Out!' yelled Ben and Foster.

'I think we're going to have to have an action replay,' I said, and we did it again in slow motion.

When Alison arrived, Foster took the bat off me like I'd only been holding it for him while he was attending to something important. Ben scratched the back of his neck.

It must've been after Christmas, because Alison was wearing a T-shirt that said 'Santa Claus is not a ROUND this year'. Santa was in the shape of a cube.

I don't know what she'd come to tell me, but after she left Donny said, 'Look out for Alison. She knows if you've been naughty or nice.'

Foster returned our visits sometimes. Once he came round when Donny wasn't there. Gary was home unexpectedly and answered the door. I could hear Foster's voice from upstairs and I had palpitations.

'Is – Erica in?'

I half-hoped Gary would say I was out, but he didn't. He didn't reply to Foster, just turned away and yelled my name up the stairs.

I was meant to be doing the laundry, so I invited Foster into the back yard while I put the washing out.

'How do you do jeans?' I asked. 'Top or bottoms?'

He had to think about it. 'Bottoms,' he decided, smiling and lighting a Lucky Strike. I turned my back as I pegged my jeans up by the cuffs. I didn't want him to see me smiling back.

When that was done, I offered him a cup of Jarrah but he didn't want any.

'Are you sure?' I asked. 'It has cinnamon.'

He shook his head. So I just sat there. My one chance alone with him before it was too late and I sat there watching him smoke. It's not that the words caught in my throat, or that I was too sober or too shy. I didn't know that I had questions then, didn't know there was anything to be said. That's how it would stay between us, my silence at least, and then his.

Foster and Ben got a new flatmate, Trent, a friendly guy about my age to whom I took an instant dislike. He put all his things in Shan's old room – his *Pulp Fiction* poster, his stereo, his bed. It was almost insulting, the way it looked like any ordinary bedroom now, as if it had never been empty.

At first I thought that spelled the end of us crashing at Foster's, but when he and Ben went on tour with Bovine, Donny managed to convince Trent to let us sleep in Foster's attic bedroom.

'Yeah, man,' Donny said. 'He's cool. We sleep over here all the time.'

'Um, I think he left some phone numbers. Maybe I should give him a call?'

'Nah, don't worry about it.'

I liked Foster's room best when Donny wasn't there. I could imagine I was Foster, sitting at his desk, thinking Foster thoughts. His room was very orderly, unlike the rest of the flat. All his CDs and tapes neatly stacked, his books flush on the shelves. When Donny put on a CD or picked up a book I was careful to note where it came from so that later, when he wasn't looking, I could put it back in the same position. I owed Foster that much: it was like he kept his best self up there. Either that or, downstairs, flat politics got in the way.

The day before Foster was due back, Donny left in the morning and I stayed behind and gave the fridge a good clean. I got pretty carried away, was at it for hours. I left a note:

This refrigerator has been soundly spanked.
Erica Nolan must be thanked.

I even washed his bed linen, but their washing machine was terrible. It banged around like it was having the worst tantrum. When I hung it out the bedspread looked a bit strange. It was batik and the dye seemed to have blurred. I thought that was probably just how it looked wet. Maybe it would come right as it dried.

When Foster got back from holiday, he called Donny at my parents' place.

'Donny,' called Gary from the hall. 'Phone for you.'

Donny got off the phone with bad news. Foster said we couldn't hang out at his flat anymore.

'He says you're kind of a handful, Erica.'

We went around to Foster and Ben's the next day to straighten things out, but Foster just stood in the doorway, blocking us. Normally he'd say hello and walk away and we'd follow him into the kitchen. He'd wash a couple of cups for us and put the jug on or whatever, pour us a whisky. That was the friendly Foster, but he didn't exist anymore.

He didn't let us in.

'See ya round,' he said to me in an older brother kind of way. He didn't say goodbye to Donny. Maybe that meant their conversation wasn't over.

'Does this have something to do with his bedspread?' I asked Donny when we were walking back to my house. 'I didn't know it needed special treatment. Who has a special handwash-only bedspread?'

'He'll come round,' said Donny.

It was only then that Alison told me Gary wasn't too keen on having 'strange men' hanging about the house.

'Strange *men*, plural?' I said. 'Trust me, it's just the one now.'

'That's as may be, but anyway. Perhaps it's time you found a place of your own.'

'Go flatting, you mean?'

'Don't you think?'

'Okay,' I said, although actually I thought that was a terrible idea. Nobody would ever accept me as a flatmate. I had a weird boyfriend, and in all respects I was very poorly qualified.

11

It takes a lot to satisfy a man, I learned. You can't just lie back.

'Don't play dead,' Donny told me. 'I'm not into that.'

If I lay still, it reminded him of when he was in the horrible place in Melbourne. (He mostly called it just that, 'the horrible place', although sometimes he called it a jail and sometimes a hospital.) These guys asked Donny to do this girl a favour. She was fat and defective mentally, and she couldn't – or wouldn't – talk. Maybe he felt sorry for her. Because who wants to die a virgin? He was young, so it was easier then, physically, but he regretted it. Sometimes he still had thoughts of himself, jabbing away at this motionless blob in her hospital gown, and it made his desire go away.

He didn't have to agree to do it with her.

And then again, you don't always know ahead of time that something is going to be a huge mistake.

Donny's first time was before I was born, in a caravan on Paekākāriki Beach. Marilyn was from California, a beautiful hippie replete with *Rolling Stone* magazines and Quaaludes. She was a teacher's wife and Donny was a fifteen-year-old boarding school dropout. They must have made a pretty pair. In those days he had golden wavy locks, he said, that Marilyn liked to plait ribbons into. Not long after that, in the horrible place, some guy pulled out his hair by the roots and it was never the same again.

There were children too, in Paekākāriki, piles of them in the caravan together, younger than Donny. 'We should all be that innocent,' he told me. Whatever that meant.

Marilyn taught him the ways. Funny, as a girl, to be taught by a man who was taught by a woman who was probably taught by a man who was probably taught by a woman. Some alternating spiral back through time of hetero initiations. At first, the other person knows more about your body than you do, even though it's the other kind. They already know where everything is and how to get things moving. In a way you're getting taught by ghosts, by some great-great-great-grandmother ghosts. Everyone's in this long chain. Like the pile of kids in the caravan with Donny and Marilyn.

12

I went to one flat interview. At the front door was a girl I knew from school. She was a year ahead of me but she also did art, and we had been billeted together on a trip to Auckland to visit Elam art school and do a tour of the galleries. Even though she was older, it would be fair to say she was more of a loser than I was. Her hair smelled like she didn't use shampoo. But now, when Donny and I showed up at her place, it was as if she didn't even remember me.

Still, I was hopeful. Maybe this was just who she was now. A year at university had turned her into a cool person. Cool people acted aloof as a sign of acceptance. I stopped flat hunting for a week, waiting for her call, but she never rang.

Donny had bad luck too, so we tried the university accommodation service. It turned out they couldn't really help singles.

'It's more designed for married people,' said the woman, frowning at Donny.

'What about if you're engaged?' he asked.

'Are you two engaged?'

He smiled coyly and put his arm round me. 'I'm working on it.'

I knew Donny was bullshitting, because we'd talked about

how dishonest marriage is. People should just be free to love who they love, and be open about it. You shouldn't have to pretend or sneak around because of some contractual obligation.

'There are a couple of one-bedroom places on the board up there,' she said, without lifting her gaze from her computer screen.

'Great,' said Donny, giving me a squeeze as we stood up. 'Let's take a look, honey bun.'

Maybe because I knew he was faking, it didn't feel that weird. It was kind of almost fun. We could be fake flatmates – a fake couple, even. It was so meaningless it was almost subversive.

So we ended up with a flat on Aro Street all to ourselves. The rent was cheap because it was in need of refurbishment. The wallpaper was coming off the wall in the living room, the window in the front door was cracked and missing a piece, and the floors were wonky and carpeted with what used to be multi-coloured stripes.

It was unfurnished, apart from a broken washing machine and a gas oven, so we had a bit of stuff to get before we could move in properly. Alison started setting aside some things for us, and Donny got on the phone to his sister Polly in Palmerston North. She and his other sister and his mother had some things he could take. The only catch was we would have to come and get it.

'Polly says she'd like to meet you. She'll drive us back with the stuff. What d'ya reckon?'

'Okay.'

Donny made a noise that was almost a laugh, somewhere between a gasp and a hoot. 'Nobody's ever met my family before. I mean, it's kind of strange.'

We took the train up on Friday night. Polly met us at the station. She was older than I expected, like someone's mum. It was weird to think she and Donny could actually be related, that she had memories of him as a little kid.

We put our bags in her spare room.

'Our mother's coming round, Plasma,' she said when we assembled in her kitchen.

'Plasma?' I said, but Donny just gave me a blank look like I should get with the programme.

'Our mother?' said Donny. 'I thought she was barely mobile.'

'She's mobile enough. Raewyn will bring her.'

'Oh what joy, all three of you at once.'

Polly shook a jar of biscuits at me. 'Have one, my dear,' she told me gently. 'You're going to need it.'

'Thanks.'

'It's hash,' she said, as I took my first bite.

'Erica doesn't do drugs,' said Donny.

'I suppose we have Nancy Reagan to thank for that. Is that true, darling? You're going out with my brother and you don't do drugs? How do you manage that?'

'I drink a lot.'

Polly laughed. 'Oh, really? Hope I've got enough wine.'

Donny adopted the haughty look he reserved for cir-cumstances such as this. 'So what's for dinner? Apart from hash cookies?'

'Don't joke. Mum had one once. She was fine.'

'You're kidding.'

'Give her a break, she's been knocking back the diazepam since the war. As well she might with that husband.'

Their dad was dead. I hadn't heard much else about him except that he'd drunkenly slammed the door on Donny's pinky when he was five. It remained crooked, however many decades later.

'What about Sister Rae?'

'Sister Rae does not partake. You any good at cooking, Erica?'

'Umm, I did Home Ec in Form One and Two.'

'Oh, good. Should be fairly fresh in your mind, then.'

'*Har de har har har,*' said Donny.

I smiled at her with what I hoped was an aggressive polite-ness. 'I'm happy to help,' I said.

'You know we're both vegetarians, don't you?'

'Plasma, you've been vegetarian for thirty-odd years. He's converted you too, has he?'

'Kind of,' I said. 'I mean I was already—'

Donny interrupted. 'She has a mind of her own you know.'

What had tipped me over into full vegetarianism was Donny's systematic destruction of the ants at Foster's flat. He'd led a whole ant army along a sugar trail to the sink where he'd anni-hilated them with hot water, despite my pleading and crying and screaming at him not to. I hated watching the transition from plucky creatures to inert dots swirling in the whirlpool. Desperate wriggling, then surrender. 'Really, Erica?' he'd said. 'If you're so worried about hurting these mindless insects, you should take a moment to think about those birds and mammals you're so fond of eating.' I'd had to admit, he had a point.

'No thanks, Erica, I don't need any help,' said Polly. 'Perhaps you two would like to go in the garden and pick some flowers for Mother?'

'I'm going to open that wine first,' said Donny.

We were getting boozed on the lawn when a car pulled up.

Raewyn got out first, a thin, unsmiling woman in a white dress. It wasn't all that sunny, but she had black glasses on anyway. She began helping her mother out of the passenger seat.

'Hello, Mother,' said Donny, as an elderly but by no means frail lady elevated herself elegantly into the structural support of her daughter's arms.

Raewyn handed Margaret her stick. It was wooden and knotty, like something that had been in the family for generations.

'Hello, dear,' Margaret said to Donny, giving the stick a gentle flick.

Donny remained in his sideways reclining position, twirling his wine glass. 'We picked you some flowers.'

Margaret stood still for a moment and regarded him impassively. 'Did you now?'

I don't know if it was the wine or the cookie, but I felt quite relaxed after dinner. I sat on the floor with one of Polly's cats and felt a reassuring sense of invisibility, patting him. *It's just you and me, Rusty*, I thought, and looked up to check no one had heard me.

'Just as well you never had any children,' Margaret was saying, looking gravely at her son.

'That we know of,' said Polly quietly.

'All my children. Barren. Aren't you, girls? Defective genes.'

Raewyn winced. 'Mum,' she said. 'Let's just sit for a while.'

'All right then, let's just sit. Wait on, aren't we already just sitting?'

'Would you like a top-up, Mother?' asked Polly, heading for the kitchen.

'No, she wouldn't,' Raewyn called after her.

'Yes, thank you, Pauline.' Margaret looked at me. 'Do you like *children*, Erica?' she asked, as if children were something pervy or absurd.

I tried a smile, knowing yet reassuring, in case I'd misunderstood. It seemed to work because she said, 'No. That's the idea. Jolly nuisance.'

Polly filled Margaret's glass.

'Thank you, darling.'

'Gizz us it,' said Donny, and took a couple of chugs from his replenished glass before refilling it to the brim.

Margaret looked at me again. 'Has she given you one of her special biscuits, dear?'

'Yes,' I said.

'Yes,' she replied. 'I can tell. You're so still. Like Raewyn here in one of her trances.'

'I don't take drugs, Mum.'

'I never said you did, dear.'

'I meditate.'

'Yes you do. The difficulty will be standing up,' she said. 'It's what they call a "body stone". What you need is a nice stick like mine. It's one of those things you can get away with as you age, a stick. It's rather distinguished I think. You couldn't get away with it, dear, you'd look odd.'

'That's probably true.'

'So you're in a new flat now, Mother? Is it to your liking?'

'It is serviceable, thank you, Roger.'

I looked at Donny. Roger?

He gave his mother a pained expression. 'Please don't call me that.'

'I'm sorry. I'm old. I forget these things.'

'My name is Donny.'

She sighed and clasped her knees with a swooping motion, as though committing it to memory. 'Right-o, Donny it is.'

'So you live in what, a granny flat?'

'It's a self-contained unit on Raewyn's property. Does the job. Yes. We keep an eye on each other, don't we, Rae?'

Donny frowned. 'What happened to all my things, Mother? Did you keep those drawings I sent you when I was in that horrible place?'

'You should see all the boxes we've got, isn't that right, Rae? There's no room in the garage yet. Have a look through while you're here, dear, I don't know what's in them.'

'Mother? Remember those drawings?' I wished he would shut up. The need in his eyes was painful.

Margaret looked away. 'Oh dear. That was a long time ago, wasn't it?'

'I have to show you, man,' Donny said, turning to me. 'You will not believe your eyes.' He turned back to Margaret, who was smiling through her frown. 'Remember, Mother? Those psychedelic drawings? You said you wanted to frame them. Remember? You thought they were beautiful.'

'Yes,' she said, her smile contracting. 'Those drawings, yes.' She went quiet after that, like she was remembering something about Donny that only a mother could know.

There was basically nothing in Palmy. Just one deserted, gusty street with empty chippie packets drifting along. Donny and I hung out in the record shop. When we came in, they were playing the Jesus and Mary Chain's 'Her Way of Praying'.

'You must know these guys, right?' he asked me, glancing at the guy behind the counter, who was smiling and nodding at us. 'No? I'd have thought you'd be the right age.'

'Oh, maybe I am,' I said, hoping the record store guy would think I was older than I was. 'I must have missed them.'

We came away with some cheap tapes for my Walkman. Then we went to the liquor store, the only other worthwhile shop in town, and took our spoils to the park in the middle of The Square.

It was a hot day, so Donny took his shirt off and I stripped to my singlet. We lay under a tree sipping our wine, listening to the tapes with one ear each.

It was all perfectly fine until I stood up. Then the park started whirling and the sweet scent of roses turned suddenly necrotic.

'You okay there, Erica?' said Donny, grabbing my arm.

I collapsed into him, but he didn't catch me. I crumpled back onto the grass.

'My ears,' I said. 'It's like they're full of padding. Can you say something? I might be deaf.'

He got me on my feet eventually, and we struggled back to

61

Polly's place at about a fifth our usual pace. I didn't vomit. I was just wobbly and spaced out.

'What happened to you?' Polly asked when she answered the door. I couldn't speak. I focused my energy on holding on to Donny.

'She's got heatstroke or something.'

'Get her naked and then we'll water her,' said Polly.

Polly kept us supplied with wet flannels, but I didn't cool down. I was like that for the rest of the day and all night, a hot log on the pull-out couch, rolling in and out of fever dreams.

Sometimes I forgot where I was. I thought I was at Foster's house. Nice of him to let us stay again. Then I remembered how he'd banned me. *A bit of a handful.* Just because I got drunk and puked. He and Ben were always getting drunk. But that was okay. When *I* got drunk it was unladylike. It was me being a silly girl. And so what if we ruined his stupid bedspread? How is a material object more important than friendship?

See ya round. Round and round. Like a circular saw.

I'd doze again and forget again and parts of my body would expand or disappear.

We'd planned to drive back with Polly the next day, but I wasn't well enough.

'Raewyn can drive you tomorrow,' she said. 'She doesn't work on Mondays.'

Donny wasn't happy.

'Just drive us back now,' he said. 'She'll be fine.'

'Can she stand up?'

'Sure, you can stand up, can't you, Erica?'

He held out his hands to me and I tried, but I had no strength.

'You're going to Raewyn's,' said Polly.

*

Raewyn was a Catholic mystic, Donny explained in the car on the way over. 'That's why she wears white all the time. She spends most of the day walking round her bedroom in figures of eight.'

That was the infinity symbol. It was a form of meditation that you could do on foot.

'She's also somewhat lacking in a sense of humour,' said Polly. 'As you may have noticed the other night. It's the religious thing. Don't worry, it's nothing personal.'

Polly and Raewyn set me up in a pale-blue room downstairs, then disappeared. Donny sat on a cane chair in the corner with a book about tarot. The room was quiet. A white marble Mary statuette prayed over me.

Raewyn was suddenly present in the room again. She cast her wan gaze over my body, then turned to Donny. 'How about euthanasia?'

At least, that's what I thought she said.

She gave Donny something that looked like eye drops because of the squeezy rubber nipple on the lid, but when I offered up my eyes to him, he told me to poke my tongue out instead. It was bitter. I hoped whatever it was would put me to sleep.

'Just had a thought,' said Raewyn, and she disappeared again.

She came back with a bottle of something called Floradix. 'Since you're vegetarian. This one's unopened. I bought it for Mum because I'm pretty sure she's anaemic, but she refuses to try it.'

She handed it to Donny, who unscrewed the cap and handed it to me.

'Get it down ya,' he said.

I hadn't eaten anything since the day before and needed nourishment, so it seemed like a good idea to drink the whole bottle. The trouble was, afterwards, I was faced with an urgent need to empty my bowel.

I felt dizzy when I stood up. Donny steadied me and I managed to get my naked body out the door, but when I tried the handle of the bathroom, it was locked.

The back door was a couple of steps away. I had to sprint outside despite my nakedness and find cover as fast as possible. There was a big pōhutukawa, which I went for first, but as I was about to crouch behind the trunk, I realised I was still in full view of Margaret's granny flat. I then saw my best option was under the stilts of the deck by the upper storey, so I ran up the hillock towards that and just in time, the shit eased out of me in the most luxuriant fashion.

I did what I could with a leaf. As I got out from under the deck, I felt a tingle spread over my scalp and under my eyes. I was about to faint. I gripped onto the chest-high planks of the deck with my hands. There was a white flash. At first I thought it was my brain switching off, but it was something worse: something entering my field of vision, here and now. When I looked up and focused, the muslin-clad figure of Raewyn Ogilvie gazed down at me from behind her French doors.

Surely if we didn't lock eyes, it never happened. I sprinted back to the room. I was a mischievous sprite, not a streaker who just shat. I was sure Raewyn would see me the same way, if she saw me at all. She would get back to her figure eights and erase everything, that's what meditators do, that's why they're so calm. They can wipe the tape, loop by loop, over and over again.

It was a long, silent drive into town the next day. I was in the back slumped sideways against the fridge, which was wrapped up in blankets and protruding in from the boot. This wasn't a very comfortable position, but I wanted to give the impression that I was still sick and possibly delirious.

Raewyn and Donny didn't have much to say to each other. I

wondered if that was normal for them or if she was particularly unimpressed with him right now. Maybe it was my fault.

When we got to our flat, I went and sat in the bedroom on the sponge mattress that Alison had given us and waited while they wheezily offloaded the Kelvinator and a few boxes of kitchen equipment.

'Goodbye, brother,' said Raewyn quietly. 'God bless. Take care of that girl of yours.'

'Yeah, bye, sister Rae.'

The flat was almost silent after that, except Donny was doing yoga, I could tell. I could hear his breathing over the hum of the fridge.

13

We ended up in the queue with Foster's new flatmate, Trent, at the enrolment office. Maybe he couldn't think of anything else to say, or maybe he didn't have many friends, because he invited us both to his moving-in party. He must not have got the memo about me and Donny being in Foster's bad books.

'Be rad if you guys can make it. Bring your mates,' he said, looking more at me than at Donny. He had very short blond hair that he was attempting to form into dreadlocks.

There weren't that many people at Trent's party. Most of the guests seemed to be friends of Foster's or Ben's. Even the elusive Phoebe was there. Maybe Trent had gone through Foster's address book phoning all the crossed-out names. Phoebe introduced herself to me in Foster's kitchen when I came in for a refill. She was confident and fashionably dressed, and no less stunning up close than I'd remembered from my first glimpse of her at the Bongo Bar the previous year.

She told me how highly she thought of Foster. 'And it's so great I get to meet people like you,' she said, squeezing my arm as if to check I was real. 'You're adorable. Any friend of Foster's is a friend of mine.'

'Actually, it was kind of Trent who invited us,' I said. 'Apparently Foster doesn't want to hang out with us anymore.'

She laughed. 'I'm sure he wants you here, Erica. Don't worry about his silly games.'

I also met June, who Donny had told me all about. He'd loved her for years before I came along, but it was not to be. She was tied to Ramon, who Donny said was an evil charlatan.

'Ramon is feeling poorly,' June told Donny when he asked after him.

Phoebe came over waggling a recently dislodged corkscrew. 'Smell it,' she commanded June, who smilingly assented. 'Don't you love a freshly plucked cork?'

'Banrock Station, I presume?' asked June.

'Banrock *Bottom*, you mean,' said Donny, but Phoebe ignored him.

'Where's your glass?' she asked June.

'You realise what that means,' Donny said when Phoebe had pulled June away. 'They're calling it quits, I betcha.'

'Who?'

He was staring off in June's direction and didn't seem to hear my question. 'They've been inseparable for years. She would never have gone out without Ramon when they were really together. He put a spell on her, you know, it was disgusting. Once when I was staying at their place I had to listen to them having sex. It sounded like she was playing a harmonica.'

Foster spent all his time out the back smoking, or up in his room. He didn't speak to me. Twice, when he went past, he pretended not to see me wave.

Then it was our turn. None of my friends from school could make it to the flat-warming. That was probably just as well. They didn't get Donny, which meant they didn't get me. Phoebe and Angelique came though, and a guy called Nick van Steen who lit up a cigarillo shortly after arriving and got to work rifling through Donny's tapes. June came later, without Ramon again. As soon as she arrived, Donny locked her into conversation and they sat side by side at the foot of his desk for the entire party.

After about an hour passing round chips and guac, I had to take my wine into the bedroom for a minute to sit quietly and drink. I was hoping Foster was just late. Although he hadn't talked to us at Trent's party, I'd behaved and Phoebe had approved of me, so maybe we were in with a chance.

There was a knock at the bedroom door. It was Angelique. She sat down on the spongy mattress on the floor with me and smiled. 'You have pretty hair,' she said.

She stroked my hair and told me it was all wonky at the back. I said, 'Oh no!' but she said, 'No, no. It's really cute. All the curls are going in different directions.'

The way Angelique looked at me made me wonder if there was something I didn't know. It was like she thought we shared some secret, something I would understand by virtue of being Donny's girlfriend.

Maybe it was the jar of Vaseline on the floor. I wanted to explain to her it wasn't like that. We didn't have sex, not really. Donny had told me how different it is for men, how their balls go blue. I helped him out as best I could, but the sad fact was, I was defective and couldn't enjoy it.

I'd started to think maybe this was just how it was for us girls. But the way Angelique looked at me made me wonder. Maybe she knew how to enjoy herself. She looked at me so intently, I thought she was going to kiss me, but she didn't.

'Let's go back in,' she said. 'Come and dance with me.'

Paul showed up, to my surprise, while I was dancing with Angelique and Phoebe to 'Suffragette City'. He was holding a Tupperware container and a single bottle of Grolsch.

I introduced him to everybody and he smiled and nodded as he shook their hands. He even exchanged pleasantries with Donny, who was still sitting with June, clutching his copy of *Things Hidden Since the Foundation of the World*.

'Is this *Ziggy Stardust*?' Paul asked when I introduced Angelique and Phoebe, who kept moving to the music. They nodded.

While Paul was in the kitchen pouring his beer into a glass, Phoebe smiled and raised an eyebrow at me. 'Sweet,' she said.

'Yes, he is.' I wanted to explain that he was the one who was really my boyfriend and there had just been a misunderstanding, but it wasn't possible. He was so self-contained, he was practically shrink-wrapped. It was plain there hadn't been any real feeling between us. That smile of his was so infuriatingly oblivious.

'Rock 'n' Roll Suicide' started and I couldn't dance again after that. I kept watching the door, but Foster never came.

14

Settling in was fun. All my childhood I'd played house, showing imaginary friends round my imaginary living room and
introducing my imaginary husband. Now I could do it with
props and a set. *Have a seat. That's our comfiest chair.* We only had
the one armchair, a lichen-green upholstered chair with bendy
wooden legs that Alison had given us. But there were enough
odds and ends for a substitute lounge suite. We had a beanbag,
plus Donny's yoga bolster and a slender camp mattress that I'd
dressed up as a bed under the bay window – 'a day bed', I'd told
Donny, but really it was so visitors could imagine we weren't
a couple, if they preferred. He'd seemed perturbed by that so
I made a point of stretching out on it every day with *Girl with
Curious Hair*, a book I'd borrowed from Foster before he stiffed us.

In the kitchen, we had a drop-sided table with actual kitchen
chairs for my pretend dinner parties. My grandmother sent me
her old smock apron, so I could put that on and pretend to be a
post-war housewife. I did bake, but my scones came out hard,
like Fimo stage props.

Even though Donny was older than me (by a quarter of a century, I found out from his birth certificate), he'd never really done
the living-together thing either, had never even lived solo in fact,

let alone with a girlfriend. He wanted to prove to himself that he could do it. 'I wanna master the practical things of the domestic sphere, man,' he said. At first, this desire of his had been uncontroversial and kind of cute. But there was another layer to it that laced his daily attendance to things pragmatic with an anxious pang. He had something to prove to his father, he said, whose long absence from the land of the living seemingly made no difference to Donny's desire to earn his respect. This same dad who'd only ever sent him away – to boarding school first, and then, when he was expelled, to a home for delinquent youth. Then to the doctors and the hospitals and maybe even prison – the story got muddy from there, but maybe it was never clear to begin with.

So every day Donny tried hard to do something – anything – clear a surface, tidy the essay drafts on his desk. He prided himself on his ability to source food for the household for free, or nearly free. He didn't have to shoplift – he just knew where to go, the right time of the day and what to say. He'd take me to Love Juice just before closing and buy a beetroot and ginger juice for us to share and – *Wow, that salad looks amazing, man!* Next we'd head to Wellspring Health on Cuba Street to check the pie warmer. *Quel dommage, slow day today, huh?* And if we had no luck there we'd go to a Turkish place further up the street where the guy would stuff a kebab full of extra falafel and potato salad and coleslaw till it was big enough for us to share. That was a last resort because it was the most expensive, at five dollars, and that was after the student discount Donny had arranged for us.

But within the home it was trickier. I couldn't hope to compete with his lust for order, and so, although I cooked and cleaned fairly often and once in a while did the laundry (which involved hand-washing things in the bath and tramping with them in a dripping pack to the laundromat), I sometimes left dishes unwashed or neglected to throw things away. Food when it expired, empty wrappers and jars – I just didn't see them. But Donny did, and for him it was a source of constant irritation and dismay. He tried to be nice about it, at first.

Donny had a few boxes he never unpacked. Once, when he was out, I saw some photos of him as a baby, about one year old. A contact sheet with pencil crosses next to most of the pictures. Were they the chosen ones or the discards? In every photo, he looked equally confused and frightened, smiling – if he smiled at all – through pursed lips and a frown. His body was facing the opposite direction from the camera, so his neck was twisted. There was a ball behind him.

I put the pictures back in the book and put the book back in the box and the box back in the closet and another box on top of that. I never looked at it again.

15

I don't know how long it was before Foster agreed to come and visit us. But when we spoke I said, 'We'll have a private flat-warming, just for you.'

'Can I bring anything?' he asked. He was so polite it was almost rude.

'Just yourself,' I said.

He arrived with a bottle of Grant's, which he gave to me.

I thanked him, and gave him the tour.

'Donny's tape collection, my books. Donny's desk. Alison gave us this comfy armchair. It belonged to her friend's great aunt or something. You can sit in it if you like. And in here's the kitchen. Enormous pantry, as you can see.'

'We're thinking of using that as a baby's bedroom,' said Donny.

'This is a fridge from the 1950s.'

'It's not that old,' said Donny.

'Donny's mother gave it to us. Margaret.'

'His mother? I didn't know you had a mother, Donny.'

'Everybody has a mother, Foster,' I said.

Donny started singing the John Lennon song 'Mother'.

Foster gave a frowny sort of smile. I led him into the

bathroom. 'Our bathroom, with fully functional bath, and handy calendar.'

'What's with the ducklings?' Foster asked.

'Aren't they cute?' I said. Margaret had thrown in the duckling calendar as a house-warming gift.

I cooked some pasta and served it with a parsley sauce I made using a tiny blender I found in the boxes from Polly and Raewyn. After that we sat in the living room. Foster and Donny talked about *Infinite Jest* while I got drunk.

'By the guy who wrote *Girl With Curious Hair*, right?' I asked, and Foster nodded.

'I've started it,' he said, 'and I thought of you guys. Donny, you especially. On the subject of addiction. It's – I've never read anything like it.'

'Yeah, man, Peanut was talking about it the other night,' said Donny.

'I guess it's based on personal experience. I mean, I don't know what kind of substances would permit you to write a book like this.' Foster grinned. 'I mean. It's not just long. It's pretty – intense.'

Donny started reminiscing about his own drug habit. 'Do you know Nick van Steen? He did a couple of years of med school. I told him how many benzos I was on at my peak and you could've knocked him flat. Enough to tranquilise several horses, he said.'

'But you quit.'

'Oh man, it was worse than the worst thing you could imagine. Epsom salts, man,' he said. 'Bags and bags of them, so many the water was thick, you know, like the Dead Sea, and I could float. I just lay in the bath at June and Ramon's house for two days straight. My whole body was contracting with pain like you would not believe.' I'd already heard this story before.

It wasn't till I started leaning decoratively on the living-room wall that I got Foster's attention.

'Talk to us, Miss Nolan,' he said.

'Jimmy, is that you?' I said, sliding slowly towards the floor. 'I'm falling down. I cannae help it, Jimmy.'

He put up a front of not finding it funny. That was how he operated, Donny and I agreed, by withholding what we wanted till we begged for it.

'You're dry, man,' Donny said to Foster. 'So fucking laconic it hurts.'

'You're the Laconic Tonic,' I said.

'*Tsch.*' Donny unscrewed the imaginary cap. 'Laconic Tonic. Refreshing, dry and simply ... superior. Best served cold.'

Foster rolled his eyes, but he put up with it.

'Laconic Tonic. Take it from me, I'm a doctor,' said Donny. 'Have you had yours today? Best with lashings of gin.'

I laughed a lot at that, but I laughed at pretty much everything that evening. There was something funny about the two of them together. Foster looked at Donny as if he was improbably stacked, liable to topple over at any moment.

It was me who fell apart. I did it in the most indelicate way possible, on the toilet with my pants down. I thought about lying in the bath instead, but it was too much effort getting in there. It's designed for elegant reclining.

They took ages to find me. I tried calling out but they couldn't hear over the Smog album they were listening to.

Eventually Donny came in. 'Erica, honey patties. What has become of thee?'

'I'm waiting to be rescued,' I said. 'Foster, now's your chance. I've broken down in the bathroom again.'

Donny took the top spot. Foster carried my legs, ignored my undies, ignored everything I was saying. It was so impersonal. He may as well have been wearing rubber gloves.

*

I lay on the sponge mattress on the floor for a couple of hours, regretting my decision to fall apart. It wasn't as if I'd actually passed out – I hadn't even vomited. It was a waste of time lying in this dark room not sleeping. But maybe Foster would pop his head round the door before he left. Maybe he'd bring me in a glass of water, maybe he'd even go down the road to get me a bottle of Lucozade.

He didn't, and even after he left and Donny came in and went to sleep, I couldn't bring myself to keep my eyes shut very long. I was spinning, but not in the way that makes you crash. It was a jittery, sick feeling and, besides that, the room was stifling. I took off my clothes. Even the sheet was too warm on my skin, so I lay there, bare, waiting for sleep.

I heard a rustle in the karamū bushes by the window. Maybe it was Foster with my bottle of Lucozade? I waited for a knock, but it didn't come. I thought I heard a sigh. Then another rustle. Perhaps it was the wind.

I suppose I drifted off. I was back in Foster's bathroom, that first night in his flat. Stooped over the sink in my sheet. *Vitreous china*. Water going down the plug hole. Round and round in a spiral. In the northern hemisphere it goes the other way. Between the poles does it stop spinning? I was on the floor. I couldn't stand up. Foster was at the top of the stairs watching me, I could feel it. I'd wanted him to see.

16

The next months passed quickly. I spent a lot of time in the bath. I went to lectures and handed in all my assignments, but in the same state of mind as when I lay in the bath getting shrivelled: I hardly noticed I was doing it. Luckily my earliest lecture was at noon, so I could set an alarm for ten to twelve and then get my clothes on and sprint up the hill. I was only ever a couple of minutes late.

Nothing much made sense about how I was feeling. Lucky for me, Donny understood what was happening to me better than I could. 'Catatonic', he called it and, sometimes, 'subsumed'. He'd seen it before in other women, like Lynette, who I knew from a photo in his album. The two of them were pointing to a sign that said 'INWARDS GOOD'. You could tell it was the '80s because she was wearing a pastel-blue shell top and had a bowl cut that was sort of whorled at the front. Lynette was a hospital nurse who'd got hold of extra Ativan for Donny when he needed it. Before she'd got subsumed, she'd liked all the things that I didn't like doing, had sought them out, even. So had Jan, after he got off the lorazepam, but she was overweight and kind of mentally inert from heroin. And as for young Calliope – only slightly older than me it turned out, and much more sexually adventurous – who

77

knew what would've happened with her, if she hadn't had to go back to Mother England the previous winter? They'd probably still be together, and I would still have been at home with Alison and Gary pining for Dieter and sitting through long phone calls with Paul. I wasn't at home though, I was in this tiny flat with crooked floors, afflicted by womanly weakness. Donny started calling me 'little mouse', not in a nice way.

'Little mouse,' he said one day, mopping himself off with a tissue, 'why don't you do it because you want to? You always wait for me to give you permission.'

He wasn't giving me permission, as I saw it, just detailed instructions. It was pointless to try to tell him that though. He'd only take it the wrong way. I concentrated on dressing.

'Why don't you ever make the first move?'

'I don't know how,' I said. 'I don't have desires like you.'

'You're like a little girl. When I so much as touch your thigh you giggle. You need to loosen up.'

'I know, I know.'

'Some girls need drugs to relax. I wonder what would be best for you. Maybe psychedelics.'

'I don't know.'

'Massage, maybe? Man, most chicks would kill to have this sort of attention in the sack.'

'I know, I know.' I wished I could be more generous with my body. Like Angelique, who, it had turned out, was a prostitute. A few months earlier, Donny had been walking towards her on Ghuznee Street and she'd flashed him. Splayed the lapels of her long fur coat – 'I'm a hooker!' She worked at a massage parlour called Pharaoh's. She'd offered to do him for free, he said.

Angelique was so gentle and sweet. But as Donny always said, sexuality is surrender, you have to give up all your defences. That's why only truly kind girls were good at it, like the ones in the magazines in Donny's desk drawer. Sex comes from the heart. I was so cerebral that wasn't an option. My shoulders stiffened at that very word, 'surrender', or his other favourite word, 'relent', like my body was determined to do the opposite of whatever he suggested.

Is this surrender? I wondered daily. Maybe the process was about to unfold. I was a mare about to be broken in. After this I'd be trotting along, in control.

17

Donny got an abscess. He was grumpy as anything and wanted me to go out to buy more whisky and I told him I didn't have enough money. He said he'd give me his bank card. He was raking in the dough that week. Foster had loaned him his mountain bike so he could start a new courier job and he'd just got his first pay.

'I don't have fake ID,' I said.

'Who cares? Have some moxie, Erica. Don't go in there all mousey and *uh, Mr Liquor Store Owner, please don't ask me how old I am, I'm just a little girl buying whisky for my Daddy*. If you give them your best Don't Fuck With Me face they won't even blink.'

'I don't have a Don't Fuck With Me face.'

'Erica, I'm in the sixth layer of hell right now. Look at me.'

He was lying on the mattress with his swollen chin cocked at the ceiling. He looked like Marlon Brando in *The Godfather*, only more dishevelled.

'Shouldn't you go to a dentist?'

'I can't afford a frigging dentist. Even the People's Centre want their pound of flesh. I went there in complete agony for my root canal but they want me to pay in instalments, for the rest of my life. It's obscene.'

'What about the hospital, then? I could get some money out on your bank card and we could get a taxi.'

'Oh, so you'll fork out for a taxi but not whisky? Never mind,' he said, rolling over to grab his jeans from the floor. He did a shoulder-stand manoeuvre and swooped to standing. His fly was already done up by the time he was vertical. 'I'll do it myself. I'll bike it. Get my own damn booze.'

He slammed the door on his way out. I waited hours for him to come home, then the phone rang.

'So you're home,' he said flatly. 'I don't have my key.'

He was at A&E. They'd drained the abscess and given him a bunch of antibiotics and pain relief and sent him on his way.

He didn't look as grumpy as I expected when he came in, despite cursing the hospital and everything it stood for.

'How come?' I asked. 'I thought you didn't want to go there.'

'I ran into Angelique,' he said, unable to conceal his glee. 'She packed me into her Ford Escort and lavished me with free liquor into the bargain.' He pulled a paper bag out of his backpack. 'Nearly said no to the codeine,' he said, throwing me a little plastic bottle. 'But you should try it. Maybe what you need is downers, and lots of 'em.'

I didn't know anything about codeine. Donny explained that people take it when they've run out of heroin or whatever, and some people, like June's Ramon, even get hooked. It sounded romantic and edgy but when I tried it that night I felt nothing. He played me the Townes van Zandt song 'Waiting 'round to Die' as I lay on the bed waiting for the downer to take effect and he stood watching, swilling whisky round his gums, gargling along. Townes sang mournfully to codeine, his voice cracking in a half-yodel of pain, as if he were singing to his dead lover. I lay there with my eyes shut, thinking that I knew just what he meant, even though I didn't love codeine or anybody.

81

18

There was one subject at university that I couldn't ghost through with my flimsy consciousness and that was logic. One day I looked at the blackboard and realised I didn't understand any of the signs except the brackets. If I wanted to go further with philosophy, I had to get this stuff into my head.

'Call Foster,' said Donny. And so I did.

It was the first time I'd been to Foster's place without Donny, and I didn't have any alcohol to blame if I did something stupid.

Ben answered the door. He didn't usually say anything, but he said hi today, even smiled. He had a nice smile.

The kitchen was more chaotic than usual. Piles of steaming rice on the table, which Foster and Ben were shunting into tubes of what appeared to be some green-black crêpe paper.

'Hope you like sushi,' said Foster.

'Isn't that like, raw fish?'

'Not today.'

Foster rolled and pressed the tubes into life.

'Use the chef's knife,' said Ben. 'On the bench somewhere.' Ben worked in a kitchen.

Soon we had piles of the seaweed tubes cut up into neat

rounds. The rice was still warm. It reminded me of when my grandmother and I made a chocolate sponge roll, when we got to the part where you roll it up in a tea towel. *Oh little baby, there there, little sponge cake,* she'd said.

'Wait,' Foster said as I started putting a piece in my mouth. 'This is the best bit.' He brandished a green tube like a tube of toothpaste.

'What's that, like avocado purée?' I asked.

'Wait and see,' he said. 'You only want a tiny dab.'

I took a bite. 'Whoa.' Sharp pangs up the nose. No shaking it out, or cooling it down with water. Nothing can extinguish it.

Foster and Ben had a competition for who could eat the biggest squirt. I guess they were getting some sort of high. Thumping the table at each other, tears streaming down their faces, tears from laughing at their pain. In all the nights of drinking with Foster, I'd never seen him fall apart like this. In fact, I'd never seen any man laughing this much before. Girls of course, when we were Giggling Gerties, as Alison liked to call us, but never men.

Eventually we got to what I'd come there for. I was lucky Foster knew this stuff and was good at it. Open brackets, close brackets. A, B. Logic through the wasabi haze.

'It's like algebra's evil twin,' I said. 'It's so abstract.'

'It's not though, that's the thing,' he said, prodding my text-book. 'You can use it to test arguments. You can use it to find out if your argument is valid or sound.'

'What if it's not the sort of argument that can be valid or sound?'

'Is there such an argument?' He asked the question not like a tutor with a model answer in mind, just like he was genuinely interested to know.

'Yes,' I said. 'Of course there is. All the important arguments are like that.' But then I couldn't think of any examples.

I pretended to find logic boring, but that was just an excuse for my failure to apply myself. I was used to being a good student. The truth was, I enjoyed it, especially when Foster was showing me. He was good at explaining things.

Foster waited till he was showing me to the door to tell me the bad news.

'So, um,' he said, scratching his neck, 'I'm going to the U S of A.'

'On a holiday, or?'

'Nah. To live. I'm doing a PhD.' He twisted the knob on the Yale lock and pulled the door open.

'Oh,' I said, swallowing. 'You got in?'

'Yeah. To one programme anyway. It's in upstate New York.'

'So, like, a small town? I mean, maybe you should wait and see who else makes an offer.'

'I want to go there.'

'But you can't leave.' A gust of wind came into the hall.

'Sorry,' he said, about the wind I suppose, and gently pulled the door shut again. 'Why can't I?'

I couldn't think of a reason, and anyway, my throat was clamping. I shook my head. 'You just can't,' I said huskily. 'I don't want you to.'

Foster considered me for a moment with a look of shocked amusement, like I was a pet lemur who'd just spoken for the first time. But his surprise gave way to sadness. 'Well,' he said, 'I'm sorry about that.'

'Congrats,' I managed, before I opened the door myself. I kept my gaze low as I closed it behind me. I pulled my hands up to the side of my head as if to hold my hair down, but really I wanted to muffle my brain.

'Foster's leaving,' I whispered when Donny got home late that evening. I said it too quietly for him to hear over the angry clatter he was making in the kitchen.

'Fuck, Erica,' he said, turning a knob on the stove. 'What did I tell you about leaving the gas on?'

'I didn't.'

'The place reeks of it. Lucky I don't light a match.'

'I didn't mean to.'

'You trying to off yourself or what?'

I really couldn't smell it. I didn't even remember turning it on.

At his goodbye party, Foster got drunker than I did. When he summoned me out the back of his flat, I thought I was going to get a telling off. He was lurching into people. I guess we both were. It was one of those parties where you can only move if someone else moves first, like a tile puzzle that you have to slide through one tile at a time. I'd been paired with Phoebe in the kitchen, who was infinitely preferable to the theatre major who'd pinned me against the wall in the hall. He had only wanted to know how old I was, which seemed to be code for something else. 'No, but how old are you, *really*?' he kept asking with what I'm sure he thought was a seductive smile and I kept repeating the same lie that I was twenty-five, which was Foster's age, until eventually he believed me and lost interest.

It turned out all Foster wanted to do was kiss me, not tell me off. He was too drunk to have any sensible conversation about anything, if he did have something to say.

'You have the reddest lips,' he said. 'You don't wear lipstick, do you?'

'No,' I said. 'Although sometimes I put Vaseline on them and mix in a tiny bit of lipstick. It's not red though. It's kind of mauvey-brown.' I could tell it wasn't the information he was looking for, but I continued anyway. I couldn't stop myself. 'I think I have some kind of viral thing in my lips, they're sore all the time. Or maybe an allergy. That's probably why they look red, because the skin is irritated.'

He frowned. I was 'importuning him with trivia', as Donny would say. But he did ask. I wished I could be as devastating as him and just say nothing. Raise an eyebrow, shake my head. He was always the one with the control. Even now, when he was drunk and saying things I wished he wouldn't.

'I feel like there's this space between us ...' He tried to gather me closer.

I put my arm out, laid my palm on his chest. Donny was in the kitchen. He could come out at any moment. 'Yes,' I said, 'there is a space.'

'But why?' asked Foster. 'Why this space?'

'We need it,' I said, tapping my palm on his chest for emphasis. 'It's like we operate better at a distance.'

'Like a buffer zone.'

'What's a buffer zone?'

He scooped me in by the shoulders, more firmly this time. A dry, fluttery kiss barely met my lips before I veered my face to one side to turn it into a hug. He smooched my cheek wetly on the way past.

It wasn't exactly how I wanted to say goodbye. But then again, if we'd really kissed, I'd have had to have sex with him. And then what? Then he'd be my boyfriend, and I'd be forced to choose between two men, and I'd probably bungle the whole thing and end up alone. Foster was going away and I couldn't follow him, not really. And Donny was complicated enough.

Lucky for me it was Ben, not Donny, who came outside during our drunken embrace. He was just having a smoke. He cast an annoyed glance in our direction and exhaled a long plume skywards before going back inside.

Foster was in the hall already packing when we came round about a week later.

He gave us each a neutral glance, then looked at the boxes with his hands on his hips. 'Thought I'd take the first batch of things to my folks' place this weekend.'

'Is that necessary?' I said. 'Why the haste?'

'Can't wait to leave us, can ya, Foz? Erica here is inconsolable.'

Foster ignored him and went up the stairs to his room with another empty box.

Donny followed him up there. 'You know where my stuff is, man? My boxes?'

'You know where my bike is?' I heard Foster reply.

I was doing a nervous jig in the hall when Ben came out of his room.

'Hi,' he said. 'How are things?'

He'd never tried to have a conversation with me before. I was kind of surprised into telling the truth. 'Oh. You know. Not great, to be honest.' I laughed.

He swallowed, dipped his head. 'Yeah?'

'Yeah. Yourself?'

'Umm. Okay, I think. I'm gonna be taking off soon too, so.'

'Oh, cool. Where to?'

'India.'

'Cool. Something to look forward to,' I said, though his news gave me an ominous feeling. Everyone I met from now on was probably going to leave. This was what guys did in their twenties, wasn't it, go somewhere far away backpacking or studying and then they'd get jobs overseas and stay wherever they ended up. That was the brain drain. At least Donny's roaming days were over. He was probably the only one old enough to stay put.

When they came downstairs, Foster looked pissed off, but he didn't say anything. He just dropped his heavy box and stood there with an ominous expression.

Donny didn't say anything either. He stormed past me down the hall. At the door, he said, 'Come on, Erica.'

I looked at Foster, waiting for him to explain what was going on, but he wouldn't look at me. He was too busy glowering at Donny, with his thumbs in the belt loops of his jeans. He kicked an empty box down the hall to Donny.

Donny kicked it back, but it didn't reach Foster. It skidded to a stop halfway.

19

Then he was gone. *I cannae believe it, Jimmy.* We wanted to say goodbye properly, because the party wasn't a proper goodbye.

We made him a mixtape to give him as a goodbye present. Donny made a cover with 'The Laconic Tonic' drawn in letters made out of green bubbles on the front and spine. I decorated the spine and wrote out the playlist. My bum got sore from so long sitting on the floor ejecting tapes and putting in new ones. I needed an opening for every closing, a clash of disharmony to follow every tidy resolve.

When Donny rang Foster's flat, Ben said he'd already moved out. When he rang Foster's folks, he wasn't home. On the day of his departure, we thought about going to the airport, but we couldn't figure out how to get out there. Eventually, we rang Wellington airport, who referred us to Auckland. His flight hadn't boarded yet. Donny said to the lady, 'We need to get an urgent message to Foster Mitchell before he boards. Can you page him over the loudspeaker?' My heart was banging in my head so loud I could hardly hear.

We waited on hold. I suggested we should just leave a message. Then the phone went off mute. 'Hello?'

'Foster my man, it's us!' said Donny.

Silence.

'Foster,' I said. 'Can you hear us?'

With a sweaty finger that nearly skidded off the button, I pressed Play on the tape recorder and held it up to the receiver. The first song on our compilation began to play: Marti Jones's 'Follow You All Over the World'.

Donny grinned at me. 'Fuckin' A, man.' Into the receiver, he announced smoothly, 'This one's goin' out to The Foz, courtesy of our sponsors, Laconic Tonic.'

I leaned over the phone next to Donny. 'You can't leave without saying goodbye!' I said.

'I have a plane to catch.'

Donny held the phone to his mouth. 'We love you, man.'

I pressed my cheek up against Donny's, leaning into the earpiece.

'I thought there was a problem with my ticket,' Foster was saying.

'We'll post you the tape,' I said.

Donny added, 'Email us your address when you find a place over there.'

We could just hear Foster say thanks to the airport lady and then it was dial tone.

Donny and I stared at each other for a moment.

'What a fucking piker,' he said.

I tuned into the Marti Jones song. It hadn't even got to the good bit yet, when Foster would entice Marti to follow him all over the world.

'Wait till he gets this tape,' I said, pressing Stop on the machine.

'He stiffed us,' Donny said.

I ejected the tape and put it back in its case. I stood up, thinking I'd put it somewhere safe while we waited for an address, and then I dropped it. Foster would never write to us, would he?

I tripped and trod on it, cracking the plastic. It looked stupid now.

20

The fights got worse after Foster left. They knocked the stuffing out of me. In the long hours I spent alone in the bath or in bed or sloth-like on the living-room floor, the flat felt so jangled with the echoes of the previous night that it wasn't possible to have coherent thoughts.

Fights about sex felt safe – I could tell Donny I needed space, or that I was just not there yet, and silly me. That bought me time. But some fights came from nowhere. I broke rules I wasn't aware of, like when I snapped the spindle adapter for his old 45s, or rules I didn't understand, like when I used a fork or a plate or a spoon and didn't straight away wash it in the sink. 'Are you trying to destroy me?' was his favourite opener, in between saying my name over and over.

Fighting was tiring. One day I broke the bathroom mirror with my hands, just slapping it. I cut myself picking up the shards. They'd sprayed out from the bathroom all over the kitchen floor and I was late for babysitting. 'Now look what you've done!' Donny said, like he had no part in it.

I didn't know I had it in me to be so violent. I hoped that maybe after the process was over it would subside. Maybe I had a tempo-rary resident of some kind. Perhaps what I needed was an exorcism.

*

We were fighting the day I broke my wrist. Donny wanted my pin number so he could spend what was left of my monthly allowance on beer and write an essay for his cultural studies class refuting the whole idea of cultural studies as a discipline. 'All I want is one crummy Belgian beer, man, so I can write this frigging thing. Do you know how hard it is for me to do this? To sit still for even one second with this grinding pain in my spine? So I can even hear the words in my brain over the typewriter? And you begrudge me that for what? Your uptight puritanical *selfishness*.' He toppled a chair. 'You little *shit*.'

With that, he grabbed me hard by the wrist and threw me to the floor on top of the chair. It didn't hurt at the time. Then he pushed over the heavy armchair with the bendy wooden legs, which I guess disappointed him for its lack of effect, so he stormed into the kitchen and brought back one of the wooden chairs and banged that down on top of my hip. It was only light, so I flung it off easily on my way back up, but then he threw himself down on me again and we were caged in by chairs in some sort of weird wrestling ring and he was grabbing my wrists again and slamming me against the floor.

Afterwards I lay on the floor for a long time while Donny paced around the flat. When I heard him go into the toilet, I got up and put my sneakers on as quickly and quietly as I could and crept out the door. Foster's bike was leaning against the wall. Donny had dubbed me on it many times but I'd never ridden it myself. *You've got to have more moxie, man*, Donny was always saying. I'd show him. I picked up the bike and carried it down the steps. I could just get over the top bar when I stood over it on the footpath. I didn't know how to mount it like Donny did, swinging his leg round from one side, so I pushed off from my standing straddle and wobbled into motion, slowly increasing my speed as I adjusted the gears – *cachung* – and headed round the corner for a ride up Holloway Road. I was an escapee, escaping into the body of a competent, unafraid person, filling my lungs with the damp leaf litter smell of the street as the cottages sped past.

I turned round where the street turned into a walking path. I'd been down it a few times with Tanya and the gang, for picnics. I didn't feel like going there today. I just wanted to coast down the road and ride back up it again, to go back and forth in loops forever, but when a car lurched out from behind a corner, I'd managed to gather enough speed that I went right over the handlebars. The driver wound down her window and asked if I was all right. I dusted my jeans off shakily. I didn't have to pretend much when I said, 'I'm okay.' I almost believed it.

I still almost believed it when I came home to no Donny and a locked door and no key under the step. Fine. I just had to pull the louvres out of the kitchen window and clamber in, but my arm had started burning by then. I thought the pain would stop after a while if I ignored it, but it didn't.

My arm was too hot for the bath.

I lay on the bed as the light slowly faded, wondering if I was going to sleep that night. When I heard the door open, I got up and stood in the doorway to the living room, blinking. He didn't look at me, just pulled off his sweatshirt and without a word turned around and placed his hands on the floor. With a slight grunt, he kicked his legs up into a handstand. He stayed like that for a long time, then, slowly and composedly, dismounted and stood in *tadasana*, eyes closed and breathing long audible lung-fuls of *ujjayi* breath as the blood drained from his face. I turned away to get myself a glass of water and when I looked back he'd descended into a downward dog.

Then I noticed the scratch marks on his back, four red parallel lines angled either side of his ribs like warpaint.

93

'You have some really big scratches on your back,' I said.
He remained silent.

The pain kept me awake in the night. I waited till the early morn-ing, when Donny opened his eyes.
'I think I've broken something.'
'Call your dad,' he said, and went back to sleep.
He didn't even get out of bed when Gary came to take me to the hospital. I guess he tended to avoid Gary. But if we'd been on better terms, he might have made more of an effort.

Maybe it was around then we had the intruder. I was playing Sinéad O'Connor really loudly in the living room when the intruder made a huge basso *galumph* that could only be a tall, thickset man jumping from a window ledge onto a toilet and into the bath. I heard it over 'Jump in the River' at full volume, two rooms away. It was impossible to miss or deny it was happening, so there was nothing for it except to go and talk to him.
'Ex-cuse me!' I said in the sort of tone a less polite person would say *What the fuck are you doing?*
The man was so tall, his stoop was just shy of a stagger, as if even standing up was hard work. His greasy curls bobbed over his eyes as he spoke. 'Oh, is this two-oh-nine?'
I said, 'No. That's not us.' I didn't tell him what number it actu-ally was, because I was thinking of the rule the self-defence teacher taught us at school about not telling people your phone number when you get a 'wrong number' call, in case they ring it again. Only I realised afterwards that didn't quite make sense for an address.
Even though he was this gigantic man and I was a skinny girl with a cast on her arm, he was the one who was acting shit-scared. I was just angry. He told me in a shaky voice he was looking for someone, and gave me a name. Did I know him? Who knows what kind of an explanation he thought that would be for

climbing in a stranger's bathroom window. Clearly his mind was no less scrambled than mine.

'You'd better go,' I said.

And then I let him out, because there was a door in the bathroom that opened onto the neighbours' steps. It was like a fire exit, although when we did have a fire and the neighbours banged on it, I was lying in the bath, and I didn't think to use it. A guy was yelling, 'Fire! Fire! Your house is on fire!' and, although I didn't really care if that was true, when I finally summoned the energy to get out and dry myself off and put a coat on, the plastic roof on the front porch was already melting, and Donny was already down the street, deep in conversation with a girl outside the video shop.

But I did have the presence of mind to let the intruder out the side door. He left without a fuss. There was an arsonist on the loose, and fires had been popping up all over our valley. For all I knew, he could have been the arsonist. That seemed unlikely though. I don't know what the relative intelligence levels are of arsonists, but he seemed far too stupid.

We got a couple of emails from Foster before the trail went cold. He sent us his address, and we posted him the tape. He wrote that he'd spent the summer (the rest of our winter) 'fighting crime with Lainie'. I didn't know what 'fighting crime' meant, or who this Lainie was. Maybe 'fighting crime' was an ironic term for something wholesome and above board. Equally, it could have been a reference to some movie I hadn't seen – or something to do with Elaine on *Seinfeld*. I quizzed Donny about it but he either didn't know or refused to explain. I came to the reluctant conclusion he must be going out with some girl called Lainie and left it at that.

Another email from Foster recommended a new album he'd been listening to over and over. I listened to it at the record store more than once trying to crack the code, but I never did.

95

21

Donny got in a fight with the dispatcher at his courier company so he went back to odd jobs. He found one gardening for Fiona Patterson, my German Literature lecturer. He knew nothing about gardens and had just abandoned German for French, but she didn't seem to mind. Quite the contrary, in fact.

'She loves me,' he told me when he arrived home after his first day. 'Her husband's old. Probably doesn't give her the attention she requires.'

'That's odd coming from you,' I said. 'She must be at least your age.'

'Age doesn't matter, Erica, it's whether you're alive or dead that matters. Nothing wrong with a mature woman. Just as long as she's alert and fully operational, which sadly is a rare and wondrous thing.'

'I'm hardly that anymore.'

'You're a stone-cold zombie mongoloid.'

'But I'm young.'

'Make the most of it. You could do worse than learn from Ms Patterson. She's read Girard, man. We spent all afternoon talking mimetic desire. I hardly got any digging done. She kept topping up my wine.'

'Her husband owns a wine shop.'

'Do I detect a little jealousy, Miss Nolan?'

'She's my fucking lecturer.'

Despite the fact that she was my lecturer, not his, it was Fiona Patterson Donny went running to after the fight when I broke my wrist. He went purposely to see her in her office the next day and stayed there for hours, he said.

'I told her what you're doing and she understood completely. It's not *acceptable*, Erica,' he said, slapping his hand down on the bench, 'as an adult cohabiting with another adult, to be so defiantly sloppy around the house. You're taking advantage of me. I'm not your fucking dad, you know, and I don't wanna be the one putting the hard word on you all the time. So don't make me. I just need to get my life in order. I was doing so well and you' – he jerked his arms above his head – 'you throw everything into disarray, you wilfully sabotage my peace of mind like a frigging – teenage leprechaun.'

'*I'm* a teenage leprechaun? What are you? A toddler on crack?'

'No. No, man,' he said, shaking his head. 'Don't do this.'

'You're fucking insane!'

'Do *not* call me that.'

'What?'

'Do *not* apply that insulting language to me.'

'What language? Insane? That's nothing. That's barely even an insult.'

A vein the size of an earthworm had appeared on Donny's temple. 'It's insulting to me. I am not insane. I have spent my entire life in a struggle against people who think they know better than I do what I'm going through and because they don't like it that I seem to *know* some things, because I actually give a *shit* about some things they'd sooner ignore, they drug me and get me hooked on shitty drugs and incarcerate me and smear me

97

with their condescending diagnoses and you know what, you're one of them, Erica. How does that feel, to be a frigging bottom feeder? No wonder you're always dragging me down, you're just trying to get me down to your scummy, shitty level.'

I felt dizzy. I considered lying down. At least if I was lying down, he couldn't push me over. But somehow I couldn't move. 'I'm too tired to fight right now.'

'Oh, you're too tired. I see. Miss Nolan's too tired. Poor Miss Nolan, poor little mouse, she's tired out. Well, *fuck*.' He gave me a shove.

Then he went out. He slammed the door. I'm not sure if he came back that night.

After the months of fighting came the freeze. During the freeze we said nothing at all if we could help it. My bones cracked and my neck seized hold of my head so I couldn't tilt or swivel it anymore. I was almost immobilised. I kept facing forwards, hoping for the best.

At university I pretended to read and write and at home I pretended to sleep until I slept.

22

Donny's work for Fiona Patterson got him a recommendation, and he started gardening for her friend, Meg Twizel. Meg was a religious studies lecturer. As it happened, Donny was thinking of ditching cultural studies in favour of religious studies, and Meg encouraged his interest.

Somehow, we ended up invited to Meg's fortieth birthday party at her villa in Highbury. It was fancy dress. We made Donny a wand out of a pencil and some foil and I assembled myself a creamy, crêpey winged costume out of some bunched-up old hippie clothes of Alison's.

I stood under the fairy lights at their bar, helping myself to whatever, pretending not to hear the man standing next to me trying to chat me up. Donny was deep in conversation with Meg, and I had important drinking to do.

I tried to contain my rage at the clueless group gathered around Meg's husband, Steve, who was reading aloud from *Infinite Jest*. I had finished the entire book, unlike Donny or Foster or anyone there, I suspected, not that any of them would've cared to know. No one even bothered to look or shuffle me an opening in their cosy circle.

When I saw Fiona Patterson arriving, I went back to the bar for a top-up.

I woke up on the deck surrounded by busybodies muttering, 'What is it? Is it drugs?'

Meg handed me a glass of water with what I'm sure she intended to be a sympathetic look.

Fiona Patterson was perched near me in a director's chair, keeping Meg company and perhaps feeling some awkward sense of responsibility for me as her student.

'*Guten Abend,*' she said, handing me a pack of tissues with the same poker face she used when handing back our assignments. A look that didn't give away if I'd got an A or a C or an F.

'You really blasted those fuckers,' Donny told me when I woke up the next afternoon. He'd brought me a plastic salad bowl to use as a bucket.

I knew I must've vomited at the party at some point, but apparently it was far worse than my usual little puke in the toilet. I'd chundered like a fire hose all over Meg and Steve's lounge.

They'd had to call the taxi company several times till a driver would take me. The cabbies wouldn't even pull up. Donny and Steve propped me up between them, trying to give the impression I was just giving them a friendly, fully conscious, end-of-the-night squeeze. It must've looked a bit like *Weekend at Bernie's*, only the body's a girl in puke-spattered broderie anglaise and fairy wings.

During my blackout, I'd bitten Donny on the arm repeatedly, and screamed at him and Fiona and Meg.

'What was I screaming?' I asked Donny between fresh pukes.

'It was pretty bad, Errorica.'

'Like what?'

'Man. I don't know. *Fuck off, you fucking cunts,* that sort of thing.'

100

'How could I have done that if I was unconscious?'

'You weren't unconscious,' said Donny. 'You were wigging out.'

He was being straight with me for once, I could tell. There are some things your mind just doesn't let you remember.

23

That was the end of my German major. I didn't pull out of Fiona's literature class officially, I just stopped turning up. After that I could concentrate on philosophy. German was a pointless subject anyway. I'd outgrown it.

On my twentieth birthday, Donny took me to the Bongo Bar. Sick asked me how old I was turning. I said, 'Twenty,' and hoped he'd take a joke, because I'd been telling him I was twenty-three for almost a year. But he looked disappointed. 'I could have lost my job.'

I'd imagined he was being nice and letting us in anyway. It was a strange thing, deceiving people. It wasn't a power I thought I had.

At my party, Phoebe and I danced to James Brown till four in the morning. 'Get Up', in particular, we rewound the tape several times to repeat.

My period was maybe a couple of weeks overdue, which was time for a test, Phoebe said. I promised her I'd go to Student Health next week. She said she'd had an abortion and it was fine, you just tell them you're crazy and they suck it right out of you like a vacuum cleaner. Maybe it would be no big deal if you were someone like Phoebe. She was wise and didn't have any regrets. Dancing with her made me feel like I could be brazen. Like I could dance till morning and till night came around again even though my legs were wobbly at three.

'Let's hit it and quit!' yelled Phoebe, shaking her money maker.

'Go ahead!' I replied.

The music teased us with repetition, finishing as if it meant to continue, as if it never really had to end.

After my birthday, I didn't feel older. I felt like I was getting younger all the time.

Donny rang Polly.

'We have *not* been at it like rabbits,' I heard him say. I could tell he wanted it to come across like he was only pretending to be offended for reasons of romantic delicacy. The truth was we hadn't been at it like rabbits or even ordinary humans. Donny only seemed to want things I was reluctant to give, and I only willingly offered the standard fare that made him speak ruefully of his 'conjugal duties'.

I'd been on the pill but, what with all the vomiting I'd been doing, there was a risk it wasn't working, so I'd stopped taking it. I didn't want to damage my unborn child, if he or she did show up.

I realised I'd have to leave Donny if I was really pregnant. Then every day would be like those dreams I had about carrying a baby in a shopping bag when I was running late for class. But maybe what I was missing was a narrative not of my own choosing. Maybe what would make sense of my life was if I made a recognisable, forgivable mistake like that. *Oh, I see what you did,* people could say. *You got yourself pregnant.* And from there the choices would be easy. I'd have to move for the sake of the baby. Leave Donny for the sake of the baby.

And all the while another part of me was saying, *Don't be so selfish. You could be having the time of your life right now. In fact, you are. So why aren't you?*

The pee began and I got the tray under me and out again. Of course it splashed my sleeve, which I tried to clean up with soap and water, but then there was nothing to dry it with, so I had to squeeze the soaped water out in the sink and dab it with that horrible crisp toilet tissue that seems to actually repel moisture.

'Would you like to watch?' the nurse asked.

I said yes. I didn't know what the other option was. So we huddled over the pottle, watching her gloved-up hand dip a piece of paper in my pee. She smiled inanely as if it was all going to be okay.

'And what are you hoping for?' she asked, still smiling. She had a lot of nerve.

'I can't say I'm hoping for anything.'

The paper strip took a long time to do anything.

'And ... it's a negative.'

'Oh,' I said. 'That's good.' But my eyes stung with tears.

I couldn't remember what I'd been feeling or expecting to feel. All I knew was that this moment was real, and everything else was something that had happened in my imagination a long time ago.

'What happened to my period, if I'm not pregnant?'

'Often it's stress – maybe you have a big test or assignment coming up or something like that?'

This was the only big test I'd worried about for weeks, and I'd failed it.

Finally, it arrived, the dull, metallic ache. A heavy one. I wondered if this was what a miscarriage would be like. It was like I was excreting redundant organs.

When I told Donny my news, he was on the beanbag reading *Things Hidden Since the Foundation of the World*. He barely looked at me. Just nodded.

'Aren't you pleased?' I asked. 'Weren't you worried I might be pregnant?'

I couldn't tell if he was pretending to be engrossed in the book, or really was, but he didn't answer. I carried on anyway. 'I was worried it could have been a false negative. You know, the test. I took it kind of early.' My voice got high. 'But it was a true negative.'

He looked up slowly, like it was a huge feat of will to even respond. 'Yeah.'

I realised I'd been crazy to worry about something so mundane. What was wrong with me? Maybe I wanted Donny to be relieved for me. Maybe I'd been wondering what kind of genetic cocktail Donny and I might mix up so much that I'd started to believe in this baby I wasn't going to have. I'd been imagining cradling baby Donny from the photos, with his chubby, doubtful smile. But now I was looking at forty-five-year-old Donny, at that tense, crooked face. He'd destroyed baby Donny, and he'd keep on destroying him.

24

I remember one other fight that year. It started in the library. Donny wanted me to liberate a book of Baudelaire poems.

'All you have to do is throw it out the window. I'll catch it.'

I said there was no way in hell.

He shoved me up against a shelf of Jean-Paul Sartre. 'You wanna destroy me? Pent-up spiteful little mouse.'

'Fuck you, you fucking mental case,' I said, shoving him back, and ran down several flights of stairs to the issues desk, where there was a queue.

He loomed up beside me with the book still in his hand. I snatched a glimpse of his expression. He was glowering, but not about to cause another scene.

'I'm *not* getting that book out for you,' I said under my breath, staring ahead at the clock. Seconds jolted past.

He said nothing.

'Roger!' An old guy with a well-trimmed beard waved sweetly at Donny as he entered the library. His probation officer, I found out later.

'Uh, hello, Pat,' said Donny, suddenly shyly polite.

'How lovely to see you here. Long time. What's that you've got there? Studying French?'

'Yes. Pat, this is Erica,' he said. 'My girlfriend.'

A glimmer of doubt crossed Pat's face just for a moment before he smiled and shook my hand. Maybe he wasn't as open-minded as he looked.

'Lovely to meet you, Erica,' he said.

It was my turn in the queue. As I went up to the desk, Donny put his hand up to wave goodbye to Pat. He backed out with his hand up waving the Baudelaire right above the scanners. You had to hand it to him. His execution was seamless.

He was waiting for me at the top of the quad when I came out. I pretended not to see him and walked off. That was what enraged him, had him scurrying up behind me and grabbing me by the shoulders and demanding to know where I thought I was going.

I was tired of having to stay in control, of being the one who didn't lose the plot, who didn't embarrass us, who dusted herself off and smiled cringingly at everyone, apologising as she did so. 'Why don't ya go fuck with someone else's head for a change,' I shouted, waving my arms around in my best Donny impersonation. 'Find some new girl to play mind games with, you Charles Manson fucking freakazoid!'

He was giving me the stunned baby look the whole time. 'Erica, Erica, what is wrong with you? What makes you say such hurtful words? You're hysterical. Look at you. You're out of your mind. Stop it. Pull yourself together. Stop!'

With that, he hit me on the side of the head with the Baudelaire. It was a heavy book. My skull stung. It felt like my brain was evaporating.

That's when I slapped him on the face.

Some guy with dreadlocks and baggy shorts stopped playing hacky sack with himself and called out, 'You okay?' I wasn't sure if he was talking to me or Donny.

'No,' I yelled back in a deeper voice than usual, stiffening my stance into an A-frame.

The guy looked scared. I wondered what he would have done if I'd started screaming.

'Yeah, we're fine,' I said, waving dismissively, and he threw the bean-filled sack at his foot.

All I did was slap him. His shock, not mine, but off I went to the counsellor for an emergency appointment.

'But you aren't in any danger right now?' she kept asking in different ways. She had a kind face, grey close-cropped hair. Probably would've looked cute when she was my age. Like the girl in *Breathless*. She tilted her head thoughtfully, glancing surreptitiously at the clock. 'He hasn't threatened to kill you? He hasn't threatened to take his own life?'

No, no and no. I stared at the jumbo box of tissues on the table between us. What was the big deal, really? I was a time waster.

Of course Donny had refused to come with me, like he did every time. He sort of promised once that he'd make his own appointment. He'd been telling me he could hardly remember anything from his childhood, about his dad. 'Sometimes when we're fighting I feel that person taking up residence in me,' he'd said. 'I hear an alien voice. His voice inside mine.'

I'd asked him if he thought there might have been more to it. Maybe there was sexual abuse?

'Maybe.' He'd nodded slowly.

'So that's something you could talk about in counselling,' I'd said hopefully. At least if my counsellor got to meet him she'd see what I meant, that this was no ordinary man you have a falling out with in public.

'But how can you talk about something you don't remember?' he'd asked.

It was a fair question.

Part 3

Breaking Up

25

My new flat was working out surprisingly well. I'd already had
some interesting chats with Darren. We sat by the TV till about
3 a.m. one night talking about unrequited love. I told him about
Dieter Cohen and he could sympathise. There was a girl he met
in first year. She was too cryptically sad for them to get together,
but then not long after she started going out with his best friend.

Bronwyn, in the room upstairs next to mine, I hardly saw.
She looked like the brunette Barbie alternative I used to have,
sophisticated, cosmopolitan, like she belonged at a cocktail party
in Manhattan. When we did talk once, she was kind. She said
her boyfriend was in the military and was currently stationed in
Bosnia. She spent most weekends at home in Napier.

Carl was my favourite. He was elusive though – he had a
friend, Ramesh, who came round often but hardly ever hung out
with the rest of us. They'd go out to Carl's 'office', as he called
his studio by the laundry, and we wouldn't see them again for
the night.

One day, Carl stopped me in the kitchen and said, 'Have you
ever thought about cutting your hair?' He pulled my hair back,
then positioned some sharp ends in downward swoops on my
forehead for a fringe.

'I did cut it, the summer before last. Kind of a bob. I've let it grow since then.'

'I like it short like this, with a fringe. Eric. Can I call you Eric?'

'Sure.'

'Eric, you'd make a cute boy. Look,' he said, looking down and lowering his voice because Darren was in the living room, 'I'm getting a semi.' I could just see the shape of his dick through his batik pants. 'Just so you know, I have my own shower out there, next to my office. It's a great shower. Any time you want to join me, just say the word.'

I wasn't sure how seriously to take his invitation. Carl had a way of seeming to be so flirtatious it didn't really mean anything.

That wasn't the only proposition I got in those first few weeks. Bronwyn had to move home to look after her mother and we had to find a new flatmate. One guy we'd agreed was a Maybe rang back the next night.

'Erica,' Carl yelled up to me, 'it's for you.'

He held his hand over the receiver and said in a dramatic whisper, 'He's asking if you're single and I said I don't know.'

'Tell him I'm not,' I said.

'Tell him yourself,' he said and handed it to me.

'Hi, Erica? We met last night. I'm the guy with the sound system that may or may not be compatible with your TV.'

I got off the phone as fast as I could. Told the guy I was flattered, but this wasn't really a good time right now.

'He must have been getting confused with Bronwyn,' I said to Carl.

'No, he asked to talk to the girl with the Yo La Tengo T-shirt.'

'But there has to have been some mistake. He's a graphic designer!' I started to laugh, which set Carl off too. He grabbed my shoulders, staring into my eyes and shaking his head like he didn't understand. 'You loony! What's so strange about a graphic designer wanting to go out with you?'

112

I couldn't explain. I was in hysterics. I nearly wet my pants. He didn't know about my boyfriend.

Amber invited me to a party at her new flat. None of our other school friends were there. I didn't know why she had invited me. We hadn't really hung out since before I moved out of Alison and Gary's place the previous summer. Things had changed for her. She was in a relationship with her new flatmate, only it was 'unofficial', she said.

'Yeah, I mean, join the club,' I said, but couldn't think of anything to back that up. There were the early days of my first real relationship and the tail end of whatever it was I'd had with Paul, but I realised I didn't know how to describe any of that.

'What happened to Donny?' Amber asked. His name gave me a start.

'We're kind of on a break right now,' I said.

'What, like Ross and Rachel on *Friends*?'

'Um, it feels a little more life and death than that, you know?' I said, pretty certain she wouldn't understand. 'If I can't sort this out, then I'm stuck in this feeble unreality and I might as well not exist. It's hard to explain.'

'Oh, wow,' she said, blankly patting the pockets of a nearby bush jacket. She pulled it off the hook and put it on. 'I'm going out for a smoke.'

It was a relief to be left alone. I wandered into the living room, where a few people were doing lines on a mirror on the floor. Amber's unofficial boyfriend offered me something pink in a tube. I shook my head. It was difficult to interact, like trying to use a mouse to draw my name on a computer screen. I was all jerky and pixelated.

I found myself a seat on a moon hopper at the back of the room. I tried to keep very still, but before long I was approached by an older guy who looked a bit gothic. His name was Zoltan.

113

'I don't really fit in here, either,' he said. 'I just get a lot of stuff on prescription that I don't really need, so. You want anything?'

'Not just now.'

'You don't look like you're having a good time. Are you sure you don't want something?'

I tried to laugh but it came out weird, like a choking sound.

'Hey, don't worry. I'm on the methadone programme,' he said. 'I get it. No pressure. Do you want to get out of here?'

He walked me all the way home. It took over an hour and he didn't even live near me. 'It's not safe for a girl like you,' he said. 'I wish that wasn't true, but it is.'

I told him I wasn't afraid. I appreciated his concern. 'It's good to have company, anyway.'

As we walked, Zoltan told me about his life, how he was managing bands and learning some kind of occult martial art. He got all of his clothes out of charity bins. I kept waiting for him to start probing me about my sex life or hinting that we were destined for each other, but he didn't. He was touchingly courteous and self-contained.

When Zoltan said goodbye outside my flat, I felt sad. It had been a comfort walking home with someone unfathomably weird, just letting him talk. I'd felt strangely at home.

26

I suppose what the counsellor told me had had some effect, though it had seemed ludicrous at the time. 'This is a form of destructive relationship,' she'd said, and, 'This is an All Or Nothing Man.' That had cracked me up. She was clearly picturing someone completely unlike Donny. All Or Nothing Man was a soap-opera actor in a baggy suit. You could tell he was consumed by passion because his tie was loose and his collar unbuttoned and he'd forgotten to gel his hair that day. But who could ever imagine a Donny?

Still, it had occurred to me that Donny and I could benefit from some time apart. It was all about Space, a word I'd perhaps acquired from Oprah Winfrey, Donny suggested. Space was the feebleness of feminine neurosis exploited as something motivational and commercially viable. Space was the kind of simple abstraction I could believe in. Only when I'd found Space could the two of us be fully distinct from each other. Then surely my desire for Donny would finally manifest itself, unmediated by my repressive impulses.

Despite the foolishness of Space as a concept, Donny had agreed the shackles of domesticity were dragging us down. If we were free agents, there would be no need to chastise me for neglecting my duties around the flat. And instead of fighting all the time, maybe finally we'd get to meet as sexual subjects. 'Erica Error,' he'd said, sipping imperiously on a Belgian beer as I separated our books into banana boxes. 'Erica Errorica, will Space become thee? Wilt thou become Erica Erotica?'

'Who knows,' I'd said.

'Or are you Miss Moneypenny, languishing in possibility? Maybe you wanna keep me at bay, like our old friend Foster, Emperor of Laconia. Desire, man. It's a mirage. Like *différance*' – he arced out an arm to demonstrate – 'always deferred, always out of reach.'

I'd said he was probably right and carried on tessellating books.

'Come on, Erica. Have some frigging spunk. The little mouse is gone, man.'

When I was ready to put the lids on my banana boxes, he'd handed me a card that must have slipped down behind his tape collection. A picture of Judee Sill, a junkie singer who sang mournfully of Jesus, the bridegroom of God, the maker of his own cross. 'Take this,' he'd said and slipped it between some philosophy readers in the box I'd just packed.

The counsellor didn't get it, of course, and she hadn't prepared me for anything. Being alone was far worse than living with Donny. I was all smudged, no sense of where I finished and other people began. We hadn't really broken up, but I was trying to believe that we had, so I could force myself into a new, less comfortable mindset. We'd meet again when I was stronger. I owed him that much.

27

Phoebe was doing her makeup and trying to think of ways to transform me. She knew what it was like to be in between men, or in between selves, if that wasn't the same thing. 'When you're single, people can tell. Your aura changes. I can tell you're single already. Fully. It's like when I broke up with Foster, for a long time I didn't have those vibes yet. It took months till I found Andy. I had to get over Foster first, and Sick.'

Sick, the bouncer at the Bongo Bar with the homemade-looking tats and the close-shaved head that emphasised his unnaturally flat-topped skull, had stolen Phoebe from Foster four years before. It was hard to believe. Phoebe was nothing like anyone you'd think would hang out with such a person.

She stood in front of the mirror, red hair glistening over her black push-up bra, pinching bits of non-existent flesh below her bra line. 'See?' she said. 'Sagging. Even with this heavy uphol-stery. There's already some sag.'

'There's no sag.' Maybe Phoebe had no idea how attractive she was, or how inadequate I felt in comparison.

She started tugging at the flesh under her chin. 'And this,' she said. 'I'm getting wattles already. For Christ's sake, I'm twenty-seven. This isn't fair. You see?' she said, picking up her glass of Merlot and pointing it at me. 'You're how old?'

'Twenty.'

'Twenty. You probably have way better genes than I do. I seem to be cursed with old crone genes. I have really thin dry skin and it wrinkles easily. So I'm probably going to be looking like a pile of crêpe paper by the time I'm thirty. I don't have much time left.'

I tried to object, but she shook her head and kept talking.

'Look at you. If I was a guy I'd jump your bones. Honestly. Make the most of it.'

Phoebe went into her wardrobe and presented me with a diaphanous red top and the shortest shorts I had ever seen. 'Hot pants, baby,' she said. 'You could totally pull it off. Me, I put red anywhere near my face I look like a car crash. I don't know what I was thinking with that top.'

To appease her, I made a show of trying the top on. I knew there was no way I could fit into the hot pants, and just as well.

'Oh, and you don't shave, I see,' said Phoebe. 'I guess that fits with the whole Earth Mother type of vibe. Some guys like that sort of thing. You just need to make sure your clothes signal it so they know up front.'

'It's not like I'm advertising for anything,' I said.

'Like hell you're not. You're advertising for sex.'

'Like a prostitute?'

'No, like a human fucking being. We're all doing it, all the time. Even Donny, probably. Although I guess the attraction with him is intellectual.'

'I don't know.'

'You don't know? You ought to know what attracted you. I think I'm going to have to pencil in my eyebrows. I look like an albino right now.'

'You do not.'

'Don't humour me. You don't know what it's like. You can get away with the natural look. I literally have to paint on a face so people can see where everything is. Otherwise guys are like, "Where's your mouth?" They don't know where to aim.'

'I mean I guess I don't even know if I want to have sex with anyone ever again.'

'You weren't attracted to someone like Donny for no reason. It must be because you have that intelligence and you saw that in him. Same thing with Foster. Why didn't you want to have sex with Foster?'

'He didn't want to have sex with me.'

'I know you guys kissed.'

'What? Did he tell you that? He was drunk.'

'Yeah, he was drunk. People lose their inhibitions when they get drunk. He would fully have sex with you.'

I took a slurp of wine and refocused. 'But I don't enjoy sex. It's like a mechanical fault. It's not something I even know how to want.'

'Wait.' She put down her eyeliner and turned to me with her hands on her hips. 'Don't tell me Donny was The One.'

'What do you mean?'

'I mean, your first time?'

'No. I mean, I had a boyfriend before Donny. We didn't have full intercourse, though.'

She raised her eyebrow.

'We liked to do other things,' I added, hoping this would sound worldly rather than pathetic.

'Oh, cool,' she said, but she didn't look convinced. 'Still, that means you've slept with like, one and a half guys. That's not even close to enough sample data to know whether you like sex or not.'

'Do you mind if I have a look in your wardrobe?' Hopefully I could find something a bit more wallflower-ish without her assistance.

'You know what, Erica?' she called in after me. 'I've decided.

119

We're going to the Bongo tonight. My shout. We can hang out. You can find yourself a new man. Maybe old Sick will be there. In any case, we can get trashed.'

As it turned out, we didn't stay long at the Bongo Bar. Sick was there, but he was about to knock off work for the night. He said he was having a few people round to his place if we'd like to join them. Phoebe said we'd meet them there, and ordered us another one for the road.

'Here you go,' she said, coming back to our table with two shots, a plate of lemon wedges and a salt shaker. Maybe she'd ordered fish and chips. 'I need a quick boost before we go. How do I look?'

'Great,' I said. 'Immaculate.' And she did, as always.

'Erica. Immaculate, is that code?'

'What?'

'It's code for old but tidy, isn't it? Like, this 1950s sofa is in immaculate condition.'

'Phoebe. You aren't old. You look—' I searched for the adjective she might be looking for. 'Hot.'

She leaned forwards over the table, fixing her squinting eyes on me with a tight smile. 'Okay, I'll let you get away with it this time, but I have a good bullshit detector, you know. *Salut*,' she said, and – to my surprise – licked the side of her thumb like a cat. I stared as she shook salt on it and licked it again.

'You've had tequila before, right?' She knocked back her shot.

'No.'

She grinned wide and slammed the table. 'Ha! No way.'

Sick lived alone in an old two-storey shop, one of those one-room-wide colonial ones with stairs in the middle. His main living area was on the ground floor where the shop had been. There was practically nothing in the place, like it had only recently been emptied of stock. Just bare wooden floorboards with the essentials of Sick's life sitting on them: some bottles, a pile of records and a record player. The other guests were upstairs – we could hear them clomping around – but Sick didn't call them down. Phoebe and I sat on the only substantial piece of furniture in the room, a couch.

'I hardly ever set this up as a couch,' he said. 'It's usually my bed.'

'You're such a gentleman,' said Phoebe.

Sick went over to his stash of drinks in the corner and held up a big unlabelled bottle of clear liquid. 'This can be either vodka or whisky. Take your pick.'

'Is that like, ethanol, or something?' asked Phoebe.

'It's just alcohol. I make my own spirits.'

'You have a distillery?' I asked.

'No, it's a kitset thing I sent away for. This is the alcohol and you can add flavours.'

Phoebe slipped off her heels, tucked her legs up under her on the couch. 'Will we go blind if we drink this?' She was smiling as if it wasn't a serious concern. It reminded me of my school friend Kathy's fifteenth birthday party when one of the boys brought out a vial of one hundred per cent alcohol and dared the others to drink it. I never knew the outcome because Kathy had switched to a different high school and I never saw those boys again.

'Come on. Would I poison you, Phoebe? I drink it all the time.'

'That's not exactly a ringing endorsement.'

Above us was a clatter like a chair falling over.

'What's going on up there?' I asked. 'Should we be worried?'

He looked at me blankly. 'No. Why should I be worried? As long as they're not damaging anything of mine.'

There was a shriek followed by the scraping of a chair.

'Why aren't they hanging out down here with you?'

'We don't need them. I've got all I need right here. Now, what'll it be, whisky or vodka?'

121

I went for whisky. He poured some of the liquid from the big bottle into a beer handle with a DB logo on it, then unscrewed a cochineal-size bottle and dripped a few drops of that on top.

'I'm going to water it down,' he said, taking it over to the tap. 'Just for you.' When he handed it to me, it was clear, like straight water.

'There's colouring you can add,' he said. 'But I don't see the point.'

'Are you sure this isn't ethanol or something?' I asked.

'Come on, Sick wouldn't give us something that's not okay to drink,' said Phoebe, inspecting her glass.

'That's right,' said Sick. 'I invite you to my house and I serve you booze that I've lovingly crafted. You better fucking well drink it.'

Phoebe took a sip. 'It's okay, actually.'

I slurped a tiny mouthful. It tasted like creaming soda crossed with nail polish remover, but there was a faint waft of something I could tell was meant to be whisky flavouring.

Three people came down the stairs. One was a barfly I recognised from the Bongo Bar. He looked like Eddie Munster. He'd been there every single minute I'd spent in that bar. Next was a woman in dark makeup and a low-cut top, laughing in a way that was oddly disconnected from the barfly, who looked as stiff and morose as usual. I recognised her from the Bongo too.

Then Angelique. She flickered her manicured wave at us on her way down the stairs. Her smile was so vague it was one-size-fits-all, as if I was just an acquaintance, not someone who had invited her to my party, who had danced with her, let her sit on my bed and stroke my hair. Donny had said she'd offered to do him for free. Had he taken her up on that offer? I recalled those scratches that had appeared on his back the night after I broke my wrist. Suddenly I wanted to scratch her all over and tear off her sexually adept lips with my teeth. Instead, I kept still and seized my face into a smile cold enough to match hers.

'Thanks, Sick,' said Angelique, draping her arm around him. 'You okay?' she asked, even though there was nothing about him that suggested otherwise. He nodded.

She looked at me and Phoebe. 'You girls okay?' she asked with a tweak of an eyebrow. *Why would we not be okay, you stupid fucking bitch?*

'Yes, thank you,' I said.

'Sick's plying us with his homemade spirits,' said Phoebe.

'Good luck with that,' said Angelique.

The barfly had gone and the other woman was already at the door. 'Don't do anything we wouldn't do,' she said as they left.

Phoebe put on her fluffy brown coat. 'Don't worry,' she said to Sick, 'I'm not going anywhere. It's just cold in here. You don't have a heater or anything, do you?'

'I've got blankets,' he said, and ran upstairs.

'Isn't he adorable?' whispered Phoebe. 'I'm lucky I've got you here as a chaperone, Erica. Otherwise I might do something I regret.'

'What about Andy?' I asked.

'Andy? Andy's not here.' She hesitated. 'You're right though, of course.'

I was relieved that Phoebe saw me as a restraining influence, because I wasn't sure how I'd respond if either she or Sick made some weird move. It was hard to know what to expect in a situation like this, I was so used to Donny's presence keeping other people's sexual whims in check.

Sick reappeared carrying a duvet and a blanket and plonked them on the floor in front of us. 'Come on,' he said. 'This is only going to work if we pull the couch out into a bed.'

'We can just wrap these round ourselves, can't we?' I said.

'If you get in under them, you can huddle for body warmth. Maybe I can join you later.'

123

So we got up and Sick pulled the couch out for us and he and Phoebe spread out a sheet, then the duvet and then the blanket on top.

'Get in,' he said, and we did. With a serious expression, he went to either corner at the bottom of the mattress and lifted it off the floor and tucked us in. 'Okay. Comfy?'

Phoebe and I nodded.

'Now how about I play some music?' He went over to his records and leafed through them for a few seconds, then pulled out a Hunters and Collectors album and held it up for us to see.

Phoebe gasped. 'He always knows exactly what to play,' she said to me under her breath.

Sick slid the record from its sleeve and put it on the turntable. Very gently, he lowered the needle. He turned to look at Phoebe as the first bars of 'Throw Your Arms Around Me' began. Phoebe stared back, tears welling up in her eyes. Her quirky smile struggled in and out of place.

With a hand on his chest, Sick began to sway gently to the music. He closed his eyes.

28

For the most part, Donny had been patient. I'd hardly seen him. Just a phone call here and there. He'd invited me round to the backpackers' he was parked up at, Windmills. I'd declined, but he was polite enough. Sounded like he was enjoying it there anyway. 'Hanging out with some French cuties,' he'd said. That was fine. He needed Space as much as I did.

It was to be expected that he would try to make contact again at some point. One of us had to. Nothing controversial about that. So I tried to remain calm when I saw the package in the letterbox.

> TO: Erica Error-Erotica Nolan
> Oh where oh where could she beeee?
> Somewhere in SPACE?

I opened it on my way to the bus stop. There was a letter in there, and the new Cat Power album on CD. I didn't read the letter. I didn't trust myself to read it in public. I shoved it all into my backpack and tried to feel optimistic – excited even. No point worrying about it.

I had a lecture that afternoon, 'Radical Politics of the Nineteenth Century'. I took ten pages of notes without hearing a word the guy was saying. I needed a distraction from Angel Face on the other side of the room. I had no idea what his actual name was but his eyes were big and soulful and he moved in this elegant yet ungainly way like a baby giraffe.

I skipped the tute I had afterwards because my brain didn't seem to be fully operational and I couldn't get away with being such a zombie in a small group. There was a girl in that class who thought otherwise though, she was always dozing. Every so often she'd wake up with a start and smile around the room complacently. It appeared she felt confident she was getting away with it. I didn't want to be that person. Or worse, be that person while appearing to be awake and fully alert. If the tutor asked me a question I'd have to pretend to have a coughing fit and leave the room or I'd just spout nonsense.

I decided I'd go to the library and force down some reading instead. I went to the Pepsi machine. A can clunked into the retrieval slot. When I turned round, Angel Face was there.

'Hello,' I said, going bright red as I pulled back the tab on my can.

'Hi,' he said. I expected him to proceed to the machine now I'd got out the way, but he just stood there smiling. He was probably a zealot of some kind.

'You're doing politics, aren't you?' he asked.

'What? Yes. No, philosophy. But it's a double one.'

'A double one?'

'That paper. We do together. I mean it's. You know. It's also a philosophy paper.' Words were getting stuck on the conveyer belt. I wanted to kill myself, swiftly and cleanly.

'Oh yeah, that must be why you're not in any of my other classes.'

'No I'm not. No that must be. You're studying politics?' A craft knife could do it. Or pills would be nice. Cosy, even, like a bedtime drink. *Here's your Ovaltine. Time for sleep now.* Blank.

'Yeah.'

'Yeah. Cool.'

I'd seen him talking to Martin, an artist Carl had met in a postcolonial history class. All I knew about Martin was that he was married, much to Carl's disappointment, to an older woman he'd met in London.

'What are you up to?'

'Nothing. Nothing at all.'

'What are you writing your essay on?'

'No idea. You?'

'Shelley. I kinda like the Romantics. I want to like the anarchists but I dunno.'

'Yeah. Same.' But as soon as I said it I remembered I liked the anarchists better. If Donny had been there, I would've remembered that. Alone, I had no fluency. My brain froze.

'Oh well.'

'Yeah.' I raised my can to him. 'Cheers to that.' I laughed.

He smiled, nodding earnestly as though I'd said something profound. 'I'm a Coke man, myself,' he said.

'Really? How disappointing.' It was. I laughed again. We could disagree on something insignificant at least. 'Well, see ya round.'

He lifted his hand up in a static wave, holding it there awhile, like he was swearing an oath, angel eyes set to stun. I realised later he was almost certainly stoned.

It was starting to get dark as I set off home. It was autumn now. Easter was over. Alison had come round with hot cross buns and chocolate bunnies. 'Come on. You're never too old for chocolate,' she'd said, and hovered. It was only after she was gone I thought of offering her some.

The wind blew leaves and grit in my face. *That's it*, I told the wind. *That's what I deserve. Spray me with dirt.* Some got in my eye and I stopped walking, blinking furiously. Some guy bashed into me running to the bus stop. 'Sorry,' I said. 'I've got something in my eye.' He was probably already out of earshot. Maybe he didn't even notice our collision. It was possible I didn't exist and my body was somehow imaginary.

Angel Face had noticed me. Kyle. He'd piped up. Broached the subjects of fizzy drinks and Romantic poets and whatnot. But I'd fucked that up, like everything else. I was midway through the first semester of my third year and still I couldn't hold down a conversation. Not only that. I'd made a complete dick of myself. No chance in hell he'd bother with me again. No. Interesting guys, guys I liked, would never like me back. They'd notice my social ineptitude. Soon enough, they'd back away. Unless they were suffering from some form of delirium like Donny.

He had such hope, such sweetness in his eyes when I opened the door. His first visit to my new flat. He followed me upstairs all deference and shy smiles. I pointed out what we'd done with the funny water feature on the landing. (We called it a water feature but it was an empty paddling pool, installed in some misguid-edly decadent moment in the seventies no doubt, surrounded as it was by shag-pile carpeting.) Carl and I had put balloons in it in lieu of the bubble bath we felt belonged there.

When we got to my room I pointed out how harmoniously I'd laid out all my things, my black-and-white sketches of hills and pylons and rocks, my books arranged by spine colour and height, my stereo I'd salvaged from Alison and Gary's place with the picture of Judee Sill he'd given me on the wall behind it. 'Hail, Queen Judee,' said Donny, pausing to pay his respects. She looked mournful, I said, but in an intellectual sort of way. It was religious, Donny said. She was taking heroin strictly as a communion thing, in place of red wine.

'Sounds dangerous,' I said.

'She got where she was going,' he replied. 'A level of devotion beyond your imagination.'

'I'm sure. Sounds intense.'

He sighed and sat down on my bed. 'Don't say that like you know.'

'Oh, don't I?'

'You have no fucking clue about intensity.'

'Oh sure, I have no clue. Isn't it your job to teach me intensity, Donny? Am I a terrible student? I thought I was A++?'

It can't have been long after that he started yelling at me. First he threw the Cat Power CD at my face. Then he started swinging at me with his backpack, which was heavy with beer cans. He threw it onto the other side of the room, where it hit the wall and thudded onto my bed. I tried to get past him but he grabbed my wrists and we stood there, twisting and resisting till I went limp and dragged myself to the floor. He didn't let me go.

'You're breaking my wrists, you mental case,' I said.

He dropped me then and I scampered over to my sneakers. I tried to slot my right foot into one.

'Nah, man. Don't be such a child.' He came over and snatched my left shoe. My hands were shaking. 'Where are you gonna *go*?'

'I'm *leaving*,' I said. 'You're making me leave my own house.'

He shook his head derisively. 'Erica. Honestly, Erica, listen to yourself. Do you know how ridiculous you sound? You're hysterical.' He held the sneaker behind his back. I tried to grab it but he held it too high. 'You just need to stop and calm down so you can hear what I'm saying.' With that, he threw it to the other end of the room. It landed on my desk.

He swooped down and grabbed the other shoe off the end of my foot and held it behind him.

'That's *it*,' I said, stomping over to the mobile clothes rack by my desk. My boots were underneath it. If I stood there and distracted him maybe he wouldn't notice till it was too late.

129

'It's over!' I shouted. 'This is fucking *over*, okay? I trusted you, I thought we could be friends. I was wrong. I was *wrong*. You're a *nightmare* and this is never going to stop.'

'*I'm* a nightmare? No.' He covered his eyes and shook his head vigorously. 'No. No. You don't know what fucking nightmares are, man. Do you have any idea of the kind of terror that nearly chokes me and stops my heart *dead* on a frigging *nightly* basis? Can you imagine for one moment the *lengths* I have gone to, to give you *space*? I lie in bed with my hard-on going *septic* trying to think of anything but you. Images don't work for me anymore. I've got half a dozen web pages I've downloaded and printed out at the computer lab. I've got new magazines from Peaches & Cream. I try to look at those succulent arses now, man, I look at the *sweetest* little pink arseholes you could imagine and I go limp. I go limp. I don't sleep. I just *weep*. I weep all night.' He started to cry. 'Is this what you want? Is this what you want, you frigid harpy?'

I bent down and put my boots on as swiftly and inconspicuously as I could, but of course he noticed.

'Nah.' He moved towards me. 'Nah. Don't do this, man. This isn't you. What happened to that sweet girl?'

'Please.'

'See?' He grabbed my shoulders. 'You scowl. You wrinkle that face in disdain. Let it *go*, Erica. *Relent*. When I met you three years ago, you had the sweetest, purest, truest face I'd ever seen. You know?'

'No,' I said. I shook my head. I didn't know. He was nuts. He always had been.

'Yes. You were the tenderest, sweetest gift a man could possibly swoon for. But you *withheld* and *withdrew*. You teased me relentlessly. You may have been on a frigging uptight power trip to the *moon* as far as I could tell, but I waited. I was so patient, man. Most guys would have lost their patience with that act a long time ago. But I knew you had that sweet girl hiding in there somewhere. I let you do your thing. I *waited*. Do you know how hard that is for me?'

'It's only been a few weeks.'

'See? You're so dismissive. You're all stiff and squinty and – forget the boots, man. Nah. Nah. Don't do this.' He snatched at my feet but they were already in. I didn't bother with the laces. I sidestepped Donny and headed to the door.

He ran in front of me and jumped around waving his arms like a netballer in goal defence. I stood very still for a moment, then dodged just quick enough to grab my bag off the hook on the back of the bedroom door and get out and down the stairs.

'You're trying to destroy me!' he shouted after me.

I purposely knocked over a coat rack at the front door as I went past, although he hadn't started down the stairs yet. I caught a glimpse of Carl's and Darren's shocked faces staring out at me from the living room as I slammed the door.

29

I ran down the hill past the Northland shops to the tunnel. My bag bounced reassuringly on my back. Ordinarily, the tunnel freaked me out. I'd imagine myself under the front wheels before a driver had time to see me, before he'd had time to brake. It was only by a series of miracles this hadn't happened yet. Tonight would not be the night though. Tonight the tunnel felt safe, a mossy hidey-hole with an exit. I slowed, balancing my steps deliberately along the narrow footpath, trying to breathe slowly. It hurt. I took air in sharp jags. It was hard to tell if I was inhaling or exhaling or both. I concentrated on walking instead, but it was slow only in relative terms, a slow clip, limbs jerking resistant micro-motions for every swing or stride forwards.

I wondered what Donny was doing, if he was still in my room or on his way. Or if he'd biked home a different route and hadn't bothered to loop round every possibility. Hard to imagine. He must still be in my room. Or in the kitchen, telling Carl his tale of woe. If he went past me on his bike I'd know where he was, for that moment at least. But even if he did go past me I couldn't trust him not to also be there waiting for me when I got back.

Out of the tunnel, I pulled my backpack round to my front, unzipped the smaller pouch. Wallet. Good. Diary, several biros, some chewing gum, a ten-trip bus ticket with no free clips. I shook the bag. No jangle. I shook it again. *Afrumph.* No tinkle of keys.

I opened up the main compartment just in case and felt around, but it was only books and exercise books and yesterday's letter from Donny that I'd grabbed from the box on my way to lectures.

As I neared the next lamp post, I looked at my watch. Not even ten yet. Good. I checked my wallet. Phonecard. Good. I could at least call ahead, but what would I say? *I've been locked out of my flat. I don't seem to have my key to your place, either. All right if I stay the night?*

It wasn't even ten yet, why would I be afraid to wake my flat-mates up? *I tried knocking but nobody's home.* No. It's a Wednesday night. Everyone's home.

I heard a bike go past. It wasn't Donny.

Someone came up behind me running, breathing heavy. I prepared my most hostile Don't Fuck With Me face and turned around. It was a woman in a tracksuit. Before she averted her gaze I could tell she was alarmed. How scary did I actually look? Or did I just look mental?

Even the cars I couldn't trust. He could've got someone to drive him. Every car that went past, I was fully prepared for him to be leaning out the window, shouting obscenities. Stopping, getting out, opening the back door, pulling me in. He'd get Carl to drive him. Carl would be on his side by now, ready to remonstrate with me, his gooey caramel eyes all disappointment – no, disgust.

At the phone box I held the phonecard out in front of me for a while, waiting for a suitable script to emerge. It didn't. I put the card in anyway and hoped, while the phone rang (*proom-poomph, proom-poomph*), the words would just come to me.

'Hello, Gary Nolan speaking.'

'Hello, Gary Nolan.'

'Hello. That'll be Erica, is it?'

'Correct. Um. I'm just on my way there and wanted to let you know.'

133

'Here? Oh, right. Did I forget something?'

'No. It's sort of a spontaneous thing. Is it all right if I stay over tonight? I thought I'd check first.'

'Sure. Everything all right?'

'Yep. Fine. Well – not really. But—' I wanted to reassure him but I had to stop. My voice was quavering.

'What's happened? You haven't hurt yourself, or something?'

'I'm fine,' I said. It was an effort to get the words out. 'It's just, you know. He of whom we do not speak.'

'Oh, God, what's he gone and done?'

'Nothing, really, don't worry. I'll be there soon.'

I hung up. I'd have to explain when I got there.

Gary opened the door and gave me a cautious hug. I glanced into my old bedroom. All the posters had been taken down and the bed and drawers replaced with Alison's flash new desk and chaise longue. It was a kind of reading room she was using for theatre stuff, people from her drama group. She called it her boudoir.

I switched on the light in the spare room when we got upstairs. On the divan was a pile of folded sheets, a continental quilt and a scratchy woollen blanket, neatly folded beside two pillows and a towel.

'Alison's gone to bed,' said Gary, and he offered me a cuppa.

We drank tea in the living room. The TV was on mute, projecting bruises onto Gary's face. I sat in front of the heater with Spongecake, who purred ferociously and submitted her fluffy side for vigorous stroking. After a while, beads of spit formed in the corners of her mouth.

'She obviously remembers me,' I said. 'Didn't run away.'

'Oh she remembers you, all right,' said Gary. 'I'm sure she appreciates the visit.'

Gary had a copy of *Birthday Letters* on the side table by his tea.

'Ted Hughes,' I said, nodding at it. 'Any good?'

'Not bad. Alison gave it to me for my birthday, funnily enough.'

'Odd choice. Doesn't she know what it's about?'

'Don't be silly.'

'Oh no, I know.'

'She knows what I like to read.'

'Bit grim though, isn't it?'

'Life's a bit grim.'

'Yours isn't, though.'

'No.'

'Not Ted Hughes grim anyway.'

'Mmm. Anyway, how are you?'

'Oh, I'm fine.' I'm a terrible liar. I just start laughing. I buried my face in the cat.

'Come on.'

I looked up, laughed straight at his face. I tried to stop it but I couldn't. He was blowing on his tea with this tense, sorrowful expression. 'Sorry. I'm sorry. I'll stop.'

He put his cup back in its saucer and sighed exasperatedly. 'Alison's worried.'

'Not worried enough to sit up, I see.'

'She gave me strict instructions that if there's any problem with Donny hanging around I'm to deposit him at the night shelter.'

'Oh, please. It's not like that,' I said, although I was unnerved by the mention of Donny. 'He hasn't been round here or anything, has he?'

'No. What's he been up to this time?'

'I just needed some space. He was at my house and he wouldn't leave. He wouldn't let me leave, either. But then I got out. So.'

'Where is he?'

'I have no idea.'

'You sure he hasn't followed you?'

'No. He wouldn't come here now. He knows he'd be pushing his luck.'

135

'Good.'

'This is not a Ted Hughes type situation.'

'Good.'

'I'm not Sylvia Plath, either.'

'Didn't think you were.'

We laughed politely. It was good to lighten the mood.

I lay awake for a few hours before I finally got to sleep. It was like old times, listening to the morepork, trying to beat the countdown to the sparrows starting their racket at dawn. *Cheep chip chip chip.* There was a nest in the guttering somewhere, or at least, there had been. It was over a year now I'd been gone, nearly one and a half, in fact. The fledglings of that summer would be fully grown now, with nests elsewhere. That's if Spongecake hadn't eaten them all. Where did she deposit her feathered trophies now I was gone? Surely not in the boudoir. I'd have to ask Gary in the morning.

When I woke up, the house was silent. No sparrows, no Alison, no Gary. I checked my watch. It was nearly midday. Alison had left a note under a box of Honey Puffs in the kitchen:

> *Be sure to snib the door on your way out.*
> *Borrow a coat if you need one. It's meant to rain.*

Under the note was a ten-dollar bill.

I stopped in again on my way back from campus. Alison wasn't home yet. She was late. Gary was about to heat up a shepherd's pie from the freezer, having received explicit instructions from her over the phone. He had them written down on a piece of memo paper.

'You can stay for tea if you want,' he said, glancing anxiously at the memo. 'I can't guarantee you'll want to eat it, but ... '

'No, that's okay,' I said. It was a relief Alison wasn't there, really. I wouldn't have known what to tell her.

'Do you think the oven is hot enough?' Gary asked.

'How long have you had it on?'

'I just turned it on.'

'Probably not yet, then.'

I must have said it more sarcastically than I'd intended because he looked hurt. 'All right, all right. She didn't bloody say, did she?'

'You got a coat?' he called out as I went down the stairs.

'It's not raining,' I said.

'It's meant to.'

I took out the letter from Donny on my walk home, tilted it into the glow of the street lamps. This was how it must be for Alison when she was rehearsing for one of her auditions. I felt the way she looked, frowning at the script like an amnesiac searching for clues.

I read it through twice. On the third read, drops of rain started to pock the paper. I put it back in my bag.

When I got home, Darren peeked out from behind the living-room door. 'Hey,' he said, frowning. 'You okay?'

'Oh. Sorry about the noise last night,' I said. 'My ex was being weird. I hope he didn't cause any trouble after I left?'

'No. Carl went up. He left after that. I wanted to call the police, but Carl wouldn't let me.'

'Oh no, is Carl okay? What did he do?'

'No, Carl's okay, worked his Carl magic, I guess. He went quietly, apparently.'

'Oh, good. Well, thanks, and sorry about that.'

'Don't apologise. Just glad you're all right.'

When I got up to my room I expected to see the Cat Power CD in the middle of the floor. It was, but what I saw first was a bouquet of flowers, big orange ones. Odd move for Donny. Did this mean he'd gone away and come back? Why hadn't Darren said anything?

There was a card inside the paper wrapping. The card had a picture of a cute puppy looking sad. Inside it said, *Erica, Just to say, we hope things get better REAL SOON. Cheers. Darren and Carl.*

I made a small yelp, somewhere between 'oh' and 'ow'. I went to the door to run downstairs and thank Darren but I stopped. I was going to cry. I couldn't run downstairs and thank him blubbing my eyes out. He'd probably think I wanted to sleep with him. Anyway, what was he thinking? What was Carl thinking? What a stupid thing to do, giving me flowers. What a fucking inappropriate move, actually.

The CD was there too. Behind where they'd put the flowers. It was like they'd laid it on top deliberately, like they were placing flowers on a grave. It wasn't even cracked. The shag pile had made sure of that.

I listened to *Moon Pix* then, and cried some more. Carl came in of course, and wanted to counsel me. I thanked him for the flowers.

'It was Darren's idea,' he said. 'He's such a sweetie, he was really worried. I told him, "She'll be fine, our Erica."'

'I am fine.'

'Bit of a heartbreaker, aren't you, m'dear?' He laughed in an embarrassed way, as if it was himself he was talking about.

'Not really.'

'Donny might beg to differ.'

'What did he tell you?'

'Just looked wrecked. In need of some pretty serious healing, that one.'

'Oh, really, you think I don't know that? I don't want to hear it. Please.'

'Sorry.'

'No, I'm sorry.'

'Let's be sorry together. This music is cool. It's very sad.'

'It is.'

'Sad in a mellow, alternative sort of way.'

'You know I want to help him, Carl, truly.'

He nodded.

'I mean, I'd help him if I actually could.'

'What's his sign?'

'His sign? Oh, his star sign. No, I don't know.'

'Let me guess.'

'Okay ...'

He closed his eyes and took in a breath. When he opened his eyes again, the playfulness had gone. 'Never mind, it's better not to discuss it. Trust me. Chaos can be very healing. So can conflict.'

'I want to believe you.'

'That's all you need to do.'

'Hey Carl, you know Martin?'

'Yup.'

'Do you know that guy he hangs round with? Kyle? The guy with long blond hair?'

'Big eyes?'

'Yeah.'

'Pretty cute dude.'

'Yeah.'

'Ooh.'

'You know anything about him?'

'Uh, I don't know. Do I? Maybe. Shit, this music is going to make me cry.'

It was 'Colors and the Kids'.

'Can I dub it off you? I wanna play it for Ramesh. He's coming round actually, I'd better go. I'm meant to be making pad thai.'

I changed my mind about not thanking Darren. I listened to the end of the album and went downstairs to thank him. He wasn't a dick about it.

I got the letter out again after that.

Are you Modest Mouse? Or Cat Power? Are you Cat Power
pretending to be Modest Mouse? Have you played long enough
with your prey? Erica, I bleed, I bleed deep pools of troubled
blood for thee. I never told anyone anything at all about this
person I only tentatively and provisionally call my Self until
you turned up and extracted him from me so gently, so kindly.
Cruel nurse! No I never told anyone about my 'true identity',
about my 'background', as impossible, yea as unlikely, as it is
to construct any 'truth' out of any of it, my wretched excuse
for a childhood, my years enslaved to Harmacy, and yet I have
thrown myself at your mercy, bodily, yea, bodily and with what
I daren't call my whole being, for in truth it's torn open and
dripping, this creature formerly known as Donny, formerly
known as R*ger, call me what you want, call me Caliban, call
me monster, call me, call me Lester Fucking Bangs, because
in spite of your scorn I haven't given up my post and remain
your obedient music-loving servant, yes, my little A++ yes,
A PS! Verily and forsooth, I have in my possession a new Cat
Power album entitled Moon Pix *. . . I hope you will allow me*
to supply and commentate it in person amid the meandering
tender chords and shaken rice and brushes of shoop shoopa doop
shoopa doop and crystal-clear trickles of purest fluted vocal
water of which I hope you will drink deep and take sustenance,
for Erica, Erica Error, Erica Erotica, I do hope to meet thee
there . . .

I had to read it again and again. I was hoping I'd get to a point
when I didn't need to look at it anymore, but whenever I thought
that moment had arrived and I'd put the letter down I found
myself picking it up again. I wanted to read it until I felt okay. I
don't know what I expected to happen.

30

'How's things at the flat?' Since the night we'd ended up at Sick's place, Phoebe had started calling me semi-regularly to check in.

'Things are good,' I said, trying to sound enthusiastic. 'Everyone's nice. We found a replacement for Bronwyn, did I tell you? Chris. She moved in last week.' Chris, a trainee librarian, had replaced Bronwyn. She hadn't come out of her room much, although she'd tried to get me interested in a Tori Amos album she was playing when I went past one day and I'd had to tell her I was busy.

I hadn't told Phoebe about the incident with Donny. I was hoping I could withhold that story for as long as possible.

'I still haven't even seen your place. I have to come see. Hey, Andy's going off on a boys' work-do thing Saturday night. They're all bonding over beers and going line dancing, he says, I don't even want to know. We should pick you up beforehand and you can come to mine. Keep me company. I'll be a lonely old crone.'

'You don't fancy line dancing with Andy?'

'Trust me. Anyway I'm sure it's all code for strippers or something.'

'Oh, no, really?'

'Who cares. Better not to know. Anyway.'

'Sure, that sounds good.'

'Also. We have a deal through Andy's work, unlimited calls to the US. Thought maybe we could give old Foster a call.'

Even though I was on the phone and no one else was around, I went bright red. The mention of his name filled me with unfathomable shame.

Every day at varsity that week, I was about ten per cent on task. The other ninety per cent of me was chattering away about ways to avoid running into Donny. Don't go to the café on campus where he gets his afghan and coffee in the morning. Don't go into town in the late afternoon 'cause that's when he goes to Love Juice and Wellspring Health in search of unsold lunch food. Don't go to the Bongo Bar. Don't go to Society. Don't go to the university library. Don't go to the quad. Don't go anywhere near Donny's flat. Don't go to the liquor store where he gets his fancy beer. Don't go anywhere near Mount Vic, where he drinks and cycles. I was going to Mount Vic next weekend to hang out at Phoebe's place. I had visions of a confrontation on Majoribanks Street, of him mowing us over with his bike, or stopping and throwing his bike at us, or abandoning his bike and shoving our bodies into the traffic. Not only would he yell obscenities at me but at Phoebe too. He'd tell her what he really thought of her and there'd be no way to stop him. I'd have to go home with him in disgrace.

We wouldn't go out this time, Phoebe and I. That was going to be my only stipulation. We'd stay in and concentrate on chatting to Foster. That was another thing for my mind to mutter away about, and it did a bit, but I was so preoccupied with avoiding Donny it softened that dread. It also meant I didn't have time to think about what I'd say. Foster had become an abstraction to me. Donny remained stubbornly and overwhelmingly concrete.

He sent more letters, hand-delivered to the box. I didn't read them. I put them on my CD shelf under the Judee Sill picture. He phoned, but I'd instructed my flatmates I was never home if he called.

The days went by. I saw him everywhere. Every awkward gait, every elegant cyclist, every expansive gesture, that was Donny. Quick. Before he sees you. Each impersonator in his pathetic normality reminded me of Donny's uniqueness, his irreplaceability, and yet, in my mind and body, each one of these imposters was also always and only him. They were all his messengers. I realised, to my horror, if I never saw him again it would be like this every day. He would always be there. I would never forget him. I could never unsee him.

I avoided most of our friends too. Seeing them was almost as bad as seeing Donny. When they saw me, when they smiled at me, they were seeing someone else. The Erica who lives with Donny. The Erica who's big enough and bold enough to be with someone like Donny, who can handle his eccentricity. Erica the intellectual. Erica Erotica.

On my way to German class on Friday, June stepped into the lift with me. There was no avoiding her gaze. She looked straight at me and bestowed on me her beautiful smile. It made me feel so guilty.

'Erica, I haven't seen you and Donny in ages!'

'No, it's been a strange time,' I said. I almost apologised, but I didn't know how. 'Donny is kind of. I moved into a different flat. It's like we're on a break, I guess.' I didn't want to say I'd broken up with him. I didn't want that news to get back to him.

'That will be a good thing for you,' she said sympathetically. 'But it must be hard.' She and Ramon had broken up recently, so maybe she was talking from experience. But I hoped she understood that ours was a temporary break, for now at least. If other people could believe in it that way, then Donny could too.

143

As I was coming out of a philosophy lecture on Friday, I glimpsed Donny on the other side of the lobby, where students were milling about after a class or ready for another one. I looked long enough to ascertain it was Donny as Donny, not an impersonator, and to see who he was speaking to: Martin and Kyle. He seemed to have their rapt attention.

Andy and Phoebe picked me up in Andy's car. I'd tidied my room for Phoebe and planned out how I was going to show her round, but in the end they turned up late and honked the horn.

'Next time,' said Phoebe, frowning through her half-wound window. 'Andy's in kind of a hurry.'

She wasn't kidding. Andy didn't look at me when I climbed in the back, just mumbled his hello and cranked his Kruder & Dorfmeister CD. Yuppie music, Donny would have thought, would have said so even, given half a chance, only he wouldn't have used that word, 'yuppie'. Only someone narrow-minded like me could be so crudely dismissive. He would have explained why such music was beneath Andy, beneath anybody, and recommended something else, the music Andy really wanted to listen to, and he would be right. I didn't know what the explanation would be, or the recommendation. I wanted to know so I didn't miss having Donny with me at moments like these. He expected a lot of people, even people he didn't like. I lacked that patience, that bold disregard for boundaries.

Andy sped all the way down the hill. If it weren't for the seat belt, I'd have been slung right across the back seat every single blind corner. When we got into town he finally stopped for a red. It was a relief, although it meant getting propelled forwards into Phoebe's headrest. A kind of suede, it felt like. It was a pretty fancy car.

Phoebe didn't say anything the whole time. One hand on the dashboard, eyes straight ahead.

The three of us went into their flat in an awkward silence, as if only coincidentally arriving at the same time. Andy got on the phone to call a taxi and Phoebe went to the bathroom upstairs. When Andy got off the phone he looked at me with a neutral expression. He obviously didn't find me attractive or interesting, which put me at ease.

'What're you girls getting up to tonight?'

'Just hanging out, I think.'

'Oh yeah, yeah, just chilling. Bet she's told you what to say and everything. You keep an eye on Phoeb for me, all right? No going out on the town. Wasn't too impressed last time you girls went out, the state she got home in. Jesus.'

Andy had been overseas when we went to the Bongo Bar and visited Sick. Maybe he was getting me confused with someone else. I opened my mouth to say something, then thought better of it.

When Phoebe came downstairs she asked Andy if she could open a particular bottle of wine. He looked annoyed but said yes.

'Give me one for the road, would you?' he asked, but when she poured his glass and put it in front of him he ignored it.

'You going to drink that?'

'It's my wine and I'll do what I fucking well want with it.'

'Fine.'

Phoebe poured us each one. The two of us clinked glasses.

The taxi cast a shadow through the flimsy curtains on the ranchslider. A polite toot. Andy still hadn't touched any of his wine. He got up without a word or gesture in either of our directions. When he was at the door, Phoebe said, 'Bye-bye, baby.' Her voice was subdued.

He said nothing. With a sour look, he slid the ranchslider shut behind him.

I remembered what Phoebe had said about him going line dancing with the boys. I hoped then it was a joke. The idea of Andy line dancing was beyond awful.

After he'd gone, Phoebe relaxed and expanded into her usual generous mode. She put on a Yo La Tengo album and started swaying a little to the music.

'This song always reminds me of Foster,' I said, when 'Autumn Sweater' came on.

The corner of her mouth curled up in affirmation. 'He's an autumn sweater kind of guy.'

'I think I heard it first at his place. No. At my parents' place. He brought it round. Do you remember when they played at orientation? Were you there that night?'

'Yeah. I like them. I was avoiding Foster, though. That's why I didn't see you.'

'Makes sense. It's cool that you two are friends again now.'

'I think so. I try to be friends with all my exes. It's not a tap you can turn off. The love is still there. You just have to learn to channel it in a different direction.'

'I guess it can be hard, though, if the relationship was difficult. I mean, if the break-up wasn't on friendly terms.'

I remembered how Donny told me he'd once walked a broken-hearted Foster home like a dog.

'Oh, yeah. It's totally okay that you aren't feeling too friendly with Donny right now.'

'Yeah I mean, I want to be friends with him, but it just doesn't seem possible yet.'

'You initiated the break-up, right? He's probably going to be feeling sorry for himself.'

'I did. But then, it's not really a break-up exactly. Not yet. I'm not sure.'

'You're not sure? Erica, if you're not sure then I don't know who is.'

'I had kind of a weird time with him the other night.'

'What? You had sex?'

'No. I invited him round and then it got weird and he wouldn't leave.'

146

'You invited him round? What did you expect to happen?'

'But it's not like that anymore. We're just friends.'

'How you stay friends is, you meet on neutral ground. You've got to keep out of each other's space. I hate to say it, but if you invite your ex into your bedroom, you're kind of asking for trouble.'

'Yeah.' Phoebe didn't get it. For her the bedroom was a place you had sex, sex you both enjoyed. She probably found it hard to say no when the opportunity arose. That's why she needed such strict rules around it. I didn't need rules because I never wanted to have sex with Donny. The temptation was never there. So I could see him and want the best for him as a friend. It was pure in that way.

Phoebe was squinting at me. In her eyes I was probably a very cruel person. She took the last gulp of wine from her glass and put it back on the coaster emphatically. 'Hey, you know what? If we're calling Foster, we have to do it now. It's late over there. Like 2 a.m. But you know Foster. It's his Friday night. He'll be up drinking or writing his thesis or something.'

'Oh, no, maybe we shouldn't bother him. I mean, does he know we're ringing? What if we wake him up?'

'Erica, if you were Foster, wouldn't you want to be woken up by us? Maybe not me these days so much, but come on.' She was getting her address book out, flipping through to F. 'Listen. It's his wet dream come true.'

She was already dialling.

'Oh my God, really?' I began to walk in small triangles back and forth.

'Erica? Calm. The Fuck. Dow – Hello? Hi, it's me. Yeah, hi. Yeah, I'm good. You good? You behaving? What? Oh, there's a delay you have to. Yeah. Just wait and. Haha. It's good to hear your voice, too. Yeah. How much you had to drink to—? Oh, no, we're way behind you, we're just starting. Well, I have a certain special guest tonight. Yes. I think you'll be. No. Wait a sec.' She angled the phone against her shoulder and beckoned towards me frantically with alternating arms.

I shook my head. 'I'm not here,' I whispered. 'Please.' But she'd already handed me the phone.

I pressed it against my ear. It was silent. If I didn't say anything and he didn't say anything, that would be that. It could all be over very soon.

Then his voice came. 'Hello?'

I felt a stab in my abdomen. 'Ha. Hello?'

Another silence. Oh God. He didn't want to talk to me. I was a disappointment. He was expecting someone else. Or worse: he didn't even recognise my voice.

'Hi, is this? Ha.'

'Yes, it's me.'

'Erica.' His laugh tore through me. 'This is a surprise.'

'It is?' I bowed my head, pivoted away from Phoebe.

'How are – you? Yeah, quite. Quite a surprise.'

I heard Phoebe open her fridge, clatter around on the bench.

'A *nice* surprise?' I asked.

Another silence. Come on, Erica. Factor it in. Don't panic.

'Yeah.'

'There's a delay,' I said. 'I can't quite.'

'So how? Yeah.'

'I can't quite deal with it properly yet.'

'It's tricky.'

'You can feel it,' I said. 'The distance. The delay. We're so close – and yet so far.'

'Yeah.'

Maybe it was hysteria, but this time I felt strangely emboldened. 'I'm gonna. I'm gonna take you upstairs.'

'You're gonna what?'

'Yeah, it's a portable phone, it's snazzy. I'm just taking you upstairs.'

148

'You're *taking* me *upstairs*?' He was laughing again. Phoebe was right, he must've been up drinking all night. It was too easy.

'You been working hard, Foster? On that thesis?' I went and stood in Andy and Phoebe's bathroom. I caught sight of myself in the mirror and had to look away. I had horrible blotches on my neck and jaw, the kind I got when I was stressed or excited. I wandered into Phoebe and Andy's bedroom, but it was full of mirrors too. A full-length one, even. This was hardly the femme fatale persona I was imagining for myself, this blotchy beanpole with long scruffy hair and boys' jeans.

'Yeah, I've been working hard, procrastinating hard . . . '

'I don't know if I approve,' I said.

'I need you here to. Maybe you wouldn't. I need you here to—'

'Stop you.'

'To keep an eye on me,' he said.

'I'd stop you procrastinating, wouldn't I? I'd stand over you and make sure you wrote at least ten pages every day before you could have a drop to drink.'

'You'd what? Stand over me. Oh, mother.'

'What's wrong with that?'

'No I'd get no words written at all with you standing over me. What a thought. Erica—'

'Now, don't be silly.'

His voice saying my name caught up with me then. I felt hot. I said his name. 'Foster?' His name in my mouth. In his ear.

'It's nice to hear you,' he said.

'Did you ever get that tape? You know, from Donny and me?'

'That tape. Yeah.'

'It was a pretty good mixtape, wasn't it?'

'Yeah, I guess it was. I had a hard time with that tape.'

'I'm sorry.'

'I had mixed feelings about that tape. It was a strange. Time. Don't be sorry. I mean, I'm sorry.'

149

There was a silence.

'Uh. I'm sorry about so many things,' I said. 'I'm sorry for keeping you up. It must be time—'

'No.'

'Your bedtime.'

'No. Time to sleep? No. That's not even remotely. No. What I feel—'

'Hey, I haven't told you yet I moved. I should give you—'

'Yeah, I heard. Phoebe—'

'Oh, you know?'

'Yeah. Phoebe told me.'

'Yeah. I should give you my new number. And address. In case you ever.'

'Yeah.'

I thought I heard him sigh, but it might have been static.

31

Carl came into my room when I was just out of the shower. Not *just* out. I was doing that thing where I sat on the floor in a towel for a long time, thinking about what to wear, or if it's too late to put clothes on, or if I should get into my nightie, when really I needed to be sitting up writing my philosophy essay that was due the next day. It was the last assignment before midyear exams, and it was worth fifty per cent of my final grade. I had to go downstairs and make myself a cup of instant coffee and a bowl of instant noodles, that was what I had to do, and come back upstairs and get my A into G but I didn't feel like talking to anybody and that, of course, was exactly the sort of time that Carl would show up in my room, and there he was, poking his head round the door, giving me the gooey caramel eyes.

He didn't wait to be invited in. My smile was enough. He wasn't embarrassed by my wearing only a towel. That was okay, that was normal. Maybe because he didn't really like girls, I wasn't embarrassed either.

'Get into bed,' he said. 'You look like you need to have a lie down.'

So I complied. I even slipped the towel off. It was more

comfortable than sitting on the carpet. My legs were getting knobbles in the flesh.

He sat down beside me and smoothed the duvet over my chest like a mother. 'Erica,' he said, 'you're like a walking womb, you know that?'

'I am?'

'You give and you give. I can feel it. You're warm and you envelop everybody and it's wonderful.'

'Uh, thanks. I'm not sure what to say. I don't feel that warm and enveloping. I feel kind of cold and – removed, I guess.'

'Are you removed from yourself, Erica? Are you taking care of you?'

'I'm trying.'

'I think you need to think about what it is that happened to you,' he said, staring deep into my eyes. 'You know what I'm talking about. You need to think about that.'

That was the thing with Carl. His knack for knowing.

Before I'd had any time to respond, he was on to the next thing. He put his hands either side of me on the bed and leaned in, bracing himself for what he was about to say. 'Erica,' he said. 'I really like your ex-boyfriend.'

This was a surprise. 'My ex-boyfriend? You mean Donny?'

'Aha. What is he, is he Latin? Māori? Italian? Unusual face. Lot of character. Lot of mana, in that face. You know?'

'I don't know. I think he has fairly ordinary colonial ancestry.'

'These things are often hush-hush. I come from a missionary family and, yeah – they don't call it the missionary position for nothing.'

I broke eye contact. His face was still so close to mine.

I addressed the stubble on his dimpled chin. 'I don't think I can deal with Donny just yet. I need some space to sort myself out.'

'Donny's got a full-on masculine energy, eh?'

'I guess so.'

'I can see the attraction. You two must've been like magnets. But did it get too close? Too intense?'

'We just fought all the time. And then, the other day when he came round—'

'Yeah, you've got baggage, the two of you, I can see that much. But you also must have an amazing connection. Something keeps bringing you together. Nothing like this happens by accident, I believe.'

'I know.' His handsome body was so near. If only he could turn into Angel Face now. Kyle could tell me nonsense about Donny all the dee-long day if he wanted.

'I'd love to broker some healing between the two of you sometime, if you'd let me. I'm really interested in the balance of masculine and feminine. You two are such extremes in that regard, I can see a lot of potential for harmony when you reach alignment.'

'Well—' The way Carl spoke it sounded so straightforward. It was also distinctly unappealing. Harmony sounded great, but did I have to stick to my patch of abject femininity to achieve it? I wasn't sure I could do that. Maybe I was more masculine than Carl realised.

'You don't have to decide right now,' he said. 'Anyway, to be honest I'm probably just horny for your man. I'd love to have a threesome with you two if you were open to that, once you're back together.' He sat up straight, beaming broadly like he knew he'd gone too far.

I laughed. 'I guess I'm ... flattered?' I was, and I was also confident it would never happen. Carl was strange and had the wrong end of the stick about so many things, but at least I felt safe with him.

He extended a hand. 'Shall we dance?'

I pulled the sheet to my chest and sat up. 'What music would you like?'

Carl selected a Madonna greatest hits album, which I had on loan from Paul. I tried not to look at the pile of unopened envelopes behind the stereo as he put the CD on. He helped me wrap the sheet round myself in a mini toga and we danced to 'Express Yourself' and 'Vogue', watching each other in the window, two couples in a dance-off, evenly matched. Carl and Carl making me and me laugh, swivelling hips in unison like Madonna's smoothest back-up boys.

All you need is some beats, an imaginary string of pearls. No one cares if you like it, this impossible connection, it's always here anyway, dipping and cresting, posing unanswerable questions.

Hold the plates, drop the plates, dip and switch.

Running man. Let's pretend it's this easy, laughter as bravado, laughter as a kind of dare.

Arm, arm, frame, frame, dip, dip, switch.

As if it's this easy. But what if it is?

32

I had been right not to read Donny's letters. My mistake was keeping them, because after a week or more with those cream envelopes looming so potently behind the stereo, I couldn't help it. I got my Stanley knife and, one by one, I slit their paper throats. I submitted myself to Donny's pleading, remonstrating, beguiling voice, convinced I was strong enough to take it now.

I wasn't. With each word, he tore painfully at me. All right, then. He'd never do in person what he did on paper.

I was forgetting. I forgot a lot.

We arranged to meet on what Phoebe called 'neutral territory', at the café on campus.

'Let's let ourselves off the hook for a change,' I said on the phone beforehand. 'I promise not to get all resentful if you don't inflict that mournful look on me.'

'Erica, your narcissism is astonishing. I don't inflict a *look* on you.'

'Yes, you do.'

'That *look*, as you callously refer to it, is nothing but undiluted despair.'

'Fine. It's okay to look sad if you're feeling sad, that's not what I mean.'

'I see. I see. Thank you for your *permission* to express emotion, Frau Maus. I know how *unpleasant* it must be for a fastidious emotion-hoarder such as yourself.'

'Don't be like that. It's just those – puppy dog eyes. It's like a guilt trip kind of thing. Maybe you don't know your own powers.'

'Maybe I don't.'

He was wearing dark glasses when I arrived, an ugly wraparound pair that completely obscured his eyes. He hunched himself protectively over his afghan and coffee. There weren't many people in the café, thank goodness. It was late in the day and the midyear break had just started.

'Herr Donnmeister, I assume,' I said.

'Frau Maus.'

His lips were pursed. I'd never seen him look so remote, or so ridiculous. He didn't take the glasses off. I started to laugh. I walked away and pretended to look at the blackboard behind the counter.

When I returned to the table I tried not to look at him. I blew on my coffee.

It was Donny who broke the silence. 'You had a nice time?' he asked slowly. 'Yakking it up with her royal honking twittiness? Aunty Feeble?'

'Phoebe is my friend. I don't see what's wrong with that.'

He leaned across the table and hissed, 'I am your goddamn friend, Erica, in case you haven't noticed. I have been for two years. Are you out of phase or just being stupid?'

'Excuse me?'

His face was contorted with vehemence, but with his eyes blacked out the effect was disastrously comical. I had to hold my breath to stop myself from laughing again.

'Do I have to remind you that the person with whom you have chosen to chafe my most intimate concerns once almost destroyed one Foster Mitchell? Whilst about the business of recruiting him as a so-called friend? She has *honked* that foul reference to him like a trophy ever since.'

'For fuck's sake. Is it so difficult for you to believe that they're actually good friends, now?'

'They're actually good friends? What are *good friends*, actually? I'm sure Phoebe's told you. I'm sure she's told you all about her adventures in the friend trade.'

'Can you please take off those stupid fricking glasses?'

'It is a deep and profound embarrassment to me that you are gossiping with this woman.'

'What do you mean, talking to her about our relationship?'

'Our relationship? Erica, listen to yourself.'

'No, you listen to me. It's not gossip to want clarity. I'm just trying to make sense of it for myself, so it's not all you and your interpretation clanging around in my—'

'Yes, yes, Erica.'

'I mean, what kind of sick power dynamic would that be, that I can't even think straight without you?'

'Oh Lord, have mercy. She's infected you with her fetid psychologising. *Clarity*, Erica? *Power* dynamic?'

'Would you prefer it if I only talked to *you* about yourself?'

He slid over the plate with the afghan on it. 'Eat it, Erica. I can't. My body is a lie. Your denial has turned my entire being into a lie.'

'My denial? My denial of what?'

'The very real business of what has taken place between us, Erica. That which you have spun into a collective untruth.'

'Donny, you have to ask yourself why you keep having to convince me of your reality if it's so true. All I ever wanted was your friendship.'

'Listen to yourself. It's patently ridiculous. These words are not your own, Erica. Every word you say is a down payment on some hideous bourgeois convention. Sometimes it sounds to me as if you wish to be married.'

'Well, I don't.'

'I don't know what makes you so sure.'

'This is a ridiculous conversation,' I said, and took a bite out of the afghan. 'Mm, bloody delicious actually, my denial.'

He took off the sunglasses and stared abjectly at me. Of course he'd make me pay. 'Here it is, Erica. My only weapon. My puppy dog eyes. See what you've made me do? It's all I have. Why don't you disembowel me on the spot? It's all I'm good for, is it not? I'm just a scapegoat to you. An excuse for all your excesses.' He slammed the table for emphasis as he recounted my crimes: 'Your transgressions, your social ineptitude, your mental infirmity, your frigidity. Why not take this to its logical conclusion? Put me out of my misery, Erica, commence puppy sacrifice forthwith!'

The disadvantage of having so few people around was that ours was by far the loudest, if not the only, conversation, louder than the Pixies album playing on the sound system and probably the sole focus of attention, whether people were interested or not. The coffee guy, Amon, was on first-name terms with Donny, sometimes even sneaked him his coffee for free. He was wiping down tables now, studiously not looking.

I got up, slung my backpack over my shoulder. 'I can't handle this,' I said. 'I'm going.'

'Me too,' he said, and followed me out, yelling, 'I'm going to Auckland tomorrow. You'll be rid of my puppy dog eyes for the midyear break at least.'

I didn't turn round till I got to the fifth floor of the library and sat down at a table overlooking the port. The harbour was empty and all around me was an eerie quiet. My head was loud. I felt guilty for disturbing the peace.

33

I got myself a job cataloguing the estate of a dead professor during the midyear break. Heavy books, textbooks, leather-bound books with gilt lettering, trashy paperbacks, scholarly journals, porn.

'We want all of it,' said Sonya, the woman in charge. 'Even if it's going in the skip, we need to catalogue it first. Write it all down.' She had a terrible haircut and no sense of humour. Mostly it was just me in the garage alone surrounded by boxes, inhaling dust. I wore fingerless gloves and a hat and scarf and still it was freezing. The only thing that kept me going was my Walkman, but blasting that meant getting startled out of my skin every time Sonya came to check on me.

There was a guy who came in for a couple of hours each afternoon too, a proper librarian who translated my folk taxonomy into something more precise. Unfortunately for me he was unattractive and smelled of sperm. Even when he sat on the other side of the garage from me I could smell it. Sometimes he'd laugh nervously under his breath when presented with another pile of *Jail Bait* or *Pleasure Chest*, but I refused to interact.

My only entertainment apart from music was thinking about Angel Face, and that was insufferable. I had weeks to wait before

I had a chance of seeing him again. I planned out conversations for every conceivable condition of our next meeting. Then I made myself imagine what those encounters would really be like.

I hadn't seen a friend for weeks. I started to check the letterbox a lot, hoping for postcards from Donny. None came. When my first cheque cleared, I went to the liquor store and treated myself to a bottle of Grant's.

My room had big windows. By night, they became mirrors. I poured myself a glass, raised it. 'Cheers,' I said to my reflection. We laughed together. Sad really. What was I, a budgie? Budgies have mirrors in their cages so they can delude themselves they have company.

That was when I heard the voice calling my name. *Erica!*

It sounded like Alison. Like she was down in the street, calling me.

Erica!

Like she was angry, or worried. But when I pressed my face up to the window, the street was empty, as far as I could see.

Erica!

Anyway, Alison would phone ahead. She'd knock. And why was she shouting? No, it was telepathy. She was afraid, I was afraid. *I can hear you, Mum,* I transmitted back.

I wasn't afraid. I put on the radio and started jumping to the beat. *If I keep jumping will you shut up?*

Silence.

Mum, if you're there, I'm sorry I worried you. Everything will be okay.

34

I could handle physical pain better than other things. Migraines blended effortlessly with hangovers. They were a good excuse to lie in bed for a day or so. The vomiting was cathartic and my head would be suspended in a pleasant void, before the pain resumed. There was a rhythm to it, a cycle of verse, chorus, verse, chorus, a song that spun round in my head for days, distracting me from any form of linear thought.

Still, when I tried taking Disprin, then Panadol, and they didn't do anything, and I took a couple of Voltaren that I had left over from when I broke my wrist, and they didn't do anything either, I got annoyed that all these things that were supposed to help didn't. And even if they did, I'd just puke them up anyway.

'Fine,' I whispered to myself, crawling round the room with my eyes shut. 'I *relent*. I surrender. I fucking *relent*.' Then I staggered downstairs and croaked at Carl that I was going to be in bed for a while sleeping off this migraine. 'I'm not here,' I said. 'If you know what I mean.'

He said, 'Okay, babe,' but didn't look up from the pot of broth that he was sniffing. I grabbed a glass of water and took it back upstairs.

I had Donny's codeine stashed behind the stereo below the

Judee Sill picture. A tiny bottle, a doll's rattle. I sprinkled pills in my palm like sweeties, gagged a little as I chugged them back.

Relent. I lay on the floor and looked at the carpet. It was covered with strands of hair. Some glinting, some dull. Some wavy, some straight. A pubic hair or two. A piece of fingernail I'd bitten off and spat. Dead parts of me. Dead even when they were attached. Just cells. All of me. Nothing but shed cells on the floor.

I lay still. *I surrender.* What to?

Known unknowns.

I woke up hot with my tongue fused to the roof of my mouth. The sun was too bright through the crack in the curtains.

I still felt terrible.

It was two days later, but nothing had changed.

The room was quiet. I lay on the floor waiting for my mother to yell my name again.

Now's the time, I said on the phone in my head. *Go on. Yell at me.* What I needed was a good telling off. *Alison? Mum?*

She was silent, because no one knew, not even telepathically. It occurred to me I could be dead. Maybe death was like this awful separation. Maybe you lived on, alone and broken, in an empty place.

I rang Windmills. I had a strong suspicion Donny would be back by now. The guy said, 'Who?'

I described him.

He said, 'That guy. Haven't a clue, but he owes us money on the room.'

'Can you tell him Erica rang?'

'Do I sound like an answering service to you?' He sighed. 'When you find him, tell him to see me.'

Perhaps Donny's days at that backpackers' were numbered.

*

162

I went to the computer lab after that to check my email. It had been a couple of weeks since I last looked.

I asked for the seat furthest away from everyone else. I sat down unobtrusively and logged on. I waited while the machine ground through its various duties and opened up my inbox. There were a bunch of messages listed, but they were ones I'd already seen. Annoying. I asked it to retrieve the new mail. There was none.

Fuck him. *Fuck* him. I felt like yanking the stupid humming box off the desk and smashing it on the floor.

But I couldn't do that and I couldn't get up and leave either. I'd only just sat down. So I wrote an email.

From: nolaneric@scs.vuw.ac.nz
To: ogilvroge@scs.vuw.ac.nz
Date: Friday, 30 July 1999 15:43
Subject: your answering service

Herr Donnmeister,

This is your answering service. Erica called. The guy
at the backpackers called. We don't know what either
of them wanted. We don't pry. Only maybe the guy at
the backpackers wants money. What does Erica want?
Honey? Party? An overdose of sweets? Does she have
a death wish? Does she have a thing for older men?
Be careful, note the year. Y2K approaches. Erica has
designs on the new millennium. Are you mixed up in her
technopalypse now?

Faithfully yours,
Miss Moneypenny

I hit Send. *Light fuse and retire immediately.* I scurried out of the lab and out across the quad and bounded up the steps on a giddy, guilty high. Maybe if I ran fast enough I could escape what I just did.

35

I checked and rechecked the Philosophy noticeboard. Kyle wasn't in any of the same classes as me. Not even the same lectures, let alone tutorials. It was the last semester of our third year. The end of our degrees.

'Get his number from Martin, or I will,' said Carl.

'Please don't do that.'

'Come on. Don't pretend I wouldn't be doing you a massive favour.'

'If I have to ask him out, what does that say? He's the guy. If he's at all interested in me, he should make the first move.'

'Jeez, Louise. Do you have any idea how lucky you are? You've got a hot ex who still wants you and here I am lusting after Martin and what hope do I have?'

'A *hot ex*? Dunno about that. And Martin's *married*.'

'He's married and he's straight, okay?'

'I suppose so.'

'Sure, I'll take an interest in your straight girl–straight boy melodrama, but please don't ask me to feel sorry for you.'

'Sorry. I didn't know you had feelings for Martin. What about Ramesh?'

'What about Donny? Don't think I don't know what you're

doing here, darl. I know how it is. A little jealousy can be a powerful aphrodisiac. Bit of rebound fun into the bargain. Listen, Martin's in my lectures on Wednesday afternoon. Meet me for coffee after class. I'll invite him to join us. Maybe we can engineer a little Angel Face manifestation.'

I went to meet Carl that Wednesday without much hope of seeing Kyle, but any chance, even an outside one, was better odds than I could hope to entertain on my own, so I waited outside the lecture theatre at the appointed time, sweating into my corduroy jacket, planning casual conversation starters for Martin that would be suitable as subtexts to relay to Angel Face in some subsequent analysis of our encounter that I knew they'd never have.

Carl raised his eyebrows suggestively at me when he came out with Martin behind him. 'Erica, you know Martin, eh?'

'Yes we've met, hi.'

'Hi.'

'He's joining us for coffee.'

'Oh, sure,' I said, feigning surprise. 'That'd be nice.'

'Did you know Martin's an artist?' Carl asked when we were in the queue. I smiled blandly at Amon the coffee guy, when he was taking my order, as if I didn't recognise him. I hadn't been back to this café since Donny and I had our last fight. Or since I scoffed all the sweeties and slept for two days.

'Oh, yeah,' I said. 'You're a photographer, eh?'

'Kind of. One of the strings to my bow anyway. Mostly a painter. But I'm experimenting with film at the moment.'

'Like movies?'

'No, like photographic film. Exposure. Treating the film directly and developing it to see what happens. My friend has a darkroom. We're doing a project together.'

'Oh, really, is that – what was his name?' Carl asked innocently. 'Long blond hair?'

'Kyle, yeah. He works in a photo studio so he gets all these offcuts and stuff to play around with. And he's got a darkroom in his flat.'

'Right, is that the place on Tory Street?' Carl asked. 'The warehouse?'

'That's the one. You interested in art at all? Photography?'

'Of course, I love it. I'm a very visual person. So's Erica. You're a bit of an artist, aren't you, Erica?'

'No, I'm not.'

'Yes, you are. I've seen your drawings.'

'I mean I did art at *school* ...'

'Great!' said Martin. 'You'll have to come and see our stuff sometime.'

'Oh, I wouldn't like to impose or anything. I don't know anything about photography.'

Carl kicked me under the table. He didn't need to. I was well aware of how wrong my words were.

'Suit yourself. I mean, it's not like we have an entrance exam or something. We just like company. But.'

'Yeah I'm terrible company, though.' I laughed.

Martin looked disappointed. 'Oh, well, never mind,' he said, turning to Carl. He talked to Carl the rest of the time.

I drank a lot of Pepsi that semester. It was all I had to go on. After a few weeks, it worked. As I was fishing in my wallet for coins, I heard my name. And again. I looked up, sure I was hearing things but looking just in case. To my surprise, I saw Martin waving at me from the other side of the lobby. And beside him, Kyle.

Once you've made eye contact, there's no walking away pretending to be oblivious. I put my fifty-cent pieces in the machine and considered ways of pressing the cold, wet Pepsi can to my face without being seen. Ways that didn't draw further attention to my lunacy. Perhaps if I touched my hand to my face? I swept a hand over my neck as I crept across the lobby, pretending to adjust my scarf. My neck warmed my hand, but my hand didn't cool my neck.

'Hey, Erica,' said Martin, smiling as if I hadn't completely stiffed him last time we spoke. 'What you up to?'

'Oh, you know, mooching around. Trying not to do any work. Ha.'

'Yeah? You know Kyle, eh?'

'We haven't – officially met.'

'Hi, Erica,' he said, nodding in a cool, jerky way, in and out more than up and down.

'Hey.'

'Hey, Erica's an artist, you know?' said Martin. 'I invited her round to the studio.'

'The studio. Yeah. You should come round. Hang out. Check out our weird art.' Kyle was giving me a look that was making my internal organs expand and collide in thrilling yet unpleasant ways.

Martin frowned. 'It's not weird. It's experimental.'

'Yeah. You probably won't like it, but anyway. We need visitors,' said Kyle.

'We need an exhibition, is what we need. I'm working on it.'

Kyle sighed. 'I don't know about that. It's not exactly exhibition material. It's kind of – wilfully obscure.'

'Maybe you need to think better of the gallery-going public,' I said.

'Maybe I need to think better of what we're actually doing,' said Kyle. 'Maybe if I don't really get it, I can hardly expect other people to like it, either.'

'Don't be a dick,' Martin said to Kyle. He turned to me. 'So what do you say, Erica? Do you wanna swing by? Settle this argument for us. Meaningful or not.'

'Ha. That sounds like a lot of pressure. I mean, I wouldn't depend on me as any kind of objective judge, but—'

'We don't care if you hate it, in fact I'd *love* it if you hated it, I'd be honoured to stir such a strong feeling in you, you know? If people hate it maybe we're onto something. I just want Kyle here to stop being so negative. We need to get into a dialogue, Kyle. That's what good art should be about.'

Kyle rolled his eyes.

I laughed. 'This is obviously an ongoing conversation.'

Martin gave me the address of Kyle's warehouse on Tory Street, and both their phone numbers. He said they'd be there later that day.

'We will?' said Kyle, grinning at Martin.

'Yeah, I'm coming round with my new negatives,' he said. 'I told you.'

'Okay.' Kyle looked at me. 'Don't get your hopes up too much. We're kind of pretentious.'

'Hey, you should bring your stuff too, Erica,' said Martin. 'I want to start something like one of those turn-of-the-century salons, you know, where everyone gets together and talks about art and philosophy and stuff.'

'One of *those* salons, you understand,' said Kyle. 'He's explaining so you don't think we're hairdressers.'

I laughed. 'Sounds good. A turn-of-the-twenty-first-century salon.'

'Fuck, yeah. No, seriously, bring your work, Erica,' said Martin. 'It'll be great.'

'Yeah, do it or he'll take your photo. Everyone's a participant.'

'Oh, no. That sounds scary.'

'It is.' Kyle nodded his jerky nod. 'It's intense.'

We said goodbye. I was one of the gang. Nothing major. So casual. So freaking casual it wasn't even funny.

I folded the piece of refill paper with their details on it into a small wad and went away clutching it. I walked all the way home with it in my hand.

Against my better judgement, I went to Kyle's warehouse that night. Like jumping into a cold swimming pool. Better not to stand there waist-high, swishing your hands around daintily. Go under. Go way down. Then it's done.

I got changed into a cute dress and admired myself in the mirror and then took it off and put back on exactly what I was wearing earlier. I didn't want them to think I'd got changed for their benefit. No, no.

I hesitated over my drawings. I flicked through the folio I kept of my faves. Boring sketches of rubbish and streams and imaginary empty streetscapes. I put them back. Better to have them imagine I was shy than know I was shit. Maybe it would be cool if Martin wanted to photograph me anyway. His camera might pick up something in me I didn't know was there.

I walked all the way. Plenty of time to talk myself out of it, to talk myself into a frenzy of self-loathing, but I didn't turn back. I kept going. I was thinking of Kyle's big angel eyes. I'd accepted his invitation to bathe in his golden light. I'd accepted it, goddamnit, I hadn't turned it down. I was going to look at his art and listen to his self-deprecating remarks.

I found the main door easy enough. It was down the back of a shop. Their flat was hard to find though. I knew it was B, and the downstairs flat was labelled A, but when I got upstairs there were three doors and none of them were labelled. I put my ear up to the door with the sticker on it that said 'Hang Ten'. Faint reggae. I listened to the door across the hall, a green door with no stickers on it. No sound at all. I guessed this was probably not their door, so this would be a good practice round. I knocked. Martin came to the door just as I was wandering away to listen at the next one.

170

'Hey, Erica. Great you could join us. Annie'll be pleased. It's turning into a sausage sizzle. My wife, Albertine, refuses to come here, she says it's too dirty.'

The place was huge. Like the size of an assembly hall or Blenheim airport. There were cactus plants everywhere, and blotchy black-and-white prints pegged to twine. In the middle of the floor was a rug with cushions on it and beanbags and frayed armchairs all around with people – too many people – maybe ten – sitting statically and quietly in a ring, passing a bong around.

Kyle was amongst them. Behind him was a life-size cardboard cut-out of Princess Leia, who was pointing a ray gun at me. He barely glanced in my direction, which was just as well. One thing at a time.

'Everybody, this is Erica. Have you met Annie? Kyle's sister.' Martin gestured in the direction of a woman with long blond hair. She had big eyes like Kyle's, though not as angelic. She waved in a polite but bored fashion.

Everybody looked like they'd just witnessed a horrific car accident. Staring straight ahead. I wondered if I'd intruded on something private, something Martin was too nice to mention.

I recognised two of the people in the circle besides Martin and Kyle: a guy with dreads from philosophy and, next to him, Mandi, from school and the yoga class I took in seventh form. Her hair was in two plaits and she was wearing a short pleated skirt. I wasn't sure if she'd seen me. Her eyes were gloomy and very red.

'Have a seat,' said Martin, gesturing towards an armchair. He sat down on a cushion beside it. I flopped into the armchair and forced myself to smile. For once I didn't have to worry about finding something to say. Nobody would care if I stayed silent. Still, I heard Donny's voice in my head telling me *have some moxie, drag these poor potheads out of their complacent hell one word at a time.*

I didn't. It was Martin who spoke first.

'So you go out with that Donny guy, eh?'

'He's just a friend,' I said.

'I thought you were his girlfriend.'

'We used to live together,' I said, hoping 'living together' would be sufficiently ambiguous for Kyle to interpret as 'flatting'.

The guy next to Martin passed him the bong. He didn't take a hit. 'Here,' he said, passing it up to me. 'You smoke?'

'No, thanks,' I said, and passed it to the guy next to me.

'Hope you don't object,' said Martin.

'No,' I said. 'I'm just not in the mood tonight.'

'I get a bit bored with it myself. Hey, Donny comes round here sometimes. He's an interesting guy.'

'Yeah, I'll give him that. He's certainly interesting.'

'Do I detect some post-break-up resentment there, Erica?'

'No. It's not like that.' I was conscious that everyone in the circle, stoned or not, could be listening to me now, including Kyle.

The next time the bong came round I had some. I needed to dull the impulse to converse.

There was an older guy in the group who looked out of place. He didn't look like a student or a businessman, exactly. He had a burgundy leather jacket and an earring and dyed black hair and a grim expression like he wasn't there to socialise. When he got up Mandi stood up too, blankly, like she was hypnotised, like standing up when he did was some involuntary reflex. We didn't admit we knew each other, but I waved as she left, arm in arm with the leather jacket guy. She nodded back.

'Is he your dealer?' I asked Martin after they'd gone.

He shrugged. 'Nothing to do with me,' he said.

Kyle hadn't said a word the whole time. Just sat there gripping the arms of his chair like he was at risk of sinking. Was he in some sort of trouble? There was an empty seat beside him now.

Rather than go over to it, I stood up with my back to him and took a close-up look at the string of photos that intersected the seating circle.

The photos were abstract splotches that reminded me of biology slides. There was something vulnerable and secret about them. You could tell they were burning, but in a controlled, slow reveal, like they were burning from the inside out. You couldn't see flames, only soft bursts of damage. I felt glad I'd decided to leave my drawings at home. These were really good.

'Go on,' said Martin, standing beside me. 'Be brutal.'

'I love them,' I told him.

'Don't lie.'

'I do.'

'D'you hear that, Kyle?'

He put his arm on my shoulder and turned me to face Kyle, who remained motionless and unimpressed.

'She's only being polite,' Kyle said.

'Come on, give the girl a little credit. Does she look like the sort of girl who'd say she loved it if she didn't?'

'Yes,' said Kyle. 'No offence, Erica.'

I blushed.

'Dicks,' said Annie, glowering at Kyle, then Martin. It was the first thing she'd said since I'd been there. 'Leave the poor girl alone.' Her kindness made my shame worse. I was pitiful, so pitiful that someone as self-contained as Annie felt compelled to step in and protect me from her harmless brother.

'Yeah, fuck you, Kyle,' said Martin. 'Why don't you get us all something to drink?'

The conversation turned to bickering over who paid what for the bottle of ouzo and who drank all the vodka. It was in the midst of this that there was a rap at the door.

I felt dizzy when I heard his voice. If I passed out I wouldn't have to look at him. I wouldn't have to acknowledge his presence

173

in any way at all, because I'd be on the floor with my eyes shut. Kyle would be bent over my body clasping my wrist, pressing his ear to my mouth, gently slapping my cheek.

Too late. Donny's twisted face was tilted at me like a sick flower. He lurched over to me with a mocking stare. *Little mouse,* his eyes said. *I've come to your rescue. You'd better be grateful.*

'Miss Moneypenny, I presume,' he said out loud.

'Hi, Donny. I was just going.'

He came right up to me and narrowed his eyes. 'Don't do this, man,' he said quietly, jutting his chin.

I walked to the door anyway and put on a grotesque smile for my hosts, waving childishly. 'Bye – bye – see ya – thanks!'

Martin followed me to the door, frowning. 'Oh, no, Erica, you don't have to—'

'Nah, it's all right.'

'You don't have to go,' he said under his breath at the door. 'Don't be silly. He's harmless.'

'No, no, it's fine. Thanks for the photos. I mean, it was great to see them. Thanks.'

He leaned in and gave me a kiss on the cheek. 'Ah well, then, *au revoir, à bientôt!*'

'*Auf Wiedersehen!*'

Donny was still scowling when I gave my final wave, but he didn't follow me out. It was one thing to be thankful for.

36

I didn't see Donny for a few months after that, although I went to Kyle's warehouse a fair bit. One time, Martin played me and Kyle an entire Hawkwind album, *Space Ritual*, in Kyle's room. I sat on the bed and Kyle sat at his desk and Martin alternated between sitting and standing, pacing to the music and waving his arms to get our attention.

He was trying to get Kyle interested in the exhibition he was setting up for their photos. 'Everyone will be there,' he said. 'It'll be great. I want to make a film of it, a film of us. It'll be like *The Last Waltz*, you know, we'll have interviews with Kyle and me and Erica and Annie.'

'Wait, what do you mean?' I asked. '*The Last Waltz* didn't have women in it.'

'It had Joni Mitchell.'

'Not as an interview subject, it didn't. Anyway, I don't see you getting Annie into it. And I'm definitely not coming if you're turning the camera on me.'

'But I want it to be about all of us. Art is a social expression, we build meaning together. Just by going to the opening, you're an artist.'

'That's like saying groupies are rock stars,' I said.

'You're hardly a groupie, Erica,' said Kyle.

'I'm as significant to your art as a groupie is to the music.'

'Donny definitely needs to be in a film,' said Martin. 'Eh. Is he a guru? Is he a shaman? Is he a madman or a genius?'

'I don't know,' said Kyle. 'They say don't work with children or animals. I can't imagine Donny's the most cooperative subject.' He was looking at me with his alarming blue eyes. Like an erotic knife attack.

'Yes,' I said.

The exhibition was a success, but Kyle was distracted. His sister had taken off to LA with no warning, abandoning her thesis.

'What's in LA?' I asked. We were standing at the top of some dark stairs near the entrance to the gallery space.

'I dunno. Beaches. Movie studios. Traffic jams. You know as much as I do.'

'She just took off?'

'Disappeared. Classic Annie move.' Kyle looked down at the camera he had round his neck. 'I just need to check the light,' he said, and pulled it up to his eye. Then the flash went.

'Hey,' I said. 'You tricked me.'

He shrugged and looked down the stairwell to greet another newcomer, sticking his hand out for a high five that turned into a semi-hug. They shook hands and patted each other on the back. 'Hey, man,' Kyle said, 'glad you could make it.'

I went inside to get another drink. He followed and I watched him discreetly, trying to gauge whether he was on the verge of tears. I decided he wasn't like Foster, who looked angry when he was sad. He was just angry. With Annie, most likely, and possibly his dad.

His dad was drunk already, swaying morosely in a corner near the drinks table. 'It's bloody brilliant what you boys have done here, Kyle,' he said, 'considering it's what? Damaged film.

176

I like it a lot. We could all learn from that. Now you, Erica, I've heard all about you. Jesus, Kyle. Get a load of that.' He lurched in my direction, boring his squinty eyes into me. 'How old are you, twelve?'

'What?'

'Dad.' Kyle rubbed his forehead.

'What's your story, freckles? You remind me of a Balthus painting. Those waifish girls. You know Balthus?' He was leaning towards me, breathing fumes on my face.

'No.'

'Painter. Specialises in nudes. Pubic girls.'

'You mean *pubescent*,' I said and walked into a room with a short film playing. It wasn't the documentary that Martin had hoped to make, but an animated version of the stills I'd already seen. Splotches appeared from a pinhead speck and grew and changed shape cancerously and gyrated in a melancholic frenzy. I was grateful for the dark to hide my tears. The room felt like a sanctuary until Kyle's dad staggered in.

'Please leave me alone,' I said.

'A man's allowed to look. Or are you against all aesthetic representations of the female form? Is that it? You're into abstractions, like my son's here. Do these splotches light your fire, darling?'

'What the fuck is your problem?' I said, leaving.

'All right, keep your wig on,' he called after me.

Some other boomer guy stood in the doorway looking shocked. An uncle perhaps. Kyle's mum came up behind him and smiled apologetically at me.

'Sorry about Ray,' she said kindly. 'He's had a bit much to drink. I know it's no excuse, but it's been a stressful week.'

I hadn't talked to Martin properly yet. I eventually caught sight of him at the other end of the room, gesticulating to someone. The room was crowded. I had to concentrate to avoid

177

spilling my drink. It was only when I got closer that I realised who he was talking to.

Donny bowed his head and peered up at me intensely, a finger on his lower lip.

Martin gave me a half-hug and said, 'I'll leave you guys to it.'

'What?' I said. 'I came over to talk to you.'

'We'll talk later,' Martin said, patting my shoulder as he departed.

Donny narrowed his eyes and smiled coolly. 'I see what you're doing,' he said. 'Very good.'

'What's that?'

'I think you know.'

'I'm attending my friends' art opening, is what I'm doing. Not sure what your interpretation is on that, but—'

'Ah, Erica,' he shook his head. 'You're lucky I'm so patient.'

'You're what?'

'I'm biding my time,' he said.

'What for?'

'For Erica Erotica. I know she's going to make a spectacular entrance any moment now.'

37

It was unusually hot for early spring. Kyle was painting a house up the road from my flat. Most days, I went round to watch his back, broad and rippled with lean muscles. Occasionally, I got the special bonus: a glimpse of his chest, with its flat pink nipples and thatch of red hair in its centre, like a cosy for his heart.

The first time I tried talking to him he zapped me with his ray gun eyes. This must be all in my head, I thought, because if he felt anything like me, he would surely fall off his ladder.

'What are you up to?' he asked.

'Not much. Just thought I'd better keep an eye on your progress.'

Neither of us said anything for a while. I didn't want to look away in case I missed something.

'Heard from Annie?'

'She's okay. Not giving much away, mind you.'

'Mysterious girl.'

'Yeah.'

There had to be some way to escalate this conversation. Maybe staying silent would do it. Maintain the intensity. But he just turned back to his painting.

'Well – see ya,' I said.

I banged into the gate on my way out. Got a bruise on my hip that lasted for days.

'Bye,' said Kyle, applying gentle dabs and strokes of paint. It was so quiet I could hear it even after I got through the gate. Fibrous like a cat's tongue.

On campus, I only managed to catch Kyle alone one time. He was standing at the tuck shop in the quad. A guy came up to us and said, 'You want to make thousands of dollars easy cash on your computer?'

Kyle said, 'No.'

'Are you crazy?'

'No,' he said firmly.

The guy turned to me, zealous eyes darting around like he was speeding. 'You wanna be rich, eh?'

'No,' I said. 'I'm okay, thanks.'

He retreated, just like that.

'I wish it was always that easy to get rid of people,' I said. 'Hey, I'm going to town for cheap pies. You heading home soon?'

'Yeah, why not,' he said, grabbing his own greasy paper bag and thanking the tuck shop guy.

When we got to the Allenby Terrace steps, he said all of a sudden that he'd been thinking of going overseas.

This again. It was the perfect move, of course, for someone like Kyle, to put an ocean between us – a buffer zone, as Foster liked to call it. Miles and miles and miles. My knees and ankles felt as if they could bend badly, like bones soaked in vinegar. I focused on securing a foot to each step, one by one, releasing quickly each time like I was ready to break into a jog, not in the slightest bit concerned about tripping and tumbling to my death.

'Anywhere in particular, or?'

'Just anywhere. This place is suffocating. There's a reason

everybody leaves and it's because nobody wants to be festering in a small town ad infinitum.'

'Wellington is hardly a small town.'

'Might as well be.'

'What about Auckland? Have you thought of moving there?'

'No. Why would I?'

'I like Auckland,' I said. 'You know. The pedestrian crossings on Queen Street where all the traffic stops and it's this massive free-for-all for a couple of minutes. The harbour. Yachts and everything. The traffic.'

'It's not exactly Singapore.'

'No,' I said, although I had no point of comparison. Auckland was the biggest city I'd ever visited.

'Our aunt died. Dad's sister, Jenny. She didn't have a husband or any kids so she left us a bunch of money. That's how come Annie ended up going to LA. So you know. I might as well use it.'

'I'm sorry. When did that happen?'

'A while ago. It doesn't matter.'

'I didn't know. Don't you want to stay and do Honours? Or an MA even?'

'No. Academia and I – it's time we parted ways.'

'Don't be silly. You're a good student.'

'I get good marks. So what? Doesn't mean I have to carry on, does it?'

In Cuba Mall, we stopped in at Wellspring Health where I grabbed a couple of spinach and feta pies for two dollars each.

'Two pies?' he said as we left the shop. 'Really?'

'Don't you want one? These are the best pies in Wellington.'

'Wouldn't say no.'

It gave me great pleasure to hand it to him.

He sank his teeth too fast into the steamy pastry, jerked his head away. 'Fuck! That's fucking hot.' Flakes of pastry dusted his lips and fluttered off as he fanned his tongue.

181

On Ghuznee Street we waited awhile to cross the road. The traffic wouldn't clear. Kyle made a disgruntled noise and started walking along the footpath. 'Come on. Let's go this way.'

I half-ran a few steps to catch him up. 'We can zigzag,' I said as I approached.

He was frowning, looking up the street.

I saw the beanie first. That ominous dome. I'd forgotten how big his head was. A heavy protuberance. I froze. He was talking to someone in a shop doorway, doing his groovy little moves and kicks. It was the doorway to Pharaoh's massage parlour.

'Shit.' I turned back the way we came, ducking back into Cuba Street to find a place to hide. The only thing that could make this worse would be if Donny had already seen me.

Kyle caught up and tapped me on the shoulder. I jumped. 'Fuck you!'

'What's your problem?'

'He was going into Pharaoh's.'

'So? He's gone in now. The coast is clear.'

'Fine, whatever.' Tears started welling up. I looked away.

'What's the big deal?' He took a bite of his pie and shook his head. 'I don't think he saw us, if that's what you're worried about.'

'It's a massage parlour.' I still had my pie in my hand. I'd hardly touched it. 'Wait there,' I said and ran over to a bin and chucked it in. *Be a tidy Kiwi*, the bin said. My pie made a satisfying thud. I glared at Kyle. *See what you made me do?*

He rolled his eyes at me. 'Oh, come on.'

Stupid Kyle had no clue about Angelique or anything. He didn't know anything about prostitutes. He'd probably never even had sex. As we walked I tried to explain. 'It's not the fact that it's a *massage parlour*, it's the combination. Donny plus massage parlour just doesn't make sense. It's not right. It goes against everything he stands for.'

'I didn't realise he was such a man of principle.'

'It's not like that.'

'A fine, upstanding member of the community.'

'Shut up.'

'He's kind of a pain in the arse, don't you think? Wouldn't you rather he was going into Pharaoh's than accosting us?'

'Why do you have to be so *stupidly* logical?'

Of course he was right, which made it all the worse. I carried on trying to justify my repulsion all the way into his building, until we were up the stairs and approaching his front door, when he stood still and put his palm out like a traffic officer.

'Stop,' he said. 'If you want to come in and hang out I must warn you, there will be no talk of Donny on the premises.'

'Okay,' I said, my voice thick. I hung my head. He was fishing around for his key. I realised then that no one else was home. We'd have the place to ourselves. I panicked. This couldn't happen now. Tears started to flow down my cheeks. While he was unlocking the door, I ran down the stairs.

At the building entrance, I hesitated. Maybe it wasn't too late. I listened for his footsteps running after me, or his voice calling my name. Silence. I started up the stairs again, wiping my eyes with my sleeve and taking a long breath in. Perhaps I could pretend I'd just dropped something and had to retrace my steps?

No. I couldn't face him. I turned back, and then I heard his door slam shut.

I went out onto Tory Street. This was bloody ridiculous. In an alternative reality, we were sitting on his bed right now. He was giving me The Look, and I was pulling his hands towards me and his warm breath was caressing my neck and we were—

I retraced my steps, aimless and disoriented.

This city was such a fucking wasteland. Here we were at the bottom of the earth, subsisting amid a bunch of broken concrete. *Bypass My Ass*, the posters said, but you could hardly blame them for wanting to destroy it all and start again. If they built a motorway, nobody would have to look at this mess, they'd be driving too fast to even notice. If this was a proper city, there'd be cool galleries and nice bars and delicatessens. People would fill the footpaths, there'd be traffic. But there was nothing, no one, just a bike courier and a grubby van spewing out diesel fumes and some gross-smelling coffee roasting place and these buildings and the shattered remains of buildings.

I was shaking. It felt like an earthquake, but it was me.

38

My birthday was coming up. I was going to be twenty-one. I dreaded it, even though exactly nothing was about to change.

When I turned sixteen, Alison had taken me out for dessert at Strawberry Fare and told me quite plainly that I was about to embark on a process of decay. 'The furrow in your brow deepens, other lines appear, your hair becomes wiry and unruly and all mousy, there are flecks of grey, then streaks, you get podgy or flabby. Of course, later on, the process accelerates dramatically.'

I'd found it odd that it was Alison telling me this when it was Gary who was balding and getting a spare tyre and pouchy wrinkles on his face. Also, it was my mother, not me, who was entering middle age, and she looked to me like she always had – perfectly fine.

'At a certain age,' she'd said, stabbing her gateau with a fork, 'at forty or fifty. My age, whatever that is. Your desirability plummets and that crushes your ego. There's actually no end of silly things you might be driven to.'

I'd felt panicked that I didn't have a boyfriend yet, a panic that persisted till Donny rendered it obsolete, but otherwise nothing she'd said had bothered me. Approaching twenty-one was different. It wasn't for want of a boyfriend that I dreaded crossing the final bridge to adulthood. It was the sense that the life I was meant to live was eluding me, that the pathways to it were getting further and further away. Maybe I'd passed them already. Maybe it'd be nothing but dead ends from here on in.

In the weeks leading up to my birthday I waited for an email or a phone call from Donny. Apart from spotting him on Ghuznee Street, I hadn't seen him since Kyle and Martin's art opening. This made me strangely sad. I knew he'd scoff at the bourgeois dorkiness of it all but, without him, I wasn't sure I knew how to party.

Gary and Alison arrived at my party early. Alison sat in the living-room window seat with a bottle of wine. Gary went into the kitchen and did a stocktake of my liquor supplies and kept asking who was coming, doing mental calculations to gauge how well I'd planned as far as booze went, and offering to go out and get more beer.

'You can never have enough beer. Go on. While you've got me here. A willing driver.' He was desperate to make himself useful.

Alison, on the other hand, I could see through the servery hatch, sipping from her paper cup of Chardonnay and staring into the empty room. They didn't stay. The first people arrived, friends of Donny's I'd invited to make up the numbers. I introduced them.

Gary said, 'Well. Happy birthday, daughter. See you on the other side.' He blew me a kiss and left.

Alison got up slowly and took one last gulp of her wine. She hesitated at the door. 'Have fun,' she said, and gave everyone an anxious wave.

The people I wanted them to meet, like Martin and Kyle and June, didn't come till it was dark. Gary and Alison were long gone by then.

Phoebe gave me a card that said *Happy Fucking Birthday!* and a pocket spray of Issey Miyake perfume. 'This suits your personality, Erica. This is you, to a tee.' It was a very sophisticated perfume. I was deeply flattered.

June gasped at the cards when she came in. 'I didn't know you were turning twenty-one.' She rummaged in her bag and with a surreptitious look slipped me a pack of clove cigarettes. 'I hope you'll accept this in lieu of something more appropriate.' She laughed mischievously and gave me a squeeze.

Martin gave me a small print, one of his and Kyle's experimental splotches. Two spots of burning joined in the middle like Siamese twins. 'Happy twenty-first, my dear,' he said, and gave me a kiss on the cheek. His wife, Albertine, came with him – an honour, as she was rarely seen outside their apartment. She wore a huge brocaded shawl swept sculpturally around her shoulders in such a way that she looked exposed, as though she'd only recently succumbed to pressure and uncovered her face and hair. I got a cold kiss from her that left a sticky residue of maroon lipstick on my cheek.

No kiss from Kyle, or even a hug. With a stiff arm, he presented me with a picture he'd taken of Donny at his exhibition opening.

'Um. Thanks,' I said, adding with an awkward laugh, 'I think.'

Trust Kyle to give me such a cryptic present. This would be fodder for hours of fretful mental exercise, sifting through each and every possible interpretation, and some impossible ones. The photo was taken from behind. Donny was framed by the door, about to disappear into the stairwell.

I leaned closer to Kyle. 'Is it weird to say I miss him?'

He jerked his head back, raised an eyebrow.

'Yeah, I suppose it is,' I said, and ran away to the toilet to cry.

Late in the party, when the guests had thinned out enough to fit comfortably on my bedroom floor, we opened a bottle of port that my grandfather had 'put down' on the occasion of my birth. Kyle and June and Martin eyed me solemnly as I poured out portions into paper cups. This was it. There'd never be any more of it.

39

And so my third year at university came to an end. I got good marks in all my exams and a letter from the Philosophy department saying they hoped I'd come back for Honours. It meant nothing, I now knew, except that I'd learned to be a good little conformist and say exactly what they expected of me in my pretty goody-two-shoes academese. The question was, could I begin to educate myself out of university bounds, as Donny had, or would I, freed from the relentless pursuit of As, collapse in a spongiform heap of neural incontinence?

I found no answer to this question, only began to realise what should have been obvious all along: there was no end to any of it. Life was a hot, tremulous hum. Uncertainty at high volume. If I carried on next year, it would be without Kyle. Donny, too. Without him or Kyle, I'd be left behind, strange, untethered.

When I heard Foster was coming back for a week or so in December, I arranged a soirée. I was looking forward to seeing him again. The pressure was off now that I had Kyle to squirm about, and here was an opportunity to get all the people that I liked in my room together at the same time. Phoebe, Kyle, June, Martin – and Foster at the centre. It was one of the last parties of the year, which this year also meant the decade, the century and the millennium.

Foster brought his girlfriend. Carmel, her name was, short for Carmelita. It was the first I'd heard of her but evidently he wanted her to meet his parents. They were spending Christmas together. Carmel hardly said a word. If Donny had been there he'd have sung her the Warren Zevon song 'Carmelita'. She'd probably never heard it, she was too square. She wasn't even good looking. No one was going to compose a love song in her honour even if they were strung out on heroin. She looked nervous and pointless. I was furious.

Phoebe was happily talking about Foster in the third person and telling him to get out his photos and, 'Ooh, guys – you have to see this one. Isn't she gorgeous?' Wafting this picture at everybody of Carm, as she called her, sitting gormlessly on a horse at some 'ranch'.

I'd wanted Kyle and Foster to meet. I'd envisaged being a shy bystander to a frank conversation between them regarding their mutual attraction to me. During this conversation it would dawn on them both how neglectful and foolish they'd been, how they'd wasted all this time being laconic and awkward when what was required of them was decisive action. How they'd proceed in light of this realisation I hadn't got as far as imagining, but two minds were better than one, and they'd no doubt encourage and advise each other in the spirit of friendship.

In fact the only conversation they had together was about books. Kyle was trying to remember the name of the book he'd started recently that had something about a Rapunzel character at the start of it.

'Was it *Fifty Favourite Bedtime Stories*?' I asked. Kyle gave me the finger.

'I know that,' said Foster. 'Yeah. Rapunzel. It's either DeLillo or Barthelme.'

'Rapunzel, Rapunzel, let down your hair!' said Martin.

'Pynchon,' said Foster. 'I think it's Pynchon.'

*

At the door, I gave Foster a hug. He told me very sternly, 'Write to me.'

'I will.' I said it twice, because he didn't seem to hear me the first time.

'Do,' he replied, with an almost menacing intensity.

Phoebe and Carmel were already in the back of a taxi. Phoebe opened her door a crack and whistled Foster a summons.

For a long time afterwards, I wondered how best to read Foster's expression, the look he'd given me when we'd said goodbye on my porch. His frown had obviously been holding back tears, which I'd done in my own way by blinking and tilting my head up. I could've been looking at the stars, if it weren't so cloudy.

Had he also been telling me, 'I haven't forgotten you, please don't forget me, either?' Or, 'Please write to me, I can't say anything in person?'

I was unwilling to accept Carmel as anything but a blatant opportunist. How Foster had allowed her to barge all the way to the other side of the world and into his parents' home was simply beyond me.

I talked to Kyle on the phone about the party afterwards.

'I wanted you to meet Foster,' I said. 'I thought you two would have a lot in common.'

'Yeah, I was sorry I didn't get more of a chance to talk to him. He seemed cool. I wanted to ask him about travel and stuff. But it wasn't a very conducive atmosphere,' he said.

'Really? Why's that? Not enough booze? Or did you want drugs?'

'No,' he said. 'I just found it all very – self-absorbed.'

'You found it self-absorbed? What do you mean? What is *it*?'

'*You*, Erica. *You* are self-absorbed.'

'I'm what?'

'Sorry, I—'

I slammed the phone down. Then I rang back to apologise and it was engaged. I tried again and got through. I said I was sorry for hanging up on him. And for being self-absorbed. He was right, I told him.

I was so ashamed. I cried a tiny bit, hoping he wouldn't hear. I secretly loved him all the more for daring to tell me the truth, but I kept that to myself.

'Hey, there's something else I wanted to tell you,' he said.

I felt sick. It was hard to tell from the tone of his voice whether it was good news or bad, but either way I dreaded it.

'Yeah, um. It turns out Donny's been up in Auckland. I don't know if he's rung you yet.'

'Oh, okay. No. What's he doing up in Auckland?'

'He was getting jobs up there, through Student Job Search. I think he might have flunked his courses down here or something.'

'Oh, no. So what, so he's – still up there or what?'

'No. He's back.'

'Right. No, I haven't heard from him.'

There was a long pause.

'I mean it's just – he's crashing at our place.'

'Oh, fuck.'

'It wasn't my idea. Martin kind of made an executive decision.'

'Martin doesn't even *live* with you.'

'Exactly. Like I say, it wasn't my idea. We've filled Annie's room now. I don't want to alienate Arthur so early in his tenancy. So – we may have to chuck him out.'

'Donny? I see.'

'By which I mean, be prepared.'

We said goodbye and I put the phone back on the hook. It was dark in the hall. It seemed as though dusk had fallen during the course of our conversation, although we hadn't been talking that long.

40

The picnic was Martin's suggestion. He billed it as a carefree summer outing. Kyle was coming, even the reclusive Albertine. 'It's about time she got out and about,' Martin said. 'Thought we could take the ferry to Days Bay, hang out at the beach, maybe go for a bit of a bush walk.' Of course I couldn't refuse an opportunity to picnic with Kyle. But when I met them at the wharf it wasn't just Martin and Kyle and Albertine. No. Donny was there too, haughtily parading the waterfront wearing a legionnaire's cap in place of his usual beanie. I nearly turned around right away, but I'd already made eye contact with Kyle and he had me hooked.

'Hi,' I said quietly.

'Hey,' said Kyle, more resigned than apologetic.

'*Willkommen*, Frau Maus,' said Donny with crisp formality. 'Hail to thee, O recently come of age!'

Martin was holding Albertine firmly by the shoulders. She had a stricken look. Maybe he was trying to stop her from jumping into the water.

We climbed the hill above Eastbourne, prickly and sweet with gorse. Zigzagged down into the bushy valley where I stood on the planks of a low bridge and yelled, 'I've hit bottom!'

At Butterfly Creek, Martin commanded us to compete to be first to touch the eel. Kyle and Donny and I duly dipped our hands in the cool water. None of us touched it except Martin, or so he claimed. 'I could have got it if I'd wanted to,' he said. 'But three of you are vegetarians. It would've been a waste.'

A gust of wind took Donny's cap away while we were picnicking and Martin ran off and caught it. Donny's face contracted with anxiety. He held his hands out as Martin knelt back down on the edge of the blanket, but he didn't give it to him.

'Hey, Donny,' he said, cocking his chin. 'Why the hat all the time? You look better without one.'

Donny reached for the hat and Martin pulled away. Kyle laughed.

'Hey,' I said. 'Give it back.'

'But why? Come on, it's a genuine question.'

'Martin,' said Albertine. 'Give the man his hat.'

We were a long way away from help, a couple of hours. Martin and Donny could get in a scuffle and end up in the creek. Donny could hit his bald head on a rock and drown.

I lunged at Martin and grabbed him by both wrists. It took us both by surprise and I inadvertently tackled him to the grass. He didn't struggle. 'Get it, Donny,' I said.

While I had Martin pinned down, Donny took the hat back.

'Mmm ... I didn't know you felt that way,' Martin muttered into my hair.

'Idiot,' said Albertine.

'Shut up,' I said, releasing him.

We sat up. Donny was holding his hat in place, as if afraid of another wind gust, or of Martin.

'Hey, man, I didn't mean to upset you,' said Martin.

Donny didn't say anything, just scowled and started peeling a boiled egg. He stood up and wandered off with it in one hand, the other on his head.

'Never touch a man's hat,' said Albertine with a shake of her head.

Albertine turned out to be a good minder for Donny. On our way back, she walked with him, nodding cautiously at his bombast, while the rest of us went on ahead, pausing every so often to check they were still behind us and waving when they came in sight. In theory, that gave me more time with Kyle, but he was cryptic as ever. The closer we were, the less he had to say. At one point, the drink bottle I was holding slipped out of my hand and tumbled downhill. He chased it a considerable way. When he handed it back he was flushed and out of breath. Our hands touched. I nearly dropped it again. He gave me The Look. It was the closest range at which he'd ever attempted it.

41

It was only a week later that Donny showed up at my door, downcast and trembling like an injured animal. I said nothing, just let him follow me upstairs.

It must have been raining because his clothes were wet. He put his bag down and stood in the middle of the floor, dripping. 'Someone stole my bike,' he said.

Foster's bike, he meant, but I didn't correct him. Donny believed in trust, not ownership, the same reason he never used a lock.

'I spent all day looking for it. On foot, Erica. The pain in my spine, man.' He reached down his back, wincing as he stretched one side of his neck. 'It's killing me. I gotta sit down.'

I helped him off with his saturated army jacket and he handed me his beanie. I took them downstairs and squeezed them out over the bath. When I came back, he was lying by his bag on the floor with his eyes shut.

I stood there shaking. I didn't know what to say, but that didn't matter. Donny would relieve me of my obligation to talk. He always did.

'Don't you understand?' he said, without opening his eyes. 'You're the only person in whose presence I can rest.'

Donny on the floor, eyes squeezed shut. If he stopped breathing, the pain would leave his body and all this tortured animation with it. He'd be a harmless wreck. I'd mourn him.

He placed one hand over his eyes, the other on his heart. I caught a glimpse of my reflection in the window. I had the same expression Alison used to use when I'd left the bathroom heater on, but I didn't feel annoyed. I didn't feel anything. I pulled the curtains.

'Kyle and his warehouse friends are crude children. Clutter my brain with schoolyard taunts. I can't think. At least when I come here, you say nothing. You expect nothing.'

'I don't know what to say,' I said. 'You seemed okay last time I saw you.'

'That was a week ago. I haven't slept. I haven't eaten. You realise I had to ditch university because of you? I'm so dejected, so damaged, so – so stunted,' he said, screwing up his face, 'can't even cry. There's no relief. This pain's relentless.'

'What sort of pain?' I asked, sitting on the floor beside him.

'It's every sort of pain!' he said, opening his eyes now to glare at me. 'Do you discriminate? Must you carve me up like a butcher his carcass?'

'I'm sorry.'

He shut his eyes again. 'Let me be still with you,' he said quietly.

And so Donny came to stay. He knew it was only temporary. Every day I'd trudge round town checking café noticeboards and taking phone numbers. I tuned in to Radio Active for the accommodation guide. I wrote everything in my notebook to pass on at the end of the day, and in return he wrote me notes of thanks or mild admonishment. It was a fragile time for him. He found it hard to phone these young folk and face rejection. He needed to recharge his cells on some Erica honey patties, he said, to lie with

196

me and accept my kindness, to gather confidence. Our year apart had been destabilising for him. He was unsteady. He doubted himself. It was horrible to see how reduced he had become. To feel in some way responsible. I became his protector – reluctant and inept, maybe, but I did my best.

Darren disapproved, of course. He stopped talking to me. If someone called, he'd say I wasn't home, even when I was, and wouldn't take a message. I avoided him and tried to forget how kind he'd been before.

Carl lent Donny his bike. He had to ask, on Darren's account no doubt, if we couldn't increase our rent now there were two of us. I reminded him that Donny was only there on a temporary basis, much like Ramesh when he came to stay. I didn't want to ask Donny for money, not only because he'd say something scathing about my capitulation to transactional thinking, but because if we didn't talk about him moving in, then it wasn't happening yet.

Nobody ever saw Chris. Now and again we heard her Tori Amos albums faintly on the landing and knew she must be home. So I doubted she had an opinion, and too bad if she did.

It was fine. Fine. Everything was fine. It's like when you're at a party, say, and they're blasting Joy Division, and everybody's smoking and you can't think or talk. You pass through. It's a cloak, the deep melancholic assurance of Ian Curtis, the smoke, the bass, the drums, yes, drumroll please, yes, it makes you taller, yes, it makes you anonymous, yes, it makes you invulner-able. No, it doesn't matter that your knees feel like they belong to somebody else. It doesn't matter if the cacophony belongs to you or this room, it doesn't matter if you want to wreck the place because you won't, this composure is what you've got instead of danger, instead of anger. You can take this anaesthetic.

42

Carl didn't mind Donny coming to stay at all. He even took us to Breaker Bay to go skinny dipping. I suspected he just wanted to see Donny naked but he proffered it as a chance for me to 'get to know Kyle a little better'. I seized the opportunity to invite Kyle but I didn't tell him about the skinny dipping part of it.

When we got out of the car, the wind was brisk. Carl took off his clothes anyway and ran straight into the surf. I could see why he wasn't shy – he had a great body. Donny laughed and disrobed down to his briefs and ran after him. He even took off his hat and his shoes. He didn't look so bad either, unencumbered, although he ran in a jerky way because of his leg. Kyle, on the other hand, seemed intent on walking to the other end of the beach fully clothed, picking up rocks every now and then and hurling them into the water. I watched him for a while, wondering if I should run after him.

'Come on in, babe,' Carl yelled to me, dog paddling amicably. 'Water's fine!'

I stripped. My undies were pale, so I decided I'd look less decent with them on than off, once they got wet. I ran to the edge of the water and then whisked them down my leg and hurled them back in the direction of our clothes.

The water was such a shock it made me gasp and gulp lung-fuls of seawater. Once I got sufficiently numb, I swooped under and undulated like a mermaid for as far as my breath would take me. Underwater was preferable to above. The cold and the bubbling sound concentrated my mind.

I was in one of my prolonged dives when I got bumped side-on by another body. I felt it slither beneath mine and away, a wash of hair caressing my chest like seaweed. When I came to the sur-face, I paddled on the spot waiting to see who it was. Carl was freestyling out to sea about a hundred metres away, and Donny was sitting in the shallows with his legs stretched out, letting surf wash over him.

Light hands gripped my right leg and then my left. Before I could respond, I felt hair passing through my knees. Coming out the other side, I could see Kyle's blond mane billowing brown under the water, followed by a brightly coloured pair of boxer shorts.

He popped up in front of me smiling, eyes squeezed shut. Instead of opening his eyes, he arranged his long hair so it cov-ered his face.

'Hello,' I said, dog paddling, 'are you Cousin It?'

It was my turn, I realised then. He wanted me to dive down and pull his pants off. I took a deep breath and went under. I tried to open my eyes but it stung too much. I felt around for his undies but before I could orient myself I got a knee or an elbow in the face. I shot back up to the surface and blinked, shaking off the seawater. Kyle popped up again, just after me. He lifted his flap of hair and squinted. 'Jeez, it's cold, eh?' he said, grinning, and swam away.

I had misjudged. He'd been in little brother mode, playing like he would if he were swimming with Annie, probably – I was nothing but a sister substitute. When he got close to shore, he stood up and began to walk. His broad back was pale compared to Carl's or even Donny's, and nothing like as muscular. His boxers had Bart Simpson on them. *EAT MY SHORTS*, said the speech bubbles.

I stayed in the water awhile, teeth chattering, attempting to calm down. By the time I got back to the sand, Carl and Donny were playfighting with a jandal.

'Quick,' said Donny, who had wrested the shoe off Carl. 'Punish her!'

'I'll punish you!' said Carl, and put him in a headlock.

I got my pants on as quick as I could with numb fingers. Kyle was already dressed and further up the beach.

'Hey, Kyle,' yelled Donny, and Kyle turned back towards us with a look of wary puzzlement. 'You need to give this girl a spanking!'

'Fuck you,' I said to Donny as I bent forwards, trying to re-attach my bra.

'Don't pretend it's not what you want,' he replied. 'Miss *Moneypenny*.'

Part 4

Moving On

43

We were thinking a lot about the new millennium, everybody was, it was on the news, in the papers. The banking systems would probably shut down. Email would stop working. Nobody had thought to set a date in the computers that didn't start with '19'. A year '20' something. A year zero. It was pretty apocalyptic but it didn't concern people like me and Donny who didn't have real jobs or much in our bank accounts. We weren't too worried about the stock market or economics. Maybe people would recognise money as an empty signifier and start talking to one another. How about that? Anarchy. Too bad if the rich kids didn't like it.

Carl had another take on it. He wanted to be on the East Cape for the new year. First to see the light. He had an idea for something healing he could do involving the twelve star signs, in which people could go to pens for their respective signs.

'You're both air signs,' he said. 'If you want to be together you can dance close to the edge.'

We had heard that David Bowie was coming to Gisborne and got excited. Carl and Donny and I began to plan a road trip. Carl's family lived in Gisborne and he knew lots of people we could visit and things we could do on the way.

'We can stop at my old boarding school,' he said.

'Where's that?' asked Donny.

Carl told him.

'You know what? I don't normally tell people about this, but that's my old school, too.'

'Aw. Old boys,' said Carl, and they gave each other an extravagant hug.

'Fuck, that was a horrible place,' said Donny. 'I'm not sure if I can handle going there.'

'Me neither, bud,' said Carl, 'but you have to face your fears to overcome them.'

Carl was nearly thirty. Back when I first met Donny, I would've thought the two of them could've been at school together. I'd had no idea Donny was so much older. Carl didn't seem to have that problem, or at least was tactful enough to keep his mouth shut.

The road trip began to take over from Carl's dance party idea. If it didn't pan out this year, he could do it next year. That was the real new millennium for those in the know. 2000 was just completing the sad story of the twentieth century. And anyway, we could see David Bowie together. David fucking Bowie!

Bowie cancelled. But the idea stuck.

Y2K was what we were waiting for, was what we'd dreaded, was vomiting on the beach at Gisborne in the half-light of a dawning millennium. The waka appeared to split. The men got out and carried the pieces to shore. That's what I saw. Kiri Te Kanawa was somewhere up the beach, wind swallowing her song and carrying it north, away from us. No trouble hearing HDU – High Dependency Unit indeed, as if our lives depended on it.

So long, 1999. I wanted to dance to Prince, but there was no Prince at the house party Carl took us to. I sat on Donny's lap. We wore the leis that were issued at the door like good party guests. We kissed. A guy said, 'That's disgusting.'

204

A woman said, 'Who here do you know?'

What a house. They'd paid attention to the lighting. They'd bought designer cushions and refurbished couches and everything was fifties kitsch or retro chic. It reminded me of the party at Meg and Steve's. These were people for whom money meant something, this was status, this was in and out and hot and not.

Not long after, Carl told us we had to go. We weren't welcome. So we went back to the beach. To the beach, pitch the tents. Donny and Carl hugging in their sleeping bags in the dunes, waiting for the dark to lift.

Y2K was stopping at a lookout and thinking about jumping while Carl cranked 'Once in a Lifetime' on the car stereo and danced on the bonnet.

Y2K was going to the boarding school Carl and Donny had both attended and finding them each in their respective line-ups of upright adolescents with their arms folded aggressively high on their chests and saying *Fuck you all, 1967, fuck you all, 1983*. We all said it and pointed. *Fuck you all. All of you.* We aren't who you wanted, we aren't who we used to be.

Y2K was having sex in the tent, Donny's sweaty body, the furtive promise of something adult and complete. Air, not water, through the fingers – never closer, this mirage.

Y2K was talking to Kyle and Foster in my head and wondering what everybody else said and justifying myself to myself and making plans and saying *Fuck you, everybody*, knowing no one cared. Thoughts were mine by virtue of being unworthy, they were rice-paper nougat wrappers, disposables that dissolved in the mouth.

Y2K was lonely, lonely, lonely, lonely and staging a sham road trip in a desperate bid for belonging. Y2K was Erica deciding, *I have to reinvent myself. I have to get out of this place. Who are these people I've come to depend on?*

Y2K was pouring sick into the sand, sand into the sick. Make a well. Like baking, stir the sand into it. Yes, you people, look away. I could be any other drunken reveller. But I'm not.

44

I began the new millennium with a migraine. Carl snuck into his friend's neighbour's garden to get a datura flower for me. 'Microdosing', he called it. He squeezed it on my tongue and showed me where on my palm to press. Nothing helped.

When finally the pain began to lift, it was a couple of days later and Donny and Carl had left the campsite for the day. I put on my jandals and sunglasses and wandered into town, where I found a secondhand bookshop. I sat for hours in the musty dark. I read *The Crying of Lot 49*. It was the book with Rapunzel in it. I'd known it all along. I wanted to assemble a summit with Kyle and Foster at once.

I found Donny and Carl at an internet café round the corner. Donny was chortling at some email he'd received. 'Man, this is great. We could stay up here for ages if we could just score us some dough. What do you think, Erica honey patties?'

'I don't know.' I was dizzy. The shop was stuffy and dark and smelled of farts.

'Carl, you reckon there's any jobs going?'

'Not much, eh.' He didn't look up from the computer screen. His timer said he had two minutes to go.

'I think I need to sit down,' I said to Donny. 'And maybe get something to drink.'

'Don't you want to lay off the booze for a day? You've only just got over that hangover of yours.'

'It was a migraine,' I said, but he was in a mocking mood and couldn't stop.

'My, what a disgrace. Erica chundering in the new millennium. What must the good people of Gisborne think? *D'you hear our lovely Kiri? Not once that dreadful girl started puking.* Isn't that right, Carl? We're three days in and she's only just woken up. *Quelle dommage.*'

'I mean I want a water or something.'

Carl looked up. He didn't appear much interested in Donny's jokes either. 'Let's get out of here,' he said.

'Why so glum, Carly baby?' Donny asked as we emerged into the sunshine.

Carl put on his shades. 'Let's go back to the camp and pack up.'

Donny and Carl started bickering back at the campsite.

'I don't get this,' said Donny. 'You gonna stiff us, or what?'

'I told you, my friends are coming home from Auckland. I'm going to stay with them for a while.'

'And who are we if not your friends, Carl?'

Carl said nothing, just shoved his tent into the boot.

'They have a whole house, man. Don't pretend there's no room.'

'They have a kid. A baby.'

'A baby? Come on. A baby doesn't take up much space.'

'I think I want to go home,' I said, folding the pup tent Carl had lent us into a puffy square and climbing onto it.

'Everyone here has a lawn. I bet they've got a lawn the size of a golf course. We can camp.'

I pressed on all fours. The air hissed quietly out. 'I've probably had enough of camping. You two can stay up here if you like. Maybe I'll get a bus back to Wellington.'

'"You two"? There's no "us two", babe,' said Carl, flashing me

208

an unfriendly smile. 'You and Donny are the couple here. I think that's quite clear.'

'Carl, man, are you jealous?'

'No, Donny. To be honest I just feel kind of used.'

'What?'

'You won't even chip in on petrol.'

'Petrol? Is that really what you expect from us, so little as that? You disappoint me, dear fellow,' Donny said, shoving a book into his backpack and pulling the drawstrings tight. 'An ungodly chill, dare I say it, has descended over your countenance. I'm afraid I must chide you in the strongest possible terms.'

Carl drove us to a backpackers'. He said it was nothing personal, just something to do with Donny's energy not being very well aligned with his own, but I could tell he was just saying that in the hopes we'd get out of the car without a scene.

Donny got into an argument with the manager at the backpackers', who insisted we pay upfront for bed linen we didn't even need. We took our sleeping bags to the beach and I tried to sit still while Donny went to get some supplies. My skin was crawling and my knees and toes were twitching and the breeze was blowing sand in my eyes. I realised I needed to take off. I had to go back to Wellington, even though the thought of it filled me with a dread I didn't understand.

When Donny came back he had Marmite scrolls and a big plastic bottle of Scrumpy. 'Get it down ya,' he said, handing me the bottle.

I jammed the cider down beside me and took off my jandals. 'I'm going for a run,' I said, and pelted down the beach on the hardest part I could find, the dark patch between wet and dry. For a few minutes, I felt good. You can't escape yourself, they say, but maybe you can. Maybe I could outrun this creeping feeling. Maybe I needed to go back to Wellington so I could leave again.

I'd go back and say goodbye to Kyle. I'd be the one going this time. I'd say goodbye to Alison and Gary. I'd make them all sorry for something. Make them notice.

We thumbed a ride the next morning in a Holden Kingswood with its front bumper scraping the road. The guy didn't have a warrant, of course, so he went inland through bushy backroads.

'Let's stop in Palmy for a week or so,' said Donny from the front seat. He had to just about shout to be heard over the juddering of the car on the loose seal, and his voice was all vibrato. 'Free-ee foo-ood,' he vibrated. 'Maybe a cheque from Mother Dearest.'

'Good idea,' I said. 'You should do it.' I told him I needed to go back so I could move my stuff out of the flat. 'Otherwise Carl will want me to keep paying rent and bills.'

'That Carl needs a spanking,' said Donny.

So we parted ways at Palmerston North. I promised I'd come and join him as soon as I sorted things out at home.

'Say hi to your mum,' I said, hugging him goodbye. 'And Polly and Sister Rae.' I'd never see them again, I thought. It was kind of a relief.

It was evening when the guy dumped me at Paekākāriki. I rang home from a phone box. No one picked up the phone, which was strange, because it was Sunday. I rang a couple more times from a phone at the railway station. The same. I took a bus to my parents' place. If they were out, I could at least dump my bag on the back porch.

They weren't out. Alison answered the door with a blotchy face.

'What's wrong?' I asked.

'Nothing,' she said.

'Are you sure?'

I went upstairs and put my backpack in the spare room. The divan bed was set up already, like they knew I was coming.

When I got to the living room, Gary was pacing in front of the bay window.

'I tried to ring ahead,' I said. 'I was wondering if I could stay here.'

He sighed and ran his fingers through what remained of his hair. 'This is—' he said. 'Your mother—'

'Your mother, what?' Alison came in blinking, her eyebrows wet. She'd washed her face with cold water. That old trick.

'Oh, shut up, woman,' Gary shouted. 'What do you think I'm—'

'What? Your mother, your mother, your mother, what?' she said, shaking her head furiously.

'Alison. Would you please be quiet.'

'Your father and I—'

'Stop it.'

'Right. I'll leave you two to it,' I said. I went up to the spare room. I sat down on the bed and turned on the lamp. There was a jar of pills with Alison's name on it on the side table.

Gary followed me in.

'Your mother is going away for a while,' he said.

'Okay,' I said, waiting for more information.

'She's going to stay with your aunt, I think.'

I searched for something polite and non-committal to say.

Gary perched his bum on a sliver of bookcase. He was hunched right over. 'I'll stay here with the cat,' he said.

'Good,' I said. 'I think I'm gonna move to Auckland. I just need somewhere to stay for a few nights.'

He made a grumpy gargled sound like I'd woken him up from an unpleasant snooze.

'What?' I asked. Now I'd announced it, moving to Auckland felt like the only sensible thing to do. Of course I would move to Auckland. I would move as soon as possible.

'Sorry,' he said. 'It's a bit chaotic here, right now.'

'You don't want me to stay?'

'Don't you have somewhere else? I'm not going to be much company.'

'I'm not looking for company.'

His face was a guilty crumpled mess. 'We weren't expecting you.'

'Okay, fine. I'll go.' I put my backpack on. I was crying. Gary was crying. What the hell was going on?

'Don't go,' he said. He pulled himself off the bookcase and stood up straight for a minute, finding his balance and wiping his face roughly with his hands. 'Sorry. Oh, God.'

'Gary, what's wrong?'

He shook his head. 'You're not getting any sense out of me right now, I'm sorry.'

'This is horrible,' I said.

Alison showed me to the front door. 'Look after yourself,' she said. 'I'm sorry about all this. Did your father tell you I'm off to Mel's?'

'Yeah.'

She patted my shoulder. 'Be good,' she said. 'Keep an eye on him when I'm gone.'

I shook my head. 'I'm going to Auckland.'

'What? Another holiday?'

'I'm moving.'

She frowned. 'To Auckland?'

'Yes. I'm sick of Wellington.'

'What are you going to do up there?'

'My master's, I guess.'

'Okay,' she said vaguely. 'You've got Mel's email address?'

'You can get your own one, you know. It doesn't have to be attached to your computer.'

'I'd call you, but I never know where you are these days.' She put her hand up to her mouth.

I nodded and gave her a hug.

'Your hair's getting long,' she said sadly, tucking a hank behind my ear.

I trudged downtown to Kyle's warehouse on Tory Street in a daze. Nothing felt real. The streets, the shops, the racket of birds addressing the twilight – surely fake. Being Sunday, there was hardly any traffic, so I didn't bother with the footpath. I roamed brashly in the gutter, in the left lane, across the centre line.

When I got to Kyle's, Martin was there alone, drinking beer under the watchful eye of Princess Leia.

'How come you're always here?' I said. 'It's not even your place.'

'I could say the same to you. What's with the backpack?'

'Yeah, I'm kind of homeless, I guess.'

'What happened?'

'I don't really know.'

'Kyle's away. You should crash in his room.'

I looked over at the shut door to Kyle's room. So many times I'd imagined spending the night there. I'd had my chance, of course, but I'd blown it. Lost my cool all over his stairwell like a total dick.

'I dunno. We should probably get permission from someone who actually lives here.'

Martin nodded. 'Ask Arthur when he gets back.'

I felt an urge to get out of the warehouse. 'Do you want to play pool or something?'

'I'll take my camera,' said Martin.

We went to the pool parlour on Courtenay Place and played a few games. Martin beat me every time. Then we went downstairs and played air hockey. I beat him at that.

'I may have bad aim,' I said. 'But I have fast reflexes.'

Arthur had no objection to my staying a couple of nights. 'This place is kind of huge for one person.' The others were all away. He gave me a phone number for Kyle, who was staying at his grandparents' house in Nelson.

213

I sat on Kyle's bed with the cordless phone. The sheets were recently changed. They smelled only of Persil.

'Your parents turned you out of the house?'

'Not exactly. Kind of. It was pretty shit. I just wanted to have something to eat and go to bed, I was so tired. But they're in the middle of this weird thing and couldn't handle my presence.'

'Really? How come this is happening to your parents and not mine? Fuck knows why Mum puts up with Dad, but they never fight.'

'I know. I don't know.' I knew it was horrible – it should be shocking, even to me, but I couldn't feel anything.

'Do you think your mum had an affair or something?'

'What makes you say that?'

'If one of them did, I'd take bets on your mum. She's the one who's into drama.'

'Please.' Maybe Kyle was right, but it wasn't a thought I wanted to entertain.

'And she's still pretty hot.'

'Shut up. They're having a break, okay? Not even that. Alison's just going to stay at my aunt's place for whatever reason. Maybe Gary needs some space.'

'Sure,' he said. He didn't sound sarcastic, but he didn't sound sure, either.

'When are you getting back?'

'Dunno. See how long the jobs last. Doing a bit of painting and maybe some orchard stuff later.'

I took in a big breath. 'I think I'm moving to Auckland.'

'By yourself?'

'Who knows? I've just decided.'

'What do you mean, *who knows*? Isn't it up to you, Erica? Your passivity is pathological.'

*

214

I told Martin on a trip to Mr Chan's.

'Cool, man,' he said, poking the button on an avocado. It was ripe. 'I can see you guys in Auckland.'

'Well, for now it's just me who's going.' I said. 'I don't want to muck Donny round. He should do what he needs to do, you know?'

'Are you serious? He'll come with you, of course. The guy'll fall apart, otherwise.'

'I kind of want to do my own thing.'

'But he loves you, Erica. You can't just abandon your post.'

'What are you talking about? We're not married. I don't have a *post*.'

'I think you do.'

'You think I have a post? Am I a post or the goat that's tied to it?'

'Whatever. I'm sorry, but he's my friend too. I feel a responsibility.' He held up a rock melon and knocked it. 'You're like this. That stable. You don't know what it's like for someone like him.'

I didn't ask what kind of fruit Donny was. I made use of my so-called 'stability' and resisted the temptation to tip over a tray of potatoes. 'Does this mean you're going to tell him?'

'No, you tell him, Erica. Honestly. It's the least you can do.'

I wasn't very good at planning. But how much did I really have to do? I had to deal with my things, that was all. Sift through them for whatever I was going to take with me, and get my bond off Carl. I rang the flat and made a time to come round.

'You and Donny owe me for some bills and rent,' Carl said.

I told him to write it down and that I'd make a deposit as soon as I could. I needed to talk to Gary about money. I was going to need funds to get to Auckland too, to get myself set up.

'I'll get you your bond back,' Carl said, 'soon as we find someone new. Bit of a tough time of year right now. They'll start calling pretty soon, though.' It was strange talking to him now we weren't flatmates or on holiday together. Donny was right. He did seem cold.

He drove me down to my parents' place. We hugged goodbye stiffly at the front door.

Thankfully, Gary wasn't home. I could leave him a note about the money situation. I pulled the cord attached to the attic ladder. It came crashing down with a screech of its deranged springs. I sat in the clean pine warmth of the roof air and went through my boxes. Exercise books full of lecture notes, angst-ridden ramblings, letters from Donny. What of this, when it came down to it, did I really need?

'Goodbye, house,' I said.

When I got to the bottom of the stairs, the cat was waiting for me.

'Spongecake,' I said, 'I forgot about you. I have to go now. Forever. Will you miss me?'

She let me pat her for a long time, even rolled onto her back so I could rub her belly fur. She was mellowing in her old age.

'Bye, Spongecake,' I said. 'Keep an eye on this place for me.'

Maybe I'd never come here again. Pretty soon it probably wouldn't be Alison and Gary's place anymore, either. It was too weird to really comprehend.

I felt adrift. I felt futuristic.

45

Martin and Albertine came to the railway station to see me off. I shook hands with Albertine. She was absurdly well-dressed in an elegant suit. Nobody but her or perhaps Helen Mirren could have pulled it off. It was unnerving.

'God bless you,' she said earnestly.

'Thanks,' I said. Martin had told me she wasn't sure how to behave around people like us. She wanted to do the right thing, which made her nervous.

Martin kissed me solemnly on the cheek.

Thankfully, the train wasn't full, and I found myself a window seat. The seat beside me remained empty as we pulled out of Wellington. I tried to breathe as I watched the stations pass. Tawa. Kenepuru. Porirua. Plimmerton. People waiting for sub-urban trains, going to parties, to town, to a late shift at the bar or supermarket. A lone guy dancing to Run-DMC. A woman with a glazed look pushing a pram back and forth on the spot. Girls in tight dresses and makeup and no jackets chasing another girl to the other end of the platform, shouting. The girl cowering in a corner, a cardigan over her face.

Auckland would be different. Auckland would be easy. It wasn't confined to this narrow strip of fault line, hemmed in by seismic hills and choppy sea. In Auckland you could go any which way, Auckland was warm and seafaring, in Auckland you could breathe.

The opening of the buffet car was announced over the loud-speaker. I considered the menu. A cup of hot chips with tomato sauce, a cup of hot tea. Tempting though it was, I didn't want to leave my place. There were plenty of spare spots, but I had a dread of losing this particular one. I couldn't be sure I would still be there when I got back.

We made our first stop at Paraparaumu. I turned away, stiffening my body into an unapproachable pose as new passengers got on. A young couple with a baby came into the carriage and went past me. I reminded myself to breathe. Nobody else came in. The seat beside me remained empty as we pulled out of the station.

I could sleep if I wanted to. Surely. This was the Overnighter. People slept. That's what people do at night on trains. Here I was, alone. I couldn't drink or play cards. It was dark. The stations stopped glowing. Maybe when we got to Palmerston North I'd shut my eyes.

At Palmerston North I shut my eyes. I tried to breathe, but my attention strayed and my breath kept stalling. Finally it clamoured into my head what I was doing here. I had escaped. I was starting again. Why did I find it necessary to sit still? I wanted to tear through the carriage yelling *I'm free, I'm free*. It wasn't a happy feeling. I thought about the emergency brake two seats up from me. What if I couldn't resist the desire to smash the glass and pull the lever? No one would stop me.

A kid shrieked repeatedly as a family moved through the carriage, shushing and shouting by turns. Other, quieter passengers went past, solo or in silent pairs. Bags were stashed in the overhead racks. The train pulled out again. I was moving to Auckland. This machine was taking me there, securely and inexorably. I was leaving the lower North Island behind. This was good. Things would be good. *Ta tum, ta tum, ta tum, ta tum.*

I felt the seat beside me compress with someone's weight. There was a pair of vacant seats in front of me, and someone had chosen the one next to me instead. I could smell it was a man. I kept my eyes shut. All I could do was pretend to be asleep. The body shifted towards me. I felt his breath on my cheek. Beer and coffee and rotten teeth. He shifted position again. Even though I could sense his arm stretching out to my face long before he touched me, when his cold hand met my cheek, I jolted in fright. Undeterred, the hand began stroking my face. The back of a hand, knuckles mostly, grazing my cheek bone, the hollow under it, my jaw.

I opened my eyes. If it had been a stranger touching me, I could have got angry, I could have jumped out of my seat. But this shock, this all-too-familiar repulsion made fresh in an instant, this I couldn't handle. Why had I not known it? I'd sat beside him, slept beside him, kissed him, wept and screamed at him for a couple of years.

'Dear Erica. My plan was to rouse you gently from your slumber.'

'I wasn't sleeping.'

'Ah, *quelle dommage*. What a blunder.'

'You scared me.'

'A nice surprise though, no?'

'Sorry. I guess I was a bit freaked out.'

It was a nightmare. No. Not a nightmare. I clapped my hands furtively, clasped them tight as if doing so could contain everything, shrink it, vacuum pack it, make me wake up in my cosy bed. No. I remained wedged in the window seat and here was my aisle-side blocker, resolutely breathing, circulating actual human blood, pressed up against my side.

'Erica, aren't you glad to see me?'

'It's just that, I thought this could be my little adventure. I know it's silly, but I wanted to see how I could manage on my own. I thought it'd make me stronger.'

'Erica, the only thing that'll make you stronger is if you stop equating being a lonely sad sack with this mythical state you call independence. Stop denying yourself.'

Donny spoke kindly, patiently, like a reasonable person who knew what was best for me. He didn't seem angry or anything. I should have been reassured by that, but I wasn't.

'Sorry. I must've been a bit on edge, being alone on the train and everything . . . ' I trailed off. I should have felt fine. This was a nice surprise, surely. It was only Donny. But I couldn't shake this odd sense of stranger danger. 'Where will you stay?' I asked after a while.

'I heard you were staying in some student apartments in the old railway station. I'm sure there's room for two there, no?'

Of course I should have known better than to tell Martin anything. Tears stung my eyes. I turned my face to the window, even though it was dark.

'No, sorry,' I said. 'They said the room is singles only. It sounds quite tiny.'

The train shuddered and chattered along the tracks. I closed my eyes. I didn't sleep. I was back where we started, an empty room at night time. If something happened, how would I know? If it was unanticipated, if I straight away forgot? It was rumour, conjecture, my word against mine. The reason you don't remember when you were a baby is you couldn't speak. No memory without language. If there aren't words you have nothing to say. Your mind goes blank. An empty blackboard. Wet the duster, wipe it clean.

I closed my eyes. I closed my fists. I didn't sleep.

46

Auckland wasn't the same as it was in my head. I was alone, almost. It was hot at inconvenient times of day. It was expensive. At least my room in the old railway station required little in the way of interaction or commitment. The big communal kitchen I loved, like a giant operating theatre, gleaming surgical steel and lino flooring under long strips of fluorescent light.

I had a phone in my room with its own number. No need to set anything up. Everything was furnished and connected and ready to use.

I went to an internet café in Fort Street. There was one email from Alison, using Mel's email address. It was vague. She said she might be there for another month or so. She was taking a sabbatical, she said, whatever that meant for a high school teacher, and asked if I was back at varsity yet.

I sent Gary a short note with my phone number. I didn't hear from him, but his name showed up on an ATM statement later. I took care of my enrolment. I found a temp job till university started. I didn't have much chance to think after that.

My escape was only partial. Almost is always worse than not at all. Nearly every day would begin with the sight of Donny

221

hovering in the garden outside the apartments. At first, I pretended not to see him and he let me pass. Then he started following me and pestered. 'Erica, Erica. Do I exist for you? Am I invisible? Am I but a figment of your imagination or you of mine? Are we haunting each other?'

Eventually we spoke. I don't remember what I told him that day.

Whatever happened was exhausting. Each day, leaving the apartment was throwing myself into the pond and not drowning. I failed. It was a failure of execution.

I was alone and I was weak. Just that. Being alone, I tripped over. Everything was murky and anaerobic and bleak. I saw nothing, I couldn't make anything out, I couldn't breathe. And there was Donny prancing around, declaring himself, questioning me, pounding my brain with his words.

How it happened hardly matters. It was the same. What else could I expect? Madness is expecting a different result.

Together we found a three-month housesit in Grey Lynn. A cramped attic flat in the roof of a dilapidated old villa. It had a boarded-up window on one side like a rotten tooth and a rat-catcher tabby called Twig. We lied to the lease-holding couple that we were together.

'We've been living together what, three years now, is it, Donny?'

'Something like that.' The adoring look he gave me made me wonder if we were still acting or if we'd turned into a mature, loving couple when I wasn't looking. Maybe we were married. Maybe we were celebrating our anniversary this evening with roast lamb and sparkling wine.

I sent everybody my *new* new number. That would be it for three months. After that, who knew?

47

Kyle called one Saturday afternoon when Donny was out. He was thinking of coming up to visit round Easter. He hadn't decided yet what he was doing with his life. Most likely going to Japan. The JET programme had some sort of evening he was going along to and then perhaps he'd have interviews or something.

'Auckland's that good, is it?' he asked. 'Like a permanent vacation.'

'Yeah. No wait. No. That's some gangster term for getting taken out, isn't it? For getting whacked?'

'Oh yeah. I was thinking of the Jim Jarmusch movie.'

'Yeah, that's what they mean by it there, too.'

'Well you do have a strong death drive, Erica. All signs point towards that.'

How did he know? The voice that used to call my name had morphed. It wasn't Alison anymore. It was other voices, people I didn't recognise, asking me the same question over and over again. *Why don't you just kill yourself?*

'What do you mean?'

'Your self-destructive impulses. Explain to me why you're living with Donny again? After all the psychodrama last time?'

'We're not living together. We're just sharing a housesit.'

'That's living together.'

'Whatever. Maybe you're right. Let's say I am self-destructive. Maybe it gets worse when I'm alone.'

'Why Donny, though?'

'You wouldn't understand, Kyle, you're such a solo adventurer.'

'Solo adventurer, really? Fuck, I want that on a T-shirt.'

'I mean. Donny's always with me, whether I like it or not. He's more manageable on the outside than he is on the inside. When I'm alone he gets really out of hand. It's easier to argue with him when he's not just in my head.'

'That sounds fucked up.'

'But anyway, it's other voices as well. I don't know who they are or where they come from. When Donny's not around it seems to be an excuse for them to pile on in.'

Why was I telling this to Kyle, of all people? He'd led me down another conversational cul de sac. He was always doing that.

We had Kyle over for dinner. After our meal, we lounged on the floor with our drinks. The mood was weirdly mellow. I was drunk and Donny was having one of his good days. I suspected Kyle was stoned to begin with. He had an eerie calm when he arrived.

Suddenly I spied, jammed down the leg of Kyle's jeans, an erection so enormous I doubted my eyes. I looked at Donny. He was busy talking. I didn't listen to anything he was saying, but Kyle nodded calmly as if he was taking it all in. It hardly seemed possible, that he was harbouring such a profound distraction and managing to take part in a conversation at the same time.

Gary rang.

'Erica,' he said. 'I have bad news.'

'Oh, really? What?'

'It's about Spongecake.' He cleared his throat huskily. 'She—'

'What?'

'She had to be—'

I listened to his tears for a while, then asked, 'Is she dead?'

He cleared his throat. 'Yeah. Sorry. Yep. Sorry, Erica.'

'That's okay,' I said. 'She was old.'

I could hear him sniffing.

'Maybe you should just email me,' I said.

'Yeah.'

'Thanks for letting me know, though.'

It was such a relief to hang up.

Donny went back to Palmy for a few days, so Kyle and I got to spend some time together. We met up one day and walked all over Auckland city.

'The cat died,' I told Kyle as we went into Borders. 'Gary was really upset. Too upset to even talk. I guess he's having some sort of midlife crisis.'

'Probably. He might be lonely without Spongecake. She was his only friend. His wife has left him.'

'She hasn't *left*.'

'Didn't you say you thought maybe they were getting divorced?'

'I was exaggerating.'

'It sounds to me as though you are ignoring your good instincts as usual. Get this,' he said, shoving a book in my face. It was *The Crying of Lot 49*.

'I've already got it. I read it. I told you.'

'Oh, yeah. Get this, then.' He picked up something else from the P section. It had a garish dragon on the cover. 'And this.' This one had a dripping knife.

He piled up books at random. He put them all in my arms. He was going for physical comedy.

We went up the road to Real Groovy and argued the relative merits of different albums for a while. Then we went up to Rasoi on K Road for samosas.

225

'Let's go to the cemetery,' I said when we'd finished our samosas. We bought some Indian sweets and passed the bag between us as we headed back up to Symonds Street. Fragrant, gritty fudge.

'Mmm,' he said. 'How come we're going to the cemetery when we're clearly already in the afterlife?'

He went into the men's toilet by Grafton Bridge while I waited. Then we dipped down into the gully to wander through the leafy graves.

Every so often he'd stop to look at an inscription or take a photograph. Once or twice he took a picture of me. Never when I was looking at him, but I'd see him frame me up, hear the shutter when I looked away.

He took one such photo when we sat down, at his suggestion, in the tangled roots of a large fig tree. It had been my hope that here, finally, he'd say something. He even leaned in a fraction and brushed the curtain of hair from my face. Did he kiss me then? No. He said, 'Can you hold it back?' meaning my hair, and pointed his stupid camera at me instead.

He walked me to my bus stop after that. To the very last available opportunity I was inviting him home for a cup of tea, for dinner, for anything he fancied, really, or would he come another day, before he went? Impossible, he told me with a sad shake of his head.

We hugged goodbye with an intensity that surprised me, after all our aloof meanderings.

'Well if you—' he said over my shoulder. At least, that's what I thought he said. It was muffled, almost a whisper.

'Well if I?' I said when we came apart.

He shook his head, looked down.

'Well if I what?'

'It doesn't matter. You misheard me.'

'What did you say?'

226

'It doesn't matter.' There were tears in his eyes.

I later became convinced that what he'd said was not 'Well if you', but 'I love you'. I heard him say it that way suddenly when I was walking up Symonds Street one evening. At the Grafton Street bridge his voice just popped into my head, enunciating each word unmistakably this time. He said it again. 'I love you.' There was no joy in this love of his. He communicated it with unmitigated regret.

48

A couple of months passed. I didn't hear from Kyle, or anyone from Wellington, and the temporary comfort of living with Donny again had turned to discomfort. On the plus side, I was slowly getting to know some of the women in my classes at university, enough to say hi to them in the hall or the library, even stopping for brief chats sometimes before and after class. I smiled and waved, took notes, contributed to discussions, wrote coherent essays, and ignored the voices pursuing me all over campus. *Why don't you just kill yourself?* they wanted to know. Somehow I managed to get on with things.

I stayed longer and longer at university. I walked home instead of getting a bus. Even when it was raining, I would take as circuitous a route as possible, stopping in all the shops on K Road to browse the merchandise or, for no reason at all, walking all the way down to the ferry terminal before beginning my ascent. I would wander through Albert Park and Myers Park and Western Park and Grey Lynn Park, sitting on benches until men or the thought of men dissuaded me.

At home I refused to bow to Donny's rigorous dish-washing regimen. When he demanded to know what I planned to do with that fork once I'd finished with it I would scream at the top of my lungs, 'Who are you?' and 'What do you want from me?' and other questions to which he had no answer.

One day, Donny threw Twig the cat out the window. Twig kept purring in his ear when he was trying to sleep. Some saliva got in his ear hole and he got mad. We were three storeys up.

Donny could throw me out of that window. I had no self-righting mechanism, no spongy shock-absorbing joints. My bones would shatter. I would die. Would I? Or would I. It had to end somehow. Why not that?

Twig came back two days later, subdued but apparently uninjured. Instead of taking long walks home at night, I began to trawl the flatmate-wanted ads and call people from phone boxes about flats.

The first place I went to was a remarkably grotty house in Ponsonby. I was interviewed by two guys, Dion and Vince.

'You cool with gay guys?' said Dion. He had a London accent and an eyebrow piercing.

'Yep,' I said, 'of course.'

Vince, who was the leaseholder, said, 'We're not a couple by the way.'

Dion smirked. 'Yeah, what he means is, we're not gay.'

'What I mean is there's two guys in the flat at the moment who happen to be gay,' Vince said. 'Jeremiah and Toshi.'

'They're not a couple, either,' said Dion.

'We also have a woman,' said Vince.

'Galina,' said Dion. 'Czech girl. But we don't *have* her exactly.'

'We want to redress the gender balance,' said Vince.

A week later, Vince rang.

Donny said, 'Who's that?'

'Hi Erica, it's Vince, we're just wondering if you're still looking for a flat.'

'Yes,' I said. 'I am, actually.'

'Great. You interested?'

'Yes.'

I must have sounded super weird, but I was trying not to give away the content of the conversation to Donny.

'Are you sure?'

'Yep, definitely.'

'How soon can you move in?'

'This Saturday.'

Donny came right up to my face and asked me again who it was.

'Great. We'll sort out the bond and everything then,' Vince was saying.

'Okay, thanks, will do – see you then.'

I hung up. 'It was someone from class. She's arranging a study group this weekend.'

'Can I come?' asked Donny.

'No,' I said, 'you'll be moving furniture, remember?'

It was perfect timing. He was moving someone else and I was moving me.

I had a big wad of cash in an envelope in my jacket pocket for the bond, and just enough extra to pay for a taxi.

The taxi pulled up. I put a backpack, a box and a rubbish bag's worth of stuff in the boot, and put myself in the back seat.

I told the driver the address. I said it casually, like it was already my home and I'd lived there a long time.

This is my getaway car, I told the driver in my head. *You're helping me escape.*

Out loud, I said, 'How's your day been?' and 'Not bad.'

In my head, I said, *Pleased to meet you. I'm Rapunzel.*

49

I was suddenly a typical twenty-something of my demographic. I was a brilliant impostor. I hung out with my normal flatmates. No calls or visits from Donny. He'd never existed. I was confident and trouble-free.

I was even making friends at university: Julie, Kate and Olivia. Olivia was my favourite, the boldest, most vociferous person I'd ever met apart from Donny, although in all ways she was a vast improvement. For starters, she was rational. Olivia already had a postgraduate degree in French literature. She knew a lot about post-structuralist theory. She organised the four of us into what we called a 'book square'. We traded recommendations on books the Philosophy department did not expose us to. Sometimes it felt like we were trading in contraband.

Kate had switched to philosophy from English, having saturated herself in literary theory and decided she wanted more theory, less literature. Julie was the least rebellious of us all and said coyly she was cheating on Kant. I didn't know what my focus should be and only knew I wasn't finding it in any papers so far that year. Hanging out with the book square girls was a two-for-one deal: procrastination and education at the same time.

Julie got me a job shelving at the university library with her.

She was pretty, one of the prettiest girls I'd ever seen, and I was stunned to learn she didn't have a boyfriend. 'I don't know how to flirt,' she said, but I suspected there was more to it than that. At least two of the guys we worked with at the library had mad crushes on her, but she didn't seem to notice. Probably she had very high standards.

Kate was good looking too. She didn't have a boyfriend, either, which somehow amazed me less. She was more aloof than Julie – cool and self-contained. She lived by herself, in a one-bedroom apartment in Herne Bay, Julie said. She never invited us round.

'How do you think she does it?' I asked Julie one day. We were drinking flat whites in the quad after our shift. 'Do you think she's one of those women who's actually comfortable alone? I wish I could be like that.'

'I wish I could afford an apartment like that,' said Julie. 'I don't exactly love my flatmates.'

'Wouldn't you miss the company, though?'

'I'd get a cat.'

I tried to imagine living alone. 'I'd go crazy,' I said. 'To be honest, I'm crazy enough as it is. I wouldn't want to risk it.'

'What are you talking about?' She stood up to chuck her paper cup in the bin. 'You seem perfectly normal to me.'

After a few weeks in my new flat, Dion and Vince and Galina and I went to the Safari Lounge to dance and drink vodka, lemon and lime. They played Fatboy Slim and Morcheeba and whatever else was danceable and light.

Dion was the kind of guy who, if he was from New Zealand, would never have danced. He was the kind of guy who took the piss out of everyone and everything but dancing was off his radar. Because he was from London he was practically raised on dance culture. He was all in, moving to the beat from day one.

Vince, I was pleased to see, could also dance, though he moved more cautiously than Dion, rocking back and forth subtly with his knees and nodding his head, holding his drink up with his shoulders and elbow protectively high, taking a suck on the straw at nervous intervals. Awkward, admittedly, but not bad for a Kiwi bloke.

Galina was on the lookout for someone she saw the previous week and kept within view of the door at all times. 'Tall guy,' she told me in the women's toilet. 'Cute. Talking, talking, everything nice, but my girlfriend got sick. I went with her. Tonight I will see him again.' She grinned and raised her eyebrows suggestively. Out on the dance floor, I could tell she was conserving energy, sparing her most devastating moves for his arrival.

I'd never been out like this with flatmates. With Carl, of course, but even then, not out, out – not dancing. It was nice. I was glad I came. Glad I'd found them in the first place. What a fluke that was. First ad I tried from the paper. And here I was, three weeks in and no Donny. I was free.

We all walked back to the flat together in the early morning. Galina's tall guy never showed up. We all sat in the lounge for a while with Jeremiah, who was watching the music channel. Galina flicked through a film festival brochure and kept flashing us pictures of the ones she liked the look of.

'Slow down, Galina,' said Dion. 'You're too quick.'

'Too quick?' she said impatiently. 'Too many. You can't see, I can't see. Too many films.'

'Yeah, I always mean to go to heaps and then I manage about one,' said Vince.

'The last art movie I went to see was *Lost Highway*,' said Dion. 'That put me right off.'

'Oh, yeah,' said Vince. 'Was that the one where the guy kills his wife?'

'Or does he?' said Dion.

Vince nodded. 'There's like, video evidence.'

'But he doesn't remember. It's fucked up.'

'*Lost Highway*,' said Galina. 'Yes. Mystery Man. Video tapes. It is a pretty scary noir film.' She squinted at me. 'You know Lynch?'

I shook my head.

'You like to play with fire, little girl?'

'What's that? Is that from *Lost Highway*?'

She rolled her eyes playfully. 'We will go to the video store.'

We made fun of the music videos for a while, then Jeremiah and Galina and Dion all said goodnight in rapid succession. Vince switched off the TV. He said, 'I'm not ready to go to sleep yet, are you?'

'I dunno,' I said. 'Not really.'

'I'm wired. Hey, do you smoke?'

I hesitated. 'No?'

'I mean, do you smoke pot?' He smiled a shy smile, darting a look at the lighter on the coffee table.

'Yep. Maybe sometimes. Yes, I do.'

'Oh, good,' he said, getting up. 'Shall we?' He shuffled over to the front door. His room was in a shed down the back of the house. 'I'll just go and get my stuff.'

So it was just the two of us and Vince's marble pipe with an ineffective filter that sent seeds hurtling down into my throat.

We talked about what we did when we weren't going to the supermarket or cooking or dancing at the Safari Lounge. Vince was a chiropractor. He had gone to tech straight after school and joined a practice after that for a few years and now he had a business all his own. He was only twenty-six.

'You're all grown up,' I said.

'Yeah,' he said. 'I have an accountant.' We giggled.

'At least you don't wear a suit or anything.' He wore hoodies and Dickies work pants and skater sneakers.

'Yeah, that's one of the many pluses of being my own boss. I kinda wish I wasn't so grown up, though. I mean, I have friends who went to uni or travelled the world and stuff. I missed out on all that. It's a nice life but I kinda want this not to be me forever. I've gotta go to London before it's too late. They won't let you in after you turn twenty-eight.'

He had a band, too, only they weren't playing anymore, called Weird Science. He said if I wanted he could play me some of their music later.

'That would be cool,' I said.

'You might not like it,' he said. 'We're kinda DIY. Punky, you know? Do you like punk music?'

'Yeah,' I said, 'of course.'

We were seated next to each other on the squishy couch. It might have been the pot or just that we were getting along so well, but after a while talking we fell into a comfortable lull. Then the lull swelled into something else and I realised we were staring at each other. It wasn't unpleasant, just difficult to comprehend. This, I didn't know. I hadn't been here before.

I almost smiled.

'Erica,' said Vince quietly. 'Do you feel that something might be—'

I found myself bending towards him. We were sitting very close. With the side of my nose, I took a swipe at his. He swiped back. Then we were kissing. A melting kiss, effortless and warm.

He paused. 'Is this happening?'

'It is.'

'Do you want to go to my room?'

I must have looked worried, because he added, in a whisper, 'We don't have to have sex. I mean. It's late. I just really want to sleep beside you.'

'Okay,' I whispered. 'Only I can't promise we won't have sex.'

He laughed and took my hand.

*

'Did you finish?' he asked afterwards. He leaned over me, his hand on my upper arm, smiling calmly.

'I've never heard that expression before,' I said. 'But I can guess what it means.'

I learned another term. 'Happy ending'. As in, 'We need to give you a happy ending,' which is what Vince said. And we did.

After that, I remembered he had a girlfriend. 'Hey, what about Carla?'

'Oh, yeah.' He clapped his palm to his forehead. 'I literally forgot.'

'You are pretty stoned.'

'Maybe. Maybe you've blinded me.'

'Maybe so. No, that's no excuse. What are you going to say?'

'I'll break up with her.'

'I mean, I don't want to be the cause of your break-up or anything.'

'No. No. I want to be with you. If that's cool.'

'Yeah. Yeah, it's cool. I like you.'

'All right, then. Tomorrow I'll break up with her.'

'Really? You sure? You guys seemed happy.'

'Yeah, we're friends, but we hadn't really been having sex for a while. I dunno. She'll be fine.'

'All right, then.'

We lay back. I splayed myself over his chest, rested my head in the crook of his neck. His breath puffed my hair.

'This is nice,' I said.

'What about you?'

'What do you mean, what about me?'

'I mean, what about that guy you were with before you moved here – what was his name?'

'Donny.'

'It's only been a couple of weeks, hasn't it? Are you sure you've had enough time?'

I sat up and looked Vince in the eye. 'I've been trying to get rid of him for three years.'

'Whoa, okay. Sounds like a great guy.'

'Yeah. The less said about him the better.'

'But technically, you are probably still on the rebound.'

'Whatever.'

'Yeah. Fuck. Don't listen to me. I've just noticed with other girls that they sometimes think they're over someone and they're really not. Like Carla had this difficult ex and he kept phoning her and stuff. She felt all guilty or – I don't know. But don't worry. I'm not trying to talk you out of this or anything.'

'You better not be,' I said, and tickled him aggressively under the armpits. He was ticklish and fought back, pleading with me to stop.

I stopped and pinned him down for a while, breathing into his face. He had a beautiful face. It was so nice to gaze at each other without having a thousand hurtful things hovering between us, infecting the air. Everything was fresh.

I kissed him. We stayed in the kiss a long time. When I moved my hand down his chest to his cock, it stiffened in my hand. I leaned close to his ear, pausing to suck on the lobe – a baby-haired plump piglet of a thing. Then I gave his cock a tug and said softly, 'I'm going to rebound the shit out of this.'

'I'd better go back to my room,' I whispered when we'd finished round two.

'No, you don't. We were going to sleep together. I mean literally. Remember? That was the whole plan.'

'That's right. That was the plan all along.' I laughed. That was only what, three hours ago?

He pulled me gently into a spoon.

'But I'll sleep in and then the others will know. I'll come in when Dion's making breakfast or something.'

'Who cares?'

237

'Wouldn't you rather keep it secret for a bit? They'll laugh at us.'

'I don't care. They can laugh all they want.'

'But sneaking around might be fun.'

'Maybe. We can strategise in the morning. In the meantime, shush. Time for sleep.'

'Unless you get another stiffy,' I whispered.

'That's enough of your lip, missy,' he whispered back. 'Anyway, it was your doing.' There was a pause, during which I began to seriously consider the possibility of going to sleep. Then Vince said, 'Why are we whispering?' and we collapsed into giggles.

'Are we even going to try to sleep?' he asked when he caught his breath, resuming his non-whisper-level, normal voice. It gave me a thrill hearing it. All manly and transgressive in the sweaty 3 a.m. air. It was a level voice. Not weird, just straight up.

'I vote no,' I said.

For a while, we snuck around. Vince would head up to the house first, naked under his towelling dressing gown. He'd put the jug on and then amble back to the room and tell me the coast was clear as he grabbed his towel. One time Galina came to the door to ask for a flat meeting and kept Vince standing there in his gown with the door open for a full five minutes while I lay face down under the duvet, pressing my face into the sheet to stifle my laughter.

'I think we have to tell them,' he said after she'd gone, and so we did. Dion gave us shit but it was fine. I think he was even happy for us.

'You didn't guess?' I asked Dion after the initial embarrassment had died down.

'I could tell something was up. He's been far too loosey goosey, all squishy, he is. Look at 'im. Bless. No, I knew he had a new lady friend, but I didn't know who. I dunno. You two.'

Galina hadn't guessed either, and went all shy on our behalf. Jeremiah and Toshi we hardly ever saw, but they both made a point of sharing a drink with us the night we told them.

'To screwing the crew!' said Jeremiah.

Toshi laughed politely.

I wondered if they'd ever screwed each other. Maybe they had and we'd just never considered it. I felt stupid for making such a big deal about the whole thing.

'Do you want to go to Yo La Tengo tonight?' Vince asked in bed one Saturday morning. We were listening to the entertainment guide on bFM.

'I've already been to one of their gigs,' I said. 'I don't know if I need to see them again.' But then he asked me what they were like, and I had to confess. 'They were great.'

'So let's go then.'

'We should go.'

He jumped out of bed and put his dressing gown on. 'Do you wanna go to town? Let's go clothes shopping.'

First we went to a skate shop on High Street where he tried on a few hoodies. Then he took me to a women's streetwear place and waited while I modelled a sexy tube dress, an orange miniskirt and a close-fitting short-sleeved shirt with a retro collar.

I got back into my jeans and baggy T-shirt. 'Well that was fun,' I said, hanging the clothes up outside the changing room.

'No you don't,' he said, taking them off the rack and heading for the counter.

'What are you doing?'

He wouldn't listen to my protests. 'Anything for my girl,' he said outside, handing me the bag. 'You've got a hot body. You deserve hot clothes.'

'Man,' I said. 'You're like my sugar daddy or something.'

'Damn straight, baby doll,' he said, putting on an accent. 'Nah,

239

it's not like that. When you've finished studying and you're earning the big bucks you can buy me stuff, all right?'

'That sounds fair,' I said, although the idea still gave me the creeps. There had to be a way I could keep things how they were.

Next, he took me to the hairdresser. While we waited for my appointment he flicked through the magazines.

'Do you want highlights?' he asked.

'I don't think so.'

'Are you sure? They're kind of cool.'

'Maybe I'll cut it all off. Get a buzz cut.'

'How do you feel about layers?' He held up a picture of Jennifer Aniston. 'Not like this, but – you know?'

'Maybe.'

The process was horrible. I hadn't been to a salon since Alison took me as a sixteen-year-old, after which I'd lost interest in professional haircare, and this reminded me why. The hairdresser kept asking me what my haircare routine was and what kind of styling products I used, despite the fact that it was painfully obvious I barely bothered to brush my hair, let alone do anything with it.

The blow-drying part took forever. I closed my eyes and pretended I couldn't hear what she was saying.

When I finally met Vince at the counter, he looked appalled. 'You gave her a Remuera bob,' he said.

The hairdresser sighed like this happened all the time. 'She asked for a bob.'

'It's fine,' I said.

'We asked for layers,' he said. 'Something edgy. This is . . .'

'This is a very nice haircut,' said the hairdresser.

'She might as well be wearing a twinset and pearls.'

He was right. I looked like a rich bitch. I vowed never to set foot in a hairdresser ever again.

*

I dressed up in my tube dress after dinner. I borrowed some of Vince's hair fudge so I could mess up the Mary Tyler Moore look the salon had given me.

'Sha-*wing*,' said Vince, doing the hip thrust from *Wayne's World*.

'You don't look too shabby yourself,' I said.

It was almost dark by the time we got in his car, a sporty-looking two-door. He pressed a button on his key ring and it made a sound like a droid. I must have jumped, because he said, 'Don't worry. I just unlocked it.'

When we got into the car I felt weird. I tried to open the door. 'Hey,' I said, when he started the engine, 'I'm not sure if I should go.'

'What? How come?' He stopped the engine.

'I don't know. I think I might be coming down with something.'

He leaned over and put the back of his hand to my forehead. 'You don't seem to have a fever.' Smiling, he cupped his hand under my chin. 'Do you need a visit from Dr Vince?'

'Maybe,' I said, and gave him a long kiss. It almost made me feel better. Maybe I was fine. 'I just have a headache,' I said, which wasn't true, but it probably would be soon.

'Poor baby,' he said. 'There should be some Panadol in the glove box. Want me to run in and get you some water?'

'That's okay,' I said. 'I can have some at the bar, I guess.'

When we arrived it was already packed. The support act were setting up and it was loud with talk. Vince held my hand as we squeezed through the crowd, tapping big guys on the shoulder and pulling me through. We made it to the back of what appeared to be the queue. Vince put his arm round me and leaned in by my ear. 'What do you want?'

It was then I caught sight of his beanie across the other side of the bar. Vince was asking me again what he could get me but I couldn't answer. I pulled away and put my head down and shoved through all the bodies as quickly as I could. I made my way to the ladies' and locked myself in a toilet and cried.

Women chatted and shrieked and yelled at one another to hurry up. 'Is anyone in there?' They kept asking. Presumably they were talking about my stall, but I said nothing. 'Are you okay?' one woman asked. I didn't reply. She knocked and asked again. I stayed quiet. Stupid nosy parker. I waited until I heard the support act starting up to unlock my door.

I glared at my reflection in the mirror. It was my best Don't Fuck With Me face, but it was all mottled red. I ran my hand under the cold tap for a while and splashed my eyes and cheeks. I blinked at myself, glared again. Better. Then a stall door opened and a woman met my gaze in the mirror. She looked startled. A fraction of a second after she averted her eyes I realised she was the drummer from Yo La Tengo.

I found Vince standing near the front guarding two beers between his feet.

'Are you sick?' he shouted in my ear.

'Yeah, sorry. I'll be fine.'

All night, Donny glowered at us from the bar. I made a point of dancing more enthusiastically than usual. There was no point letting him ruin it. He was an ex-boyfriend. No big deal. If he wanted to glower at me that was his business.

When the crowd thinned out, I thought I'd be polite and mature and went over to say hello.

'Hello. Did you enjoy the gig?'

He looked at me like I'd asked him if he enjoyed being disembowelled.

'No. No I did not. Erica, Erica, how can you so brazenly assault my vision? Does not one tender thought foray into your consciousness on my behalf? Are you as callous as you seem or are you just made thick from slatternly lust and disregard for human decency?'

242

Vince came over. 'Everything okay, babe?'

'*Babe?*' said Donny. 'You're this chump's *babe* now, Erica?'

'Let's go,' I said to Vince.

'You turn up unannounced and flaunt yourself in my general direction for three hours and then Mr Doofus here whisks you off into the night? Do you really think that's any way to behave, Erica?'

Vince hugged me round the shoulders. 'Just ignore him,' I said as we left the bar.

It was only after we'd been walking awhile outside that we heard a shout. It was Donny.

'Erica! You can't walk away from me. Stop this pathetic charade.'

I turned around and got a glimpse of him, his face creased with hatred, holding a beer bottle out in front of him in anguished declamation.

'Why are you denying it, Erica? Why are you doing this? Deny, deny, deny.'

Vince turned around. 'Fuck off, Noddy.' We kept walking.

'Pretend all you like, Erica. You might fool this class B dunce here, but you can't fool me. I know who you really are.'

'Ignore him,' I told Vince.

'You know, one day it'll erupt on you, Erica. This wilful denial will grow cankerous and burst. Like a pestilent sore – is that what you want? You're a good little Freudian, Erica. Get a load of the return of the repressed!'

'You're mad,' I yelled. 'Leave us alone, you crusty old rapist.'

There was traffic on the road ahead and we had to slow down before we could cross it. I gripped Vince by the arm. 'How far off is the car?' I whispered. 'He's going to catch us up.'

Vince stopped. He turned back. 'Listen, fuck knuckle. Leave my girlfriend alone or I'm calling the cops.'

I flinched, afraid Donny was going to slug him. But he didn't. He froze. We stood facing each other stiffly, awaiting the culmination of Donny's rage. Vince got his cell phone out and pressed the On button.

'I mean it, dipshit.'

'Oh sure, invoke the law, why don't you? Run to Daddy, pretty boy. Tell the nice police officer all about it. I'm not sure just what crime is being committed here except that crime against this sad personage,' he said, gesturing at me, 'of withdrawing all meaning and dignity from the core of her very being and replacing it with this gruesome husk of social rectitude you dare call Girlfriend.'

Vince was shifting from one foot to the other like he was unsure whether to call the cops or tackle him.

'Don't,' I said suddenly. I wasn't sure if I was speaking to Donny or Vince. Probably nothing I ever said or did from now on could make sense. 'Stop.'

'Fuck you, you fucking creepy skid mark,' said Vince.

In one swift, unbending movement, Donny brought his right arm down and smashed his beer bottle on the footpath. Beer spread in a dark stain. He bent down to pick a shard of glass from it, held it out towards us like a knife.

'Let's go,' I said, yanking Vince back to face the road. The traffic was never going to clear. We'd have to make a run for it. We dashed into gaps, one lane at a time, side stepping along the white lines between the lanes. One car stopped and honked repeatedly at us. Vince gave them the finger.

When we'd made it across, we sprinted up the side street all the way to the car. Vince popped the lock from the button on his key ring and the car made a startling sound that jolted through me like an electric current. The car was unlocked now. At any moment Donny could climb in and hijack us.

Thankfully, when we got into the car it was just the two of us. Vince locked the doors. We said nothing to each other. I spent the entire journey home coming up with different ways Vince might break it to me that our relationship was no longer tenable.

Each time, I replied in my head that this was entirely reasonable. No sane person wants to get into a relationship of any kind with Donny, and Donny was part of the package with me.

But Vince didn't try to break up with me. Instead, in his room that night, he said sadly he was sorry I'd had to deal with that man, told me I was with him now and he'd always protect me.

He held my hand, squeezed it, pressed it to his chest. We kissed.

'Thank you,' I said. 'Thank you for being so understanding.' It was truly amazing, how understanding he was being. But it didn't seem real. He had to be deluding himself more than Donny or I was, if he could be so confident, so reassuring.

'I'll always look after you,' he said again when we were snuggling in bed. 'I won't let anybody hurt you, ever again.'

My stomach clenched. For the first time since we'd been together I felt like sleeping in my own room.

It's not as if he didn't mean it. He was the sweetest, kindest man I knew.

50

Olivia was married to an engineer called Ants. They owned their own unit in Mount Eden. Our 'book squares' took place on lazy afternoons in their lounge, sipping tea and trading photocopies. Julie couldn't understand why Olivia complained about married life.

'You have it all,' she said. 'A lovely husband, a great flat, a dog.'

'You think knowing about the historic oppression of women can spare you?' Olivia raised her forefinger portentously. 'Not on your life. And it's not historic. Get married, you become a chattel. Perhaps it's worse if you love him. Sex changes once you're married. You think it won't, but all of a sudden it's somehow approved, cleansed of the stain of *jouissance*, and suddenly there are your parents and your grandparents and your priest and aunts and uncles and even God all sweetly smiling over you in bed. You won't know it till you experience it yourselves.'

I wondered if the oppression I'd felt with Donny was not unusual, if, really, when it came down to it, my personal sovereignty could be safe with any man, in any couplehood. Perhaps marriage was just the logical extension of that suffocation? It was closing off all the exits and sitting there together, choking in the dark.

Olivia had brought us photocopies of Gayle Rubin's essay

about women as commodities of exchange. We were mere tokens – gestures, she explained, like money or handshakes. We brought men together.

'But it's not as if we're all just hookers, are we?' said Julie. 'Not that we're better than that, but you can hardly compare marriage and prostitution, can you? Look at you, Olivia. At least you love the man you married. And you had a choice. You chose him freely. Prostitutes don't get that chance.'

Kate was frowning and going red. She wouldn't say what was bothering her, only that you shouldn't confuse freedom and power, because sometimes you have to choose between the two. You can't have it both ways.

'What is power, Kate?' Olivia asked. 'Who gets power and who gets freedom, in your book? I'm interested to know.'

'Sex is power,' said Kate, getting redder. 'Do you have any idea how powerless most men are when it comes to sex? How fragile? How needy? The only reason you don't see it is because you've been duped, for the same reason you kid yourselves love is a Get Out of Jail Free card when really it's a life sentence.'

Julie looked stunned. 'Surely you don't think that of a nice man like Ants? Or Erica's Vince? Men our age are starting to turn it all around. They're raised by single women. They don't want to repeat their fathers' mistakes. Anyway, they couldn't if they tried.'

Olivia nodded gravely at Julie. 'Kate is correct, I think, sadly,' she said. 'It's not about individuals, of course. It's a structure we are all participating in and which we can't escape.'

'Like fate?' I ventured.

Kate and Olivia exchanged an amused look. 'Not exactly, Erica,' said Olivia. 'But just as inexorable.'

'In my opinion, the only way round it is to go against the grain,' said Kate. 'Never submit to the known paths. If it's comfortable, it's dangerous. You're getting sucked into a vortex.'

Julie was worried. 'But surely some of the dangerous things we're told to avoid really are dangerous? We can't be counter-intuitive about everything, or we'd be self-harming or – I don't know, being like whatshername, submitting to twenty-four-hour gang bangs in the name of art or feminism or whatever it is she was doing. Anyway, she went insane, and it's hardly surprising.'

'What would you know, Julie?' Kate was getting vehement again. 'What would you know if she went insane or if it was risky, or what? Who are you to tell her what's safe to do with her body and what isn't?' Her face crumpled. 'I'm sorry. It's just—'

'Oh, Kate, what's wrong?' Julie came and sat beside her on the couch. She put her arm round her and the tears started.

Kate covered her face, shrugged Julie's arm off. 'Don't.'

Julie turned to Olivia, then me. A pleading look, as if to say, *What do we do?* Or was it, *Do something?*

Olivia frowned. 'I think we have hit a nerve with Kate. Let's talk about something else for a bit.'

'Oh, fuck off, Olivia. I know you'll just tell them after I'm gone anyway.'

Olivia looked hurt.

'Sorry,' said Kate.

For a while we pretended the conversation hadn't happened and the three of us (minus Kate) began to discuss the red carpet photos in Olivia's magazine, ranking the dresses and each pro-fessing our devotion to what we thought was the weirdest, most tasteless, most outré garment.

Kate was silent until, during a brief lull in our couture chat, she burst out, 'Okay, this is ridiculous. I bang on about resistance and what do I do?' A smile crept open and was gone. 'Um, the thing is, I'm a stripper.'

Julie's face went slack. As if to mask her shock, she brought her hand politely to her mouth. 'I'm sorry.' She looked crushed, almost distressed. 'I had no idea. I feel so selfish.'

'Me too,' I said. I couldn't think of anything else to say.

Kate hadn't finished. 'Also, sometimes men pay me for sex,' she said. 'I don't believe it's particularly dangerous or that it makes me any less of a person. But there *is* a massive taboo, no matter how much you may want to deny it. And if you try to tell me it's no big deal you'll only insult me. So please. Just say nothing at all.'

The room went silent. Maybe Kate would storm out now and we could all relax and begin to make sense of it amongst ourselves, or Olivia could. She'd had longer to process it, obviously, being party to this information longer than we had. Or maybe Kate would hit Julie. Or smash her tea cup on Olivia's newly polished floor. Or start crying again.

Kate did none of these things. She began to smile again, broader this time. 'So,' she said. 'Who's gonna be brave enough to ask what it's like?'

Vince remained as sweet as ever. We had sex everywhere, or did our best. Once at the pub, in the men's, before we were called out by the duty manager; in Vince's chiropractic practice rooms while his client waited outside; down in the gully round the back of his bedroom, mixed up amid the leaf litter; several times in the shower, making ourselves late for parties, even making Ants and Olivia wait in the living room one time when we'd invited them for dinner.

He introduced me to his mother, Beryl, a hospital administrator who lived alone in Ōtāhuhu.

Beryl asked Vince if he'd been eating garlic bread when we arrived woefully late one Sunday lunch and we couldn't stop laughing. She was hurt because she thought we'd been filling up before we came, so we didn't have to eat her 'hideous food'.

'Oh, God, I got it wrong, didn't I?' she said. 'None of this is any good.'

'Beryl, no – it's lovely, it's fine.'

We couldn't tell her I was the real source of Vince's garlic breath.

'Do I really smell of garlic?' I asked when we got in the car.

'Don't make me laugh while I'm driving,' said Vince, backing out of the drive.

'You could've just brushed your teeth.'

'We were late as fuck.'

When we got onto the motorway, I put on a Buzzcocks album. Vince turned it down.

'Babe,' he said anxiously, 'I've been thinking about London.'

'Again?' I said.

'I have to think about it. Time's running out. Once I'm past twenty-seven I can't do the working holiday thing anymore.'

'But you don't have to think about it right now, do you? At least, *I* don't have to think about it.'

'But I want you to.'

'Why?'

'Because I care about you. I care about us.'

I said nothing. I felt like I had been brought to the brink of a deep pit.

'Erica?'

'If you go away, there is no us.' I couldn't look, because I could well imagine his crushed expression. I held my palm up to the side window, blinked out at the off-ramp exit signs.

'I want you to come with me.'

'I can't,' I said, shaking my head. 'I've got my studies. I have a whole thesis to write.'

'Can't you do that over there? Can't you get a scholarship or something, and transfer?'

'I don't think so, not in the middle of my degree.'

'Don't you want to?'

'No,' I said. 'I want to stay here with you. I want to carry on as

250

we are.' Even as I said it, I knew it wasn't true. It was a relief that Vince was going away. There would be an end to this.

'But we can't.'

Somehow Vince got me to agree to join him in London at the end of next year. He'd leave in March, before his birthday. I could come in November. That would be only eight months we'd be apart. He seemed to think that would be fine, and I wanted to believe him.

'I'll pay for your tickets and everything,' he said. 'I'll write to you every day.'

It was December then. I started counting down. Only three months to go.

We went on holiday together over Vince's Christmas break. We did a road trip all over the country, stopping in Wellington, where we hung out with Phoebe for a day and I showed him the sights, such as they were. The Mount Vic lookout, Oriental Bay, the Beehive, Massey Memorial. He met my tentatively reunited parents over a tense but painless Christmas dinner. Then we went to the Gathering in Tākaka for New Year's and had a strangely sober time amongst the hippies and ravers. It was like a subdued school camp gone wrong. Someone had done something to the teachers and parents and we were left to pretend to have fun, as if we actually preferred it this way, doing New Age aerobics on a boggy field or sitting politely on a bank in a chill-out zone, pretending to be stoned enough to appreciate the ambient music.

It was a relief when we returned to Auckland and Vince went back to work. I had a summer job at the university library and so did Julie. Together we were part of the lucky skeleton crew. It was hard work for Julie, who had the misfortune of fancying a fellow shelver who had recently been promoted to full-time

251

supervisor. I got the sense he knew about Julie's crush and he enjoyed telling her what to do.

'How do you flirt?' Julie asked me in the stacks one day.

'You've asked me this before.' It seemed that Julie couldn't accept that it was a question to which there couldn't be any satisfactory answer.

'Honestly,' she said. 'I never had a dad at home. My mum's such a fiercely independent woman. I don't know. I never had a chance.'

'Sounds like you had a great chance to me.'

'Don't get me wrong, she's amazing. But sometimes I wish she could just take the intensity down a notch.'

'What does that have to do with your not being able to flirt?'

'I feel so ill-equipped. It's like I need to learn how to be more compromising of myself or something. Less aggressively insistent of my own authenticity. I don't know. Listen to me.'

'You're a feminist's worst nightmare.'

She frowned. 'I feel like there's some happy place where you can be feminine and strong and fully yourself and attract the right sort of men and I just don't know how to get there.'

'Wow, that sounds like a wonderful place, Julie. Let me know when you find it.'

'Oh, come on. You've got Vince. You must have flirted to begin with.'

'Not that I'm aware of. It just happened.'

'Who made the first move?'

'I think we both did.'

'Erica! I can't tell you how frustrating you're being,' she said, banging a sociology textbook on the shelf. 'I need details.'

If I could have thought of anything useful, anything at all, I'd have said it, but truthfully it was a relief my mind was such a blank. The more we talked about me and Vince, the more I felt like my head was caving in.

51

Vince left in March, as planned. We had a tearful goodbye at the airport, him and Beryl and me.

I cried for days, immobile. I remembered things, like the fact that Spongecake was dead, like the fact that my parents had nearly got divorced.

I dripped tears. I was defrosting. Some feeling came back. There were other things I began to recall.

52

Foster rang one day in March after Vince left. Dion took a message. It was waiting for me on the coffee table when I got back from university.

ERICA, it said. *Foster rang.* And that was all.

'Did he say what it was about?' I asked. 'I mean, did he say anything else? Like, is he in town, or?'

'No. D'you want me to repeat exactly what he said? He said, "Just tell her Foster rang." I asked if he had a message or anything and he said, "It's not an important call."'

'That was all?'

Dion raised his pierced eyebrow. 'Should Vince be worried about this?'

Foster was probably visiting Auckland for a day and this was my only chance to see him. That was that. I'd never hear from him again.

I wrote to Kyle instead. Even though he hadn't written back the last couple of emails, I thought it was worth a shot. If this arrived at just the right moment, if I hit him at just the right angle, maybe I'd get a reply.

I wrote to June. *It's great being a singleton for once,* I lied. *The days feel so much longer. It's like I have so much more space, and I can reach further into it. I think I'm off men for good.*

I know just what you mean, she replied, and quickly confessed she wasn't single anymore herself, she was giddy with love. *It would be nice not to be so distracted, for once*, she said, but I knew that wasn't true.

Kyle did not reply. My days after shelving became entirely structured around going to the computer lab and refreshing my inbox. I did no work on my thesis at all. I had all year – the rest of the year – for that.

I needed someone else to write to. I wrote to Phoebe, another letter about how great it was to finally be liberated and have the opportunity to get to know myself and so much bullshit I made myself sick in the toilets afterwards.

What happened to Mr Hot Buns? she wanted to know.

He's gone to London, I emailed back. *I said I'd join him when I've finished my thesis, but I don't see myself getting through the next eight months without him. Technically, we're still together. I haven't had the heart to break it to him yet.*

You really ought to be straight with the poor guy, she admonished me in her reply.

I knew she was right, but only in some distant reality I couldn't hope to occupy. I couldn't be straight with Vince. I could hardly even be straight with myself. I was deep in unnameable terror. Nobody who knew this terror could possibly blame me for what I was doing, which, if I stopped to think about it, was simply slowly, gently placing a plastic bag over this thing and squeezing. Squeezing tight till it stopped thrashing.

53

I didn't tell poor Vince it was over. Surely any day now he'd get stoned with some English chick and tumble into bed and then he'd have to break it to me and I could be legitimately devastated and that would be that. Maybe we could even remain friends, and I could act noble and beneficent and he'd never have the faintest idea what a heartless bitch I really was. But when he phoned me from a backpackers' in Sweden, I knew I'd under-estimated him.

'Erica, why don't you sign off with love and kisses anymore?' he asked, and his voice was choked with tears.

I went to Shadows and bought three pints, pretending to read a book. A guy asked me what I was reading, but when I showed him *This Sex Which Is Not One*, his eyes glazed over and he backed away. Also I was drunk by then and didn't hesitate to scowl.

When I'd finished my beers, I went to the computer lab and wrote an email.

From: enol004@uofa.ac.nz
To: donnmeister@manmail.com
Date: Thursday, 5 April 2001 17:49
Subject: a trick question

Dear Donny,

This is hard to ask because when I last saw you, you
were not your best. You were not the Donny I knew and
the memories I think I had are confused with that, it's all a
jumble and I don't know myself so well, maybe not so well
as I know you. Isn't it swell?

Yeah. What was that then?

A question.

Oh yes. A proposition, actually. How about this: if you
could pay me, would you? I'd consider your offer. Ask
me, tell me whatever it is that you want. Whatever it is,
no matter what, no matter how big or small, profound or
profane. It can be – maybe should be – almost obscene.
Too obscene to mention. And what you'd give in return.
And I make no promises except that I'd consider. I'd
consider anything. No price too small to be considered.

Think of it as a thought experiment.

Think of it like this: let's reduce everything down
exactly how we DON'T want it, let's debase it to an
obvious extreme and Have Done With It, you see? What
happens then? Can we possibly address the gaping gulf
of What The Hell Happened?

Don't answer right away. You may surprise yourself.

Querulously yours,
Erica

I didn't hear from Donny for three days, during which I had
a migraine. I lay in Vince's old room with a pillowcase over my
head and every so often flung the back door open to be sick into
the gully down below.

I began to wonder, when my wondering capacity was

sufficiently restored, if Donny was dead. I began to wonder, what if he'd taken the shard of glass that night and slit his throat with it? If Donny was dead, would I be desolate or relieved? I tried feeling both those things. Both dead ends. I didn't believe he was dead and I didn't believe I could feel anything at all.

If he wasn't dead, and he replied to my email and complied with my request, and asked me to do whatever it is that he wanted, once and for all, then what? What was it I hoped to learn?

Donny wasn't dead. We arranged to meet at my flat that Easter, when everyone else was away. It would be the first time he'd visited me there, the first time I'd entrusted him with my address. We were starting afresh. It was Easter. A yeasty, eggy time of renewal.

A knock at the door. I felt reassured, as soon as I saw him, that this had been the right decision. Donny was changed. Time, or my email, had softened him. He'd become pliable, grown into a shy, doughy, expansive mass.

'I must say,' Donny began, lowering himself onto the milk crate across from me in my room, 'I was, shall we say, intrigued?'

'It's all you, though,' I said. 'This is only as interesting as what you choose to make it.'

'Is that so?' he said. The idea appeared to both gratify him, and – strangely – almost embarrass him.

We caught each other up on the news as we knew it. 'Been interlocuting with Martin a bit in the cybersphere,' Donny said. 'Kyle's found himself and his bodacious appendage a satisfactory sexual posting in Tokyo, I hear.'

'Oh, yes?' I said, blinking back tears in what I hoped was a convincing display of imperturbability.

'Yeah. He's doing it with *twins*.'

By way of distraction I offered him coffee, and some hot cross buns I'd made myself.

'They never rose,' I said, hyperextending my fingers. 'They're like volcanic rocks.'

'*Splendide.*'

I slipped on the bricks on the way down the path, smashing the coffee plunger and scalding my legs and hands. When I got back to the kitchen, I was shaking. Shivering. From the cold, perhaps.

We'd have to drink instant.

He was browsing my CDs like a normal visitor when I returned. I was going to have to remind him why he was here.

'So what is it?' I asked, putting our coffees down on the desk beside him. 'What will it be?'

He was frowning casually at the back of *Never Mind the Bollocks.* 'And what was the question?'

Do you want to picture something sad? Imagine Donny, of all people, hope in his heart, slowly taking off his clothes. Twenty dollars on top of the stereo.

Is it any better if Erica doesn't do as she's told but freezes on the spot and breaks down?

Alison, she whispers on the phone in her head, *Mum. I've made a terrible mistake.*

'Erica?' Donny was standing in his briefs at the end of the bed, head tilted to one side, more puzzled than outraged. 'Are you laughing?'

I covered my face. 'No,' I said, wiping my eyes.

He sat down next to me. 'I thought you'd finally found your mojo.'

'Yeah. So did I.'

'Most guys would be completely humiliated right now,' he said, tilting his head towards the ceiling.

'I know.'

He let out a long breath. 'I just feel so much sorrow.'

'Yeah.'

'I want love,' he said. 'I want us to be fulsomely conjoined.'

'I know,' I said again, and put my hand on his shoulder. 'I'm sorry. I'm not myself.'

'You're never yourself, Erica.'

I got off the bed and started picking up his things. I folded his jeans and sweatshirt gently in my arms and stroked them smooth like a cat. 'Here.'

He hugged them to his body.

'I think I need to be alone,' I said.

While he was dressing, I paced around the room pretending to tidy up. I was waiting for his rage to burst, but it didn't.

I gave him his twenty bucks back. 'Be careful going up the path,' I said. 'There's glass.'

54

Afterwards, in the bathroom, I ran the cold tap hard and splashed cold water on my pulse points. I was wearing Vince's old towelling robe. I blinked in the mirror. No one was watching me. No one was hovering outside the door, wondering if I needed help. The flat was empty. Everyone was on holiday. It was just me and me.

I threw the hot cross buns in the bin. They thudded in like rocks on a roof, possums playing a prank. I laughed, because there was nothing left to do.

It felt like an ending, because it was.

Acknowledgements

This book was conceived and (for the most part) written during the course of my MA year at the IIML. I owe a huge debt of gratitude to everyone who read it, critiqued it, and workshopped it into being, most especially the wonderful Emily Perkins, my thesis supervisor, and my classmates Andrei Seleznev, Cassandra Barnett, James Pasley, Johanna Knox, Keava McKeogh, Max Olijnyk, Michelle Rahurahu Scott, Sinead Overbye and Tracey Schuyt. I'd like to thank Tracey Slaughter, my external examiner, for her insightful reading and encouragement. I'm also very grateful to the Adam Foundation for their generosity.

Heartfelt thanks to the good people at VUP, in particular Fergus Barrowman for his kindness in championing this book and bringing it into the world. Kirsten McDougall and Jasmine Sargent – thanks so much for your patience, support and hard work. Thanks to Russell Kleyn for the brilliant cover art.

I'd like to thank my agent, Seren Adams of United Agents, for her encouragement, along with my workmates, friends, and family. Special mention goes to Agnieszka Zabicka, Joanna Merwood-Salisbury, and my dear parents, Mary Atwool and Brent Southgate.

Finally, I could not have written this book without the support of my husband David Coventry, first reader, purveyor of good writing advice and (when needed) brutal honesty. Thanks, David. This book is for you.